Blood Ties

Book 2 in the written in blood series

S. F. Rae

SUNSET WREN PRESS

Sunset Wren Press

SYNOPSIS

Bullets have been fired.
Pasts have been revealed
Secrets uncovered.
But that's only half the story.

Everyone wanted to know who was responsible behind the hit on Haven.
But they have learned much more than they had bargained for.
What started as a quest of revenge, is now a deadly chess game.
And the clock is ticking.

Blood Ties

ISBN: 9781804675106
Perfect Bound

First published in 2023 by bookvault Publishing,
Peterborough, United Kingdom

An Environmentally friendly book printed and bound in
England by bookvault, powered by printondemand-worldwide

Trigger Warnings

This is a slow burn, dark romance aimed at adults. It will be steamy and violent. A lot of topics are covered in this book, however I know that triggers can be very different for different people so if you do have any questions or queries about any of the triggers listed, please email me and I will try to ease any and all concerns, or visit my website which will list the triggers in detail. SFRaeAuthor@gmail.com / www.sunsetwrenpress.com Sometimes my characters can be offensive, and do not represent my personal views at all. They are just characters, and they are notorious for surprising me and not doing as they are told. Any offence caused is not intended, and if you wish to discuss content with me further feel free to get in touch.

<u>Potential triggers:</u>
Death - Loss of a loved one.

Rough sexual scenes.
Past child abuse.
Branding.
Mentions of sexual assault.
Male on Male violence.
Female on male violence.
Female on Female violence.
Knives.
Drowning.

CONTENTS

Previously in the Written in Blood Series

This book takes place directly after the events of Bloodbath, and is meant to be read in order. If you haven't read Bloodbath I implore you to stop so you don't spoil it for yourself. There will be spoilers from this point onwards.
Seriously.
Go read the first one.

Okay, that should hopefully be enough, for the rest of you I've included a little refresher but if you can't remember Bloodbath just go back and read it. Most of you seemed to binge read it anyway (no judgement, I'm flattered) and you never know you might find stuff you missed the first time.

Previously in Bloodbath

Blood, murder, and mayhem.

Nyx wakes up surrounded by the bodies of pretty much everyone she's ever loved. But just what do we know happened at Haven? Well, we don't fully know at the moment. X had that weird dream, and clearly he has something to do with it. He's clearly harbouring a lot of guilt. Probably need's a shoulder rub or something. Maybe a cookie?

Nyx is the unluckiest person on the planet.

Not only does she lose everyone she cared about, she then gets kidnapped. I think Creed is still feeling the nut shot she gave him, when he scurried away with her on Kaiden's orders. When she meets Kaiden she goes a little batshit, let's be honest. The push and pull between these two. I think that car scene was a good start but damn that arrest warrant. I'm still bitter. Don't worry, totally make up for it I promise.

Keith Ryker.

Can I get a collective URGH? I hate the man, and writing his dialogue makes my skin crawl. The guy is a prick. The voice Nyx remembers when she visits Haven belongs to him. Is he bothered? Nope. Instead he shoots Creed (NOOOOOOO) and chases Nyx through the woods while remembering how he killed his wife. I am not writing it out again because blergh but it was all in the last chapter. He killed Maria, because she was trying to prove the truth about Evelynn's death.

<3 Jason and Maria <3

How many of you saw that they were in fact Nyx's parents? Any ideas on why Maria never said anything? Or who she actually was? One day you will find out but until then I'd love to hear your theories. Obviously she isn't who she said she was from the start.

X

Did you manage to figure out his identity? It was subtle, but we will recap it in the early chapters so if you didn't get the whole picture I am not going to spoil it here. Mwahahahaha. Bloodbath ends with Nyx falling into his clutches, and Creed bleeding out, or dead, in Kaiden's office. What will Kaiden do when he discovers the girl he swore to protect is missing?

Let Blood Ties begin.

CHAPTER ONE

D riving back to the Ryker mansion with Kaiden might have felt a little ironic, if I could feel anything at all.

Everything I knew, everything I've strived to be, means nothing any more. No wonder Kaiden had laughed at me, he could see my effort, my entire career, and it didn't amount to anything more than a colossal waste of time.

How can I have been so blind?

For a bitter old man, I sure had some fucked up rose-tinted glasses on. With every arrest, I'd felt like I was stemming the tide of violence and corruption just a little, even if I was powerless to stop it completely. I might have saved a life, let someone breathe easier, at least for a short while. But now I'm seeing Blight in a completely different light, and the world is a lot more complicated when I don't have my head stuck so far up my own ass.

How could Maria be so fucking optimistic all the fucking time?

Maria . . .

I can't even begin to unpack the revelations which have come to light. Everytime I think about it, I have even more unanswered questions.

Why did she never say anything? To either of us?

Why did she always act like Nyx wasn't her child, just a stray she picked up?

I feel my anger rise.

How could she pretend she isn't our little girl?

I remember the look of soul shattering pain on Nyx's face when she found out the truth. I'm hurting, but it's a completely different kettle of fish for Nyx.

How could she do this to us?

To her own daughter?

"Daughter?" The word slips out of my lips without conscious thought. The term feels foreign on my tongue. I never imagined myself as father material, but to have that choice taken away from me . . . Seeing an independent woman stand before me, not needing a father in her life . . . What am I even meant to do with that?

Does she even want a dad?

Would she want . . . Me?

Luckily Kaiden ignores my slip up, or just doesn't feel like making a comment, too lost in his own thoughts. I've slowly changed my opinion of the man beside me, just a little. Maybe he isn't just a carbon copy of his shifty as shit father, maybe he was just dealt a bad hand and did what he felt he had to, just to survive.

I glance at Kaiden again.

How can a father who has been there, right from the very beginning; seen the tears, the scraped knees, the first words, every achievement and failure, every single raw, precious, unfiltered moment . . . just throw it all away?

Prison is no place a parent should ever consider for their child, it's not a time out or a lesson that needs teaching. Brightside prison isn't a camp, or a fucking holiday retreat. The entire building stinks of death and the very air vibrates with the promise of violence. You'd think in such a corrupt town the prison would be filled to bursting, but the borderline weekly riots keep the prisoner count down.

What kind of heartless monster would even think about sending their child to such a hell?

I could never do that to Nyx. Even before the truth came to light, I would never have dreamed of it. I'd always been drawn to protect her. I recognised her pain. Maybe on a subconscious level I saw Maria's feisty passion, and my hard-headed stubbornness too. I've had that gnawing ache, a need to be there for her, ever since I saw her fall apart in the hospital. I've wanted to ease her pain and dry her tears. If Nyx ever got arrested I'd move heaven and hell for her, regardless of the crime. She could probably kill a man, and I'd help her bury the body.

Is this all just a part of fatherhood? Some subconscious impulse to protect one's young?

As we pull up at the mansion, Kaiden finally breaks the silence between us.

"Look. Before we go in there, I just want to thank you." He looks awkward, as if gratitude is something he rarely expresses. The sincerity in his eyes is raw and makes me feel a little uncomfortable.

This is not the cold-blooded ice prince, the playboy bachelor. This is a Kaiden I don't think a lot of people ever get to see.

"You don't have to thank me. I was just doing my job."

That's the truth, after all. The timelines don't match up. It's not like I did him a favour or anything.

"You didn't have to stick your neck out and be my alibi, but I appreciate it all the same." There's something vulnerable as he speaks, which causes me to hesitate, dismissing him didn't feel right, so I try to downplay it instead.

"I didn't do it for you." And it's true, I have no idea who's shuffling the pieces around the board but if someone is going after Nyx, extra hands to keep her safe are something I can't pass up. I will not lose her.

"I know you're shaken up about the birth certificate–"

Here we go again.

I feel my skin prickle, with unease.

"Oh? You mean the fact I have a daughter, who was kept a secret from me until she didn't need me any more?" My voice cracks, and I hear just how pathetic and bitter I sound.

"I can't begin to understand what you are going through–" He tries to sympathise but I just can't deal with this right now.

"You're right, you can't," I snarl. *I know deep down Kaiden doesn't deserve my anger but I can't hold it in check.*

"Fuck's sake, let me finish," he snaps back. I glare at him, not saying a word. Kaiden takes a deep breath and continues. "As you can tell, family for me is something very different, but I know what it means to Nyx. She might act strong, and like nothing can phase her, but it's an act. Inside she's unsure, vulnerable, and right now she's fucking terrified. Not that she'd ever admit it. She's scared of letting everyone down, she's scared she'll disappoint Maria, disappoint her family, disappoint us. She piles all this pressure on herself, until she can barely see past it. But I know for a fact, this news has shaken her, just as much as you. So just be honest with yourself, and with her, and see what happens." Without waiting for my response Kaiden gets out of the car and starts walking for the door, leaving me scrambling to catch up. Surprisingly I actually feel a little bit better.

As I enter the mansion, I almost run into the back of Kaiden, who is frozen in place.

"Son." Mr Ryker is coming down the stairs, his eyes devoid of all warmth as he looks down at us.

"Father, I wasn't aware you were back in town." Kaiden acknowledges his father with a tone that is the complete opposite of the warm person who spoke of Nyx mere moments ago. As Mr Ryker's eyes fall on me, I feel my body tense.

"And Detective Wyatt. It seems today is a day full of surprises for everyone." He put on his best public smile, but something feels wrong. "Captain Collins informed me you had been released. What a happy occasion. We should celebrate." Every word coming out of his mouth sounds deadly, despite the smile on his face. Unease settles in my bones, making me fidget.

"As much as I'd like to, I have things to do—" Kaiden starts.

"Poppycock." He cuts Kaiden off with a wave of his hand. I stand there in shock at the blatant dismissal.

Glancing at Kaiden, you can see the anger dancing in his eyes, the throb at his temple, the tightening of his jaw, but his father is completely unaware, or just doesn't care. Instead he just drones on, his sense of self importance evident.

"You've proven you actually have a brain cell in between those ears of yours, if that doesn't call for a party

I don't know what does. To top it all off, you have the number one detective as an alibi," He brings his fingers up to his lips for a dramatic chef's kiss, "even I didn't see that coming." I bristle at his tone and what he's implying.

"The timelines didn't match up, Kaiden didn't do anything wrong. *This time.*" I aim the last words towards Kaiden expecting his signature smirk, but his serious expression remains unchanged.

"Huh, less impressive then, regardless we should be happy. My son is home at last, and it's been too long. Now, I appreciate you bringing my son home, Detective, but this is a time for family. Surely you understand?" I definitely understand a dismissal when I hear one, I turn back towards the door, but Kaiden's voice gives me pause.

"Wait, he's working with me to find out what happened at Haven, Creed should be in my office--"

"Oh you don't have to worry about it, it's sorted out now. Nothing to worry your little head about. The case has been closed." Mr Ryker's tone speaks volumes, the lives of Maria, of the dancers, of his employees mean absolutely jack-shit to the man.

"What do you mean it's closed?" I spit, my anger rising to a whole new level. "I'm the lead detective, and it's not fucking closed." Mr Ryker doesn't even flinch at my outburst, just shrugs it off.

"It is what it is, I'm afraid. If you have a problem with it, it's not me you have to take it up with." He's right, getting angry with him isn't going to get me anywhere, but there is no way I'm letting this go. I look towards Kaiden, noting his frown.

"Where's Creed?" *and Nyx.* Kaiden asks. His voice betrays nothing of his concern for Nyx, but I'm getting used to his tells, his poker face isn't as good as it once was. The way he grinds his molars, to stop himself from saying what's really on his mind is a dead giveaway. The way he digs his nails into his palms, to keep his rage in check. Right now I can tell the man is livid, but more than that, he's worried.

"Honestly, I can't believe you let that unwashed primate around here, I thought you'd just grow out of this *phase* and get some more appropriate associates, but it seems like you can't even do that for yourself. Really, Kaiden, do I have to do everything for you?" Mr Ryker's tone is really grating on my nerves. Kaiden is a fully grown man. No wonder the guy is a bit wonky in the head if the only role model he has speaks down to him like a fucking two-year-old.

"Where. Is. Creed?" Kaiden spits, anger flushing his cheeks.

I suddenly feel very guilty about the daddy's boy comment earlier. He's nothing like his father.

"That is a conversation best left for later, boy," he replies, shooting daggers at Kaiden, "Now let the Detective go on his merry little way. I need to tell you all about my trip." He grins a feral smile, as if all of his cards are turning up Aces and my blood runs cold.

That smile can't mean anything good.

"Of course, Father, I will just see the detective out." Kaiden keeps his voice steady but I don't miss the flash of anger in his eyes.

"Good boy, make yourself useful . . . Detective." He gives me a final nod, before swanning off without so much as a backward glance.

We don't say anything as we walk to my car, but I can feel the anger coiling around Kaiden with every step.

"Want to talk about it?" I hesitantly ask.

"Him?" Kaiden shrugs, "It is what it is." He sounds smaller, and I don't like it.

"For what it's worth, I want to apologise for thinking you were anything like your father. You deserve better."

"Just do me a favour, be better than that sorry excuse for a human," he asks.

I nod, I'm already planning on it.

There is no way I will ever treat Nyx like that.

He glances towards the house.

"Do you still have your notepad?" Kaiden asks

"Always."

"Pass it over." He orders, and I do it unquestioningly.

When did things start to change so much?.

He reaches a blank page and starts to scribble. "This is an address, a safe house, it's mine and Creed's contingency plan. That's where Creed and Nyx should be. I need you to find them, I need you to figure this whole mess out while I play nice with . . . *that.*" I take the notepad back, reading the address before putting it in my pocket.

"Just be careful, something about this stinks, and I don't trust your old man one bit. Call it a gut feeling," I warn him.

I'm genuinely worried, I've felt this churning, niggling gut feeling more times in the last week than I have my entire career. This sense of foreboding.

Kaiden just gives me a sad smile and shrugs.

"I'll be fine, even if it's just for appearances sake. Just find our girl, yeah?" He seems resigned to his fate, but there's something telling me that letting him go back in there is a mistake. Maybe it's just my cop instinct, but sending him back to dance with a monster like that alone, doesn't sit right with me one bit.

"Of course, I'll send you a text the moment I have eyes on them." I promise, giving him a small squeeze on the shoulder. "If you need me—"

"I will be fine. Now go." His tone leaves little room for argument, his cold facade firmly back in place.

Chapter Two

I watch Jason's car until it gets to the gate, and I keep following it until it disappears completely from view. My hope goes with him, if anything has happened to Nyx, to Creed . . . He will find them. I want nothing more than to run after him, to help him find them, but I can't. If my father were to know just how much I care, it would sign their death warrants instantly.

If they aren't already dead.

Creed had only been tolerated by my side because he's useful. He's a unique brand of twisted, oneI've come to rely on. He has the freedom I don't have, to leave this place, do anything he wants, but he's always refused to leave me behind, he stayed loyal to me, all these years. My brother in all but blood.

But for him not to contact me . . .

Dread claws at my heart, twisting my gut.

Creed is a survivor, he's fine. He's got to be. Nyx will be with him, probably teasing him, driving him mental.

Yeah, they probably just forgot to text.

I pull myself together, my emotions hidden behind a mask which is starting to feel a little bit alien. It doesn't slide on as easily as it once did. I turn, looking up at the house, before taking reluctant steps back into the lion's den once more.

There's no point putting it off, or dragging my feet, and Abyss help me if I ignore his summons. It's time to see what twisted plan he's thought up this time.

I find him lurking in his lair. At least that's what I dubbed it. It's where he entertains, where he hatches his twisted plans and feeds his sense of entitlement and ego. His very own web.

I usually avoid this room whenever possible. Most of my darkest moments are tied to this room and walking into it used to make me feel like a scared little boy all over again. I would be assaulted by various memories, things I'd prefer remained buried. The time he forced me to brand a beaten up mess of a child, when I was just a boy, the pain filled screams kept me awake for weeks. The way he told me my mum had just abandoned me while he had a whore on her knees in front of him, already erasing her memory. Those were the nights I cried myself to sleep, but eventually I had no more tears to give.

It's all part of his game, it's the reason he always drags me in here. To unsettle me. To make me feel less than But it'd stopped having the desired effect years ago. These days it compounds my hatred. The ghosts that once haunted me now fuel my rage. I do not cower, I refuse to let him make me feel small, or less than. Every facial expression, every word, is a chess game. What he doesn't know is . . . I'm playing to win.

"There you are, boy, what took you so long?" Before I can even respond he's already continuing, lost in the sound of his own voice. "Never mind, I had the most amazing trip."

And I care because?

Honestly I don't give a flying fuck about who he stuck his cock in, what he snorted and who he snorted it off, or who he screwed over. I zone out, nodding at the appropriate times while I'm trying to discreetly check my phone.

Nothing yet.

"Am I boring you, boy?" He hisses, leaning forward in his large wingback chair, he glares at me full of venom and violence.

"No, sorry, father." I try to project a weak demeanour, lowering my gaze, trying to make myself look smaller.

It makes me feel sick.

My skin crawls with how unnatural it feels, I am anything but weak.

"I'm just concerned about Creed, it's unlike him not to check in." I explain, carefully choosing my words.

Father scoffs at me.

I use the term 'father' loosely.

"Forget the street urchin. He's outlived his usefulness."

Outlived? No. Never.

"Son, you're not *upset* over such a creature are you?" His tone suggests empathy but I'd fallen into this particular trap too many times as a child. His heart is dead, his empathy non-existent. I long to tell him that Creed is my brother, the one who has kept me sane all these years, who kept my heart beating long after my father tried to rip it out. But it was a route that'd end badly for us both.

Anyone who threatens the version of me he wishes me to be gets exterminated, no exceptions. So, I bury my worry, bury my love for my sworn brother way down deep, where *his* poison can never reach it, and say the words he wants to hear.

"He's a means to an end, always has been. But finding a replacement is tedious." The words feel like ash in my mouth. Even though I don't mean them, just voicing them feels like a betrayal. I know Creed would understand, and that he'd encourage me, saying it was all part of the plan, but it just feels so wrong.

"It's okay, I will assign you someone to help, someone more fitting for your station." I fight the urge to roll my eyes.

Of course. 'Help'. More like, inform my father of my every move. Anyone my father chooses for me will be nothing more than a glorified babysitter. Crushing me under my fathers thumb so I can't even take a breath without his permission.

"As generous as that is, Father, I'd prefer to keep Creed since I know how he operates, and I've already broken him in." I can almost hear Creed's laughter at my words, the inevitable dick joke that'd be guaranteed to follow. I fight to keep the smile off my face.

"Well, we can't all have what we want, can we?" he spits, angrily, the feral gleam in his eye makes me wary.

"Please explain, Father." I ask, looking at the floor, anything to avoid inciting him further. There's something about his words which causes my anxiety to rise.

"Stupid child, I see I have to spoon feed everything to you," he snarls. "That pathetic charity case was all over one of his whores in your office. Such blatant disrespect can't be tolerated. You might be dumb and blind, but I will not allow such flagrant disregard of the name I spent so long building." I stand there, stunned.

Creed and Nyx? No. He wouldn't.

"What happened to the whore?" It breaks my heart to refer to her as such, but if she's out there alone, I need to get this over with and find her.

"Gone, scurried off like a rabbit, leaving her lover to bleed out," he explains, as if I've just asked what the weather's like. My horror must show on my face before I can school my expression. "It's okay, Son, I've already had the carpet removed in your office, the new one will be fitted soon."

As if that's what I'm upset about.

What kind of monster . . .?

I shouldn't be surprised, after all these years . . .

But Creed . . .

They were meant to be safe here.

My heart feels like it's shattering into a million pieces.

This can't be happening.

I need to get out of here.

I can't breathe.

"I . . .I" Words fail me.

"Spit it out, boy, you know how I feel about stuttering. It's a weakness. You're not weak, are you? I have no use for a weak son." The threat is clear as day.

"I apologise, Father, I was just overcome with gratitude for your proactive thinking." Somehow I manage to get the words out, hoping it's the correct response.

"Understandable." He relaxes back in his chair. "My good mood has been soured thinking of such . . . *disappointments*. I am in no mood to tolerate your presence. Leave me." He waves his arm, as if his words aren't dismissal enough for his stupid spawn.

I make my way to my office, hoping I'd misheard, praying to anyone, anything that might be able to hear me.

It just can't be true.

But no matter how much I want to deny it. My eyes can't refute the truth. Every little detail. The gaping hole in my office. The smell of blood. The unmistakable red tinge to the floorboards that will never be removed.

Blood.

Just how long had he bled for? How long did he suffer, hoping I'd come through the door? Did he feel like I'd let him down? Did he blame me?

My fingers are already dialling before I register the phone in my hand.

"Jason, please tell me you have them." I plead, my voice sounding weak and desperate, even to my own ears.

"What happened? What's wrong?" He sounds worried.

"I just need to know they're okay. Please." I'm begging, I can hear the whine in my voice, a sound I haven't heard for years.

"Okay, okay, I'll be there in five minutes, in the meantime do you want to tell me what has got you so riled?" He's gentle with his worlds, like handling a child but honestly, at this moment in time, I'm grateful. I feel so close to shattering.

"Father said Creed has outlived his usefulness, and there was blood . . . So much blood."

"Shit. That's not good. Did he say anything about Nyx?" He asks, worry lacing his words.

"He called her Creed's whore, and said she ran, leaving Creed to bleed out." I spit out the words, surprised they even manage to leave my throat, when it feels like I'm suffocating.

"I call bullshit." Jason snarls.

"But the blood—"

"Fuck the blood, did you see a body?" He asks, grounding me in logic and reason.

"No, but it's an awful lot of blood," I point out, refusing to get my hopes up.

"He's a big fucker, he probably needs a bigger blood supply to power that fucking ego of his. No body means there's hope."

"You know, Creed would've probably made a dick joke about that." I smile a little, even now Creed gives me strength, supporting me in the way only a brother can.

"And he'll have all the time in the world to make every dick joke he wants, once we find the little fucker and beat some sense into him for not calling. Okay?" Hearing the challenge in Jason's voice lights a similar fire in me. Creed's body harbours a series of scars, each scar tells a story of a time he couldn't be beaten. This will just be another story to tell.

I grip the ray of hope Jason's given me with both hands. He's right. Creed has never been a quitter, it's now my turn not to give up on him.

"Okay." I say, my voice sounds stronger, more confident.

"I'm pulling up now, did you want me to hang up, or—"

"No, stay on the line."

I need to hear them, need to know, one way or another.

I hold my breath as the engine cuts off. I listen intently, I need signs of life . . . The jingle of the keys as he removes them, the door opening and closing, every single footstep up the familiar gravel pathway, every second feels like days as my dread mounts.

Please, please be there.

I pray to every entity in those moments leading up to the knock on the door. My chest is tight, as if my own heart doesn't want to beat. I don't want to know the answer. I don't want to hear the next words from Jason's mouth. I want to hear Nyx's laughter, or Creed's surprise. I don't want to hear the words which will cement my fear.

"Sorry, Kaiden, there doesn't seem to be anyone here."

CHAPTER THREE

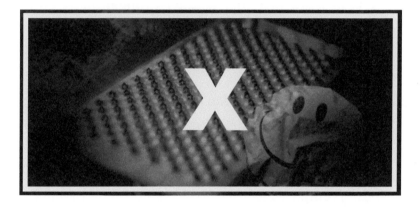

The jealousy is eating me up inside, twisting my thoughts. My monster's crying out for blood, for violence. We were so close.

Prey.

I could almost taste his screams in the air. My very blood feels like it's at war, unsettled within my veins. My mother's blood is fire, dancing and singing, crying out for freedom and retribution. My father's is cold and leaden. Silent in its encouragement to be the monster I was born to be. Who my father designed me to be. The monster which couldn't be saved. Could never be redeemed. Just a soulless machine causing misery and death . . .

It's already too late.

I can feel the monster's claw marks, echoing the scars on my back where whips bit into my flesh a lifetime ago, he wants out.

Just think . . . If it wasn't for him . . .

No.

I'm the one in control here. Not the monster.

But he came between you.

He will take her away from you.

No. I won't let him.

You think you can stop him?

You need me.

Without me, you are just a scared little boy.

I snarl my annoyance, jolting Nyx from her sleep.

Her eyes flare open with fright, I needed to pull my shit together before I did something I'd regret.

"You okay?" her voice is nervous, unsure.

"Fine," I huff.

She frowns at my abrupt tone, but she doesn't push me further. Instead her eyes trace over the source of my jealousy. Her worry is clear in her eyes as she studies him. It doesn't take a genius to realise she's *attached* to the meerkat creature.

"This is all my fault, he told me to run," her voice is barely a whisper, her grip on his hand is tight, unrelenting. I clench my jaw, as my temper flares higher.

"He was shot protecting me."

"Better than you getting hurt," I mutter under my breath, but from the look she gives me, my words are not missed.

"How can you say that?" she hisses, her temper flaring.

My angry Kitten.

I feel my lips twist into what some might consider a smile.

With the flash of her anger, I see something more. Something dark. Something familiar.

The monster inside twitches with interest.

I told you so. I told you she's perfect for us.

The demon in my head huffs its annoyance, content to let me remain in control for now. I can feel something resembling curiosity about our little Kitten. I can't let my guard down for a moment though, it's always watching . . . Waiting for its chance.

"Please be okay," she whispers over him. Clinging to his bedside, as if every breath is going to be his last.

"He will be," I offer my reassurance, not that it seems to do much.

"You don't know that," Nyx isn't comforted by my words in the slightest.

"I've seen a lot of bullet wounds—" I start to explain, but she cuts me off.

"I don't give a shit. Unless you're a doctor, how do you know? How can you be a hundred percent sure?" She watches me, a challenge in her eyes. "We should take him to the hospital."

"We can't take him to the hospital. Even in Blight they'll ask questions."

"Can't you just pay someone. That's what you do, isn't it? Wave money at the problem?" She snaps.

I am not my brother.

I want to throw the words at her, but a single tear rolling down her cheek stops me dead.

She's hurting.

For the first time ever, I don't want to revel in someone's pain. Even my monster is staying suspiciously silent.

"P-rin-cess."

The words from his throat are dry and raspy, but Nyx acts like it's the most beautiful sound she's ever heard. The tortured look instantly morphs into relief. He managed to give her more hope with that one word than I ever could.

"Creed, I'm here, it's okay. I'm so sorry," she gushes, leaning over him, but the abyss had already dragged him back under. He's out cold.

Thank fuck for that.

I'm not ready for him to be up, and asking questions just yet. I doubt he'd mistake my identity, at least not for very long. I have to come clean to Nyx before he reveals my secret. It'll be better coming from me.

I need to make her understand.

Nyx has given up trying to rouse Creed, instead she just holds his hand again, mumbling apologies under her breath.

Not that she has anything to be sorry about.

"He will wake up when he's ready. He just needs rest." I try again to reassure her, the fact he woke up is a good sign, even if it was only briefly.

She slowly nods, as if she's still struggling to believe it.

"Come on, let's get him more comfortable. There's a cot and everything set up in the basement. I think there's some medical supplies down there too."

What I didn't tell her is that it'll also keep him behind a lockable door, in a room with no escape. There's a reason Creed is Kaiden's right hand man, and I wasn't taking any chances.

"How will we move him?"

I roll my eyes, sliding my arms under his shoulders and knees. I huff in annoyance at the tightening of fabric against my arms, as my muscles strain under his weight. I doubt Nyx would appreciate me flinging the oaf over my shoulder, so here I am carrying the meerkat like a fucking princess.

I stride quickly over to the basement door, and kick it open with my foot. I never lock it when it's empty. I never know when I'm going to bring an unexpected guest home, someone who needs a more . . . *restricted* place to stay. Nyx trails behind me as I make my way downstairs, her eyes look around curiously.

As I lay the muscled mongoose down on the camping bed, it groans under his weight, but it holds.

"There, he will be safe down here." I say it for Nyx's benefit but her attention is elsewhere. Focused on a cage in the corner.

"Why do you have a cage?" she asks, suspicion lacing her tone.

Shit, I'd forgotten about that.

"Dog," I grunt out. It's a shit excuse, but the only explanation I can come up with.

"Must have been a big dog," Nyx mutters, clearly not convinced.

I walk over to the locked trunk for the promised medical supplies. We'd already bandaged him up, but from the rasp of his throat he's certainly in need of fluids. My thoughts slip back to the blood puddle, the way it spread over the carpet. It's probably thanks to his sheer size that he's even alive right now.

If it had been Nyx—

There's no doubt in my mind that if it was her, she would have been gone. Just like Maria, leaving me alone again.

First your mother.

Then Maria.

Anyone would choose death over you.

You are nothing.

The monster whispers in my mind. I shake my head trying to clear the darkness, but the part of me that always feels like a spare is too raw, it's too much. The monster has a hold.

Flashes of hollowed eyes, my mothers thundering footsteps over the undergrowth, the sharp sting of pain against my back, the sizzle of flesh. I can't tell which screams are mine as they echo in my head, bouncing, gaining in volume. The pressure behind my eyes keeps growing, my head pounding as my senses are overwhelmed.

A hand on my shoulder breaks my waking nightmare, it sears me, the touch too hot against my cool skin. I spin around with a hiss, ready to defend myself, my heartbeat thunders in my ears, my breathing heavy.

No one touches me.

No one.

"It's okay, it's just me." Nyx's speckled golden eyes are wide with fright. But she doesn't cower like she's scared of me. It's a look I haven't seen for such a long time. Concern . . . For me.

"I was calling your name, and you didn't respond."

My name?

"Kaiden, are you okay?" she asks.

Oh.

Of course.

It's always about him.

"Don't touch me," I spit, and she shrinks back from me. Tears fill her eyes but she refuses to let them fall. Instead she grits her teeth, and storms back to Creed's bedside.

I trail behind her, an IV bag full of fluids and the relevant gear. I can feel her eyes on me, digging into my skin, scraping, trying to see inside. But I'm too raw. Too broken. I avoid her gaze and focus on the task at hand.

I never thought these supplies would ever be used to save a life, the only reason I even had them was in case my monster got a little bit too enthusiastic in an interrogation, and I needed to buy time. But looking at Creed, I can't help but feel a tiny slither of gratitude. He must have known there was no outrunning a bullet, yet he'd still acted as a shield so my Kitten could run. Without him, I would have been too late. It would have been Haven all over again.

Once the IV was in and secure, there's no more putting it off. Creed will recover and wake, sooner or later, and before he does I need to tell my Kitten the truth.

Chapter Four

I was finally starting to feel safe. The initial threat has passed, and even if Mr Ryker finds this place, the basement is a fortress. Nothing is getting in here without permission.

Nothing is getting out either.

My suspicions whisper at me, not allowing me to let my guard down fully. Kaiden's behaviour is odd to say the least. I know he's worrying about Creed, and finding out about his dad must have been shocking but this isn't my Kaiden. My confident pillar of strength. This version is edgier, with an unmistakably feral gleam in his eye. I follow him up the stairs, throwing one final look at Creed over my shoulder. Seeing the rise and fall of his chest, gives me instant comfort.

It's okay.

I'm okay.

We will all be okay.

I follow Kaiden all the way to a bedroom located at the top of the house. He opens the door and waves me in.

"You should get some rest." His voice is strained, as if the words are not the ones he wants to say, but they forced their way out of his lips anyway.

What's going on?

"You're probably right," I agree. He refuses to look at me, focusing on anything and everything else. I reach out a hand to touch the one hanging by his side. Instantly he flinches, his eyes snapping to mine as he snatches his hand away.

The darkness I see in those eyes, the pain, the raw hatred takes my breath away. I've never seen such hardness, such bloodlust. Not once has Kaiden looked at me like that . . . Not once. Meeting his gaze is like looking into a frozen wasteland, nothing can survive the burning cold landscape which calls out for sacrifice and blood.

Who can blame him for rejecting me, I got Creed shot. His closest friend could have died because of me.

"In," the word is sharp. Cold.

Head down, I walk inside, one measured footstep after another.

"Kitten–"

"Don't . . . Don't call me that."

He cocks his head to the side, and watches me, waiting. But what can I say?

I'm sorry? That isn't going to cut it.

I'm sorry Creed got shot.

I'm sorry I ran and just left him.

I'm sorry you have a father like him.

I'm sorry about what happened to you mum.

Wait. His mum . . . He doesn't know.

"I need to tell you about your mother." I close my eyes trying to pull forth the courage to tell him. But how can I? It's one thing to think your mother left, it's another thing entirely to know she was brutally murdered.

His body tenses, his eyes softening a little.

"No, you don't, Kitten."

"But—" I try to explain.

"I already know."

"How? How can you possibly . . ." I look at him, I mean really look at him. Ever since he'd found me in the woods I've felt safe, but as I replay the events in my head, something doesn't add up. I initially wrote it off as the heat of the moment, but there seems to be something almost unsure about his gaze when he looks at me. It's not the same possessive, all consuming, confident look Kaiden gives me. It's raw, it's monstrous, like he can barely hold himself back. I feel myself flush at the thought.

"You . . . You're . . ."

"Yes, Kitten?"

I stare at him.

No, surely not?

He closes the distance between us, dwarfing me with his height.

Kaiden's height.

He traps me in those wintery eyes.

Kaiden's eyes.

But that smirk.

That's not Kaiden's smirk.

That smirk is cruel, not teasing. Lethal, not flirty.

And it was fucking hot.

I frown at the voice in my head, before leashing it tightly.

I'm not sure what flashes across my face, but his smirk drops and he steps away.

I stand there stunned, my heart thunders in my chest, my cheeks flushed.

"You're the brother. A twin." My voice is barely more than a whisper but he hears me. His posture shifts, his jaw tenses.

"Yeah, the spare. Clever Kitten, you figured it out."

"But how?" I'm so confused, why did Kaiden never say anything?

"Well, when a mummy and a daddy love each other very much—" he mocks.

"Fuck you, you know what I mean." I hiss, feeling my temper flare.

They are certainly brothers. Dickheaded, frustrating, little fucking know-it-alls.

"That's a story for another time," he replies, totally shutting me down. I can tell from the look on his face I'm not going to get any more answers out of him right now.

"Fine." The word sounds bratty to my ears, childish, but I can't help it. Maybe it's because they look the same that the rejection stings. "Let me ask one more question instead." I reason, trying my luck.

"I doubt you're going to give me a choice in the matter," he mumbles.

Too fucking right.

"Why did you rescue Creed?" I don't know what he's expecting me to ask but it certainly isn't that.

"What do you mean?" he asks, looking uncomfortable. Shifting under my gaze. "Isn't that what people do? Help others?"

It's my turn to scoff.

"No. People are arseholes. Hungry, greedy little fuck-wits. They don't swan into danger to rescue someone they don't even know. Not in this town." I know he feels the same, when the corners of his mouth curl and amusement sparkles in his eyes.

"You asked me to," he replies, with a simple shrug of his shoulders.

What.

The.

Fuck?

My vagina already decided to do fucking backflips while my brain scrambled to make sense of his words.

He risked his life, risked everything, just because I asked?

I'm stunned, probably gaping as I just stare at him.

Who the fuck is this guy?

"But . . ."

"But what, Kitten?"

"You don't know me," I whisper.

"Is that what you think?" His voice is harsh, as he closes the distance between us again, "Are you sure about that?" He looks down at me, judging my reaction, before his jaw softens.

"Oh, Kitten, I know you better than you know yourself." He leans down, his breath against my neck. "I sense your bloodlust, I sense your darkness, I sense your pain. It screams in my veins, fuelling me further." His words tease my skin as he growls against my throat, it takes all my self control not to tilt my head, to bare my neck to him.

Problem is, he's right.

I know it, I just don't want to admit it.

I'm just as much of a monster as Kaiden, as Creed. Hearing Jason's vow of revenge filled me with glee. Not once did I flinch. Not once did I feel scared when their eyes filled with shadows, their lips curled in menace. No.

I want to go to war with all of them. I want to bathe in the blood of my enemies. I want to delight in their screams.

"There's my Kitten," he whispers against my throat, his tongue darts out to run over my pulse. "Don't you ever hide away from me."

Those words.

Kaiden.

Fuck.

Guilt slams into me like a fucking freight train, and I push *him* away.

"Who the fuck do you think you are?" I snarl.

"I'm the little boy who protected you all those years ago when Maria was threatening to take you over her knee, and I am the man who protects you now. Or are you forgetting the whole 'alone in the woods' thing. Come on, Kitten, you know me."

I laugh a cruel laugh.

"Oh sure, my hero," my words drip with sarcasm, "and just where were you when I woke up surrounded by blood, after everyone I'd ever cared about had been ripped away from me? Where were you when my heart was ripped open and raw? Where were you when Creed ate that bullet protecting me from a monster you knew all about?" As my rant comes to an end, I don't have the strength to look up and meet his eyes. I know it's unfair, but I need to put some distance between us. I need him to stop invading my senses. He looks exactly like Kaiden, except he was all fire to Kaiden's ice.

Kaiden.

Kaiden.

I have to keep thinking of Kaiden.

His possessiveness makes my toes curl, his generosity makes me feel cared for, his strength makes me feel like I can do anything.

My Kaiden.

"Get out." The words are cold, said with a deathly chill which causes him to frown. "I'm done, I'm done with this conversation. I'm done with whatever fucked up mind games you are trying to pull. I. Am. Done. Get out." I walk over to the door, and hold it open.

He stands watching for a while, studying me before he sighs in annoyance, and walks towards the doorway. He stops in front of me, before slowly turning towards me, the cruel smile back on his lips.

"I'm letting you have your rest, for now. But don't mistake me, Kitten, we are far from done."

Chapter Five

The door slams behind me, making me flinch. I want to turn and beat it down, to somehow convince her of the truth. That our monsters are destined to rule this pathetic world.

I can wait though.

She knows the truth.

She's always known the truth.

It's what lured her to my bedroom that night.

When the darkness and violence still clung to me.

When my raw, broken soul was put together by her gentle hands.

Her bloodlust leaked out even then, just enough to sing me a lullaby of redemption.

I have waited years to be reunited with her, what's a little while longer?

Still.

I can't deny her words hurt.

I have failed, and that failure still looms over me every waking moment, and haunts my dreams every time I close my eyes.

You are nothing.

You are worse than nothing.

"Shut up." The words bounce back at me, mockingly.

I walk round the house, locking doors and windows, and setting up the alarms. I toy with the idea of booby-traps but I can't risk it, not when I have no guarantee my strong willed Kitten won't be the one to set them off.

My feet eventually lead me all the way to the basement door, opening it, I flick on the light switch and head down the stairs to check on our *guest.*

Play. The monster's interest calls to me.

Screams.

Blood.

Chaos.

Always Chaos.

No. I can't. Not now. He saved her.

He also took her.

Took her to him.

He tried to steal her.

He who keeps her from us even now.

No.

Before I realise it, my feet are leading me to his bedside. The rise and fall of his chest is steady, his pulse growing in strength.

It's no fun when they're sleeping.

No screams.

No panic.

As I feel the monster fall into a slumber once again I breathe a sigh of relief. Ever since I heard my father's voice, and heard the way he called to my Kitten in the woods, my inner demon had been riding me hard. Crying out for vengeance and blood, and they weren't picky about who they'd claim it from.

I retrieve the restraints I have hidden in the locked trunk and tie him to the bed. I neglected to do it earlier because I didn't want to scare Nyx but I can't afford him getting loose. Even with a locked door, this human mountain could probably just bowl right through it. Knowing he isn't going anywhere finally allows me to relax just a little, giving into the soul weary ache which has settled deep into my bones.

I trudge back up the stairs, stopping in front of Nyx's room, my ears strain as I try to pick up any sound. I'm not sure how long I stand there waiting, not hearing a single peep.

She left you.

Everyone leaves you. My monster sing-songs in my head.

I gently open the door, needing to see her.

She wouldn't leave me.

Maybe not yet.

I can feel the smirk of my monster as it stretches under my skin, testing its leash for when I lose control again.

As soon as my eyes fall on her sleeping from, the monster's venomous words lose their power.

She's still here.

I gently close the door behind me as I leave her to her slumber, but I struggle to take a single step down the hallway, knowing the moment I do the monster's voice will grab a hold once more. I'm too raw, too tired.

So fucking tired.

I lean with my back against her door, before sinking down to the floor, head in my hands.

If she wants to escape me, she's going to have to do it over my cold body.

Picturing her face, I gently let go, surrendering myself to the whims of dreams and nightmares.

The phone is heavy in my hand, it's the emergency burner.

Usually silent.

Day after day.

Week after week.

It was what we agreed upon.

It was a last resort.

Our scheduled check-ins, and drop offs were enough.

Usually.

The missed call icon taunts me, filling me with something that feels an awful lot like fear.

Not again.

I tried to phone back, but the phone just rings, and rings before the automated voicemail kicks in.

Growling at the stupid device, I phone again.

And again.

Dread claws at my insides.

Something is very, very wrong.

The monster perks up, mocking me, taunting me, poking at my weakness. Delighting in my fear.

I can't stand it.

My thoughts are consumed by Maria as I race back to my hometown. She is my only connection to my old life, the only thing I have which resembles humanity.

We are going to expose him together.

Lay my mother's tormented spirit to rest.

She's the only one who knows the truth.

She wants justice just as I do

But she tethers me when my demons cry out, thrashing in their need for vengeance.

She is the one who was determined to do this the right way.

Without her . . .

Without her all bets are off.

I run around Blight like the hounds of hell are nipping at my heels. I need her, and I know right now, she needs me. She would never have phoned otherwise. It risked too much. Every second my fear grows. There's only one place left to check, and going there will risk everything. I hesitate, the urgency to find her causes my heart to pound wildly in my ears. I remain rational enough to try her phone one more time, all the while I make up hundreds of scenarios in my head, a million harmless excuses as to why she can't answer, but I know deep down it's a lie. Every echoing ring in the still night air is heavy and undeniable.

Haven is somewhere I'll be instantly recognised, but I've exhausted all other options. I need to know she's okay. I need to see her with my own two eyes. As soon as I lay eyes on her I'll slip back into the shadows. Becoming a ghost once again.

As I stealthily cross through the quiet car park, I make my way to the back of the building, slipping through the backdoor to the club. As soon as I break the sound suppressing seal, I realise just why my instincts have been going haywire. The sound of men leering, and having fun wouldn't be unusual for Haven, it was a den of debauchery and lust after all, but the screams. Those are different. The air reeks of terror, desperation and violence. Being mindful of my presence, I sneak forward.

The first thing I see is Maria's head slumped forward, her wrists restrained, hanging between two stripper poles. My breath catches, such stillness can only mean one thing. I move towards her, hoping, praying I'll see the slight tremble of a breath filling her lungs. I keep my eyes on her, as I creep for-

*ward, frightened that if I blink I'll miss the breath I'm willing
her to take . . . Any minute now . . . Right fucking now.*

Still nothing.

*It's been too long. I quicken my pace, she can't be dead.
I trip as I make my way around her, glancing down to find
a pair of glazed eyes staring up at me. I don't recognise the
face, but from the clothes she wears she must be one of the
dancers. Already dead, the other women are soon to follow.
But I'm not here for them, I can't be here for them. I have
one goal, and revealing myself now will derail the entire plan.
I shouldn't be here, but at the same time I can't stay away.
My thoughts imagine the blue eyes staring at me could be my
favourite shade of hazel. But she wouldn't be here. She couldn't
be. Maria would keep her far from a place like this.*

*Shaking the image away, I look up. Only for my gaze to
rest on hollowed out sockets, and a face forever twisted in a
never-ending scream.*

No.

No.

It can't be.

I can't be too late.

*I scramble to my feet, reaching for the pulse point I already
know will confirm my worst fears.*

She's dead.

Heartbreak is rapidly replaced with anger.

Who else will he take from me?

Who else will pay the price for his insanity?

Red tinges my vision, I focus on the men still laughing, taking, maiming, killing.

They still hadn't noticed me, too lost in their own pleasure and bloodshed to realise the danger they're in.

The hunters are now the hunted.

Licking my lips, I let the monster take full control of my body, giving them a taste of their own medicine, their screams replace those of the women, my manic laughter a haunting sound as I bathe the club in their blood.

Until . . . After what could be hours or mere minutes, I'm the only one left standing.

Blood soaks my clothes.

Taints my skin.

I wake up, instantly alert, as a shout disrupts my slumber.

Creed is awake.

I throw a worried glance at Nyx's door, but it remains closed, she's still asleep. I fight the urge to go check on her, but the noise from the basement is getting more and more insistent. I want to spend a little bit of time with our guest before Nyx wakes up, so I hurry downstairs.

As I unlock the door and open it, the volume increases. I can hear him straining to get free as he screams profanities.

Fuck, it's too early for this. Creed certainly has a set of lungs on him. Wonder what they'd look like mounted on my wall.

"And then I'll put a traffic cone so far up your fucking ass, it comes out of your head. And then I'll cover it in peanut butter, and put it in a dog park, so every dog in a twenty mile radius will come piss all over you. And then–" He stops mid sentence, as I walk into his line of sight.

"Is Princess okay?"

His concern for her confirmed my suspicions. He can play the loyal soldier all he wants, but he wouldn't throw himself in front of a bullet if he didn't care about her.

"Princess?" My tone is deadly.

It would be hard enough to hear her name on his lips, but Princess?

No. She's mine.

Something must show on my face, as Creed looks at me, watching, studying, his eyes slanted with concentration, his body on high alert.

"You're not Kaiden."

"Ding-ding-ding! We have a winner. Maybe demoting you to a ferret of fuck ups was a little harsh. You don't appear to be as stupid as you look."

"How is this possible?" he asks.

His intense gaze on me feels like a million tiny legs, creeping across my skin.

Invasive.

Unwanted.

Creed backtracks, "You need to calm the fuck down." He struggles against his restraints again. He can sense the danger. His helplessness. I can taste it. He can't stop me. He'd soon stop judging me. Stop comparing me to my twin, the golden boy. All because of a few fucking minutes.

I'm deaf to all but my own insecurities.

My own bitterness.

My own failings.

The monster chuckles darkly.

"Kaiden, this. Kaiden, that." The words came out of my mouth but they sound so very far away, as the monster stretches, filling my skin. "I'm so fucking sick to death of Kaiden. A real chip of the old block, taking things that don't belong to him. Acting like he controls the world, pulls all the strings. Well how controlled do you think he'll be, when I peel off your skin, and send it to him. Think he'd use it as a blanket as he cries himself to sleep over the pet he couldn't save?"

He scoffs but his eyes betray him, showing his uncertainty.

The hard ones always like to put on a show, but it always ends the same way.

49

As I close the distance between us, my cruel smile increases as I fasten my hands around his throat.

He looks at me with defiance, not the fear I'm expecting.

I increase the pressure on his throat, the only clue I have that he feels it is the tightening of his jaw. No thrashing, no panic.

Huh.

I tilt my head at him as he fights to keep his eyelids open, but still he doesn't flail. I can't help but respect him, the man has nerves of steel. And an uncompromising will, that overrides mortal instincts. He's a fighter, if you take away the possibility of a win, he's the type who'll still fight you any way he can. Defying you until the very end.

I lose focus when a hand grabs my wrist, little claws digging into my skin. It's almost laughable how small her hand is compared to mine.

"What the fuck are you doing? Let him go!" she snarls, all venom and vengeance.

It's . . . Cute.

She pushes against me, and I humour her, taking a step back as she shoves my chest. Fire burns in her eyes. She's fearless, sheltering Creed, using her body as a barrier between us.

"Princess . . ." Creed's voice is a plea, a plea for what? I don't know, but it makes me want to reintroduce a bullet to his body, this time making it stick.

I snarl at him, and pull Nyx towards me.

Mine.

"Princess!" Creed's voice breaks, finally the fear I seek leaks into that one word.

"It's okay, Creed. He won't hurt me. Will you?"

She tilts her head to the side to look at me, the rage is still there, but there's no fear.

"You protected me. You saved both of us. You don't want to do this." Her words soothe me somehow. Suddenly I don't even remember why my hands were around his throat, as I feel her back press against me.

Even the monster is purring under the feel of her as I hold her close to me. The smell of violence still clings to her, reminding me I'm doing a pretty shitty job of taking care of her.

I can give her this.

I glare at Creed one last time, warning him that this isn't over, but he just gives me a knowing smirk. I growl my annoyance as I release Nyx, walking to the door. I need to get my head on straight before I do something I'll regret.

"Wait," Nyx calls to me, stilling my steps.

"What?" I hiss, not wanting to turn around.

"You never told us your name."

"Kaleb." I answer. "Kaleb Ryker."

The name feels clumsy in my mouth, it's been such a long time since I've been asked my name, and even longer since I've answered honestly. Without waiting for a response, I head out of the room, my soul flayed open with that one truth. But there's no escaping it, I am a Ryker.

Chapter Six

I watch him slink out of the room. Part of me wants to follow him, but I'm hyperaware of Creed's eyes on me, carefully watching in the way only he does.

"Kaleb, huh? Am I the only one freaking out a little right now?" Creed mutters. "There's fucking two of them and Kaiden is the sane one."

"Can you be serious for one fucking second?" I hiss, turning around to face Creed,

"Oh, Princess, were you worried about me?" he teases, a cocky smirk on his stupid face.

"Urgh!" I exclaim.

What is it with these stupid, egotistical little fuckwits? Creed with his cocky, fucking know-it-all attitude, Kaiden with his smirks and filthy words, and now Kaleb.

"I'm dead, I had an aneurysm caused by stress . . . I can't possibly know this many assholes."

"Oh don't be like that . . . Don't lump us in with him. He called me a ferret . . . Do I look like a ferret to you?"

"That's what you're going to focus on? Really?" I put on a stupid macho voice, "*Look at me, I'm Creed. Almost kill me, fiiiine, but calling me a ferret is taking it too far.*"

"Well?" he asks.

"Well what?"

"I don't look like a ferret, do I?"

"Creed." His name came out as a whine. I can't take much more of this.

"Okay, okay. I'll drop the ferret thing, besides, a ferret would have wriggled out of these ties already, and as much as I love my knives, I do not like the way they're currently stabbing me in the ass."

I roll my eyes, but start loosening the restraints holding him down.

Silence hangs between us until he's free.

As soon as the last restraint falls off his wrist, he sits up, pulling me down onto his lap. He crushes me against his chest and just holds me there for a moment. I relax into the warmth of his hard chest, allowing the beat of his heart to comfort me.

"I'm so glad you're okay, Princess."

He's alive.

We are alive.

We escaped.

I start to sob into his chest, the scent of leather still clings to his skin despite his jacket being long gone.

He's okay.

"I thought . . . I thought . . ." I babble incoherently

"Shhh, it's okay, Princess. I'm here, I'm okay," he soothes, stroking my hair as he holds me.

"You're not okay though, you were shot," I mutter.

"I am okay, it's not the first time I've gotten friendly with a bullet, and I doubt it will be the last."

I wriggle out of his grip, elbowing him in the side.

"Oof, gentle, Princess."

"Still going to tell me you're okay?"

"I am. Just sore. Promise." He wears his normal easy smile, so I give in for now. I'm just glad he's okay.

"You scared me," I whisper.

"I know. But it's okay. We're okay," he comforts me. Finally, I feel the last bit of stress leave my body as he presses a small kiss to the top of my head.

We're okay.

"Don't tell me to run like that ever again. Even your ego can't cushion a bullet," I scold.

"If anything happened to you, and Kaiden found out, a bullet would be the least of my worries," he teases.

"Shut up." I feel the heat of a blush warm my cheeks.

We sit like that for a little while, side by side on the little cot.

"Princess?"

I jump at the sound of his voice.

"Yes?"

"I know you probably don't want to talk about it, but how did we get here?" Looking up at him, I see a frown on his usually carefree face.

"It's a bit of a blur to be honest but when you said run, I ran." I hesitate slightly, feeling the guilt creep up. I look down at my feet trying to stop the tears from falling again. Creed notices my hesitation and brings his arm up around my shoulders again, squeezing me tight.

"You did what I asked, if you didn't we would both probably be dead right now."

"I know, but-"

"No buts, Princess. I'll be your shield anytime, without hesitation. Every bullet and every blade will hurt a lot less than the pain I'd feel if you got hurt." He stares at me with a softness and vulnerability I'd never seen before. He gently tucks a strand of hair behind my ear, reverently gliding his fingers against my skin. Before I could question it, his normal expression was back, making me feel as if I imagined the whole thing.

"I mean, Kaiden would probably skin me." He laughs, back to his normal self. "What happened after you ran? I vaguely remember him leaving the room, and I tried to follow, I swear I did—"

"It's okay, I know. You're my knight, remember?"

I smile up at him, and he quickly looks away, clearing his throat.

"Yes, of course. Me and Kaiden will always try to protect you."

"He's going to lose his shit when he finds out what happened."

"Probably," Creed agrees.

"After I ran, he followed me." Creed tenses beside me. "He wanted me to run, he wanted to chase me. He . . ." I take a breath and Creed pulls me closer, to the point I can barely tell where one of us ends and the other begins. I inhale his scent, and draw strength from the warmth of his chest under my palm.

"Take your time," he murmurs into my hair.

"He told me how he was going fuck me in the dirt as he rung the life from my neck." I whispered the words into Creed's chest, but he heard every single one.

"I'll kill him," he snarls.

"You can't he's—"

"I'm going to fucking kill him." Violence swirls in his eyes, a promise of things to come. I shiver, but not in fear, never in fear.

"You are going to have to get in line," Kaleb snarls from the darkness, causing us both to jump. Creed instantly gets to his feet with a wince, putting himself between Kaleb and I. I put my hand on his arm to make sure he doesn't do anything rash and stupid, but the way Kaleb's eyes focus on the connection makes me drop my hand almost immediately.

Okay. No touching. Got it.

We stand there for a little while, in some sort of stalemate before the most amazing smell hits my nostrils.

Pizza.

My stomach lets out a god-awful rumble at the scent, which I'm pretty sure echoes in the confined space, making me flush scarlett with embarrassment.

Creed laughs, and even Kaleb struggles to hold back a smile.

"Here," Kaleb says, revealing three boxes of heaven, "I didn't know what—"

He stops speaking as I practically rip the boxes from this grasp, taking my plundered booty back to the cot. He gives me a sad smile before turning away again.

I freeze, that smile's filled with such longing and pain it takes my breath away. No one deserves that level of pain. However, before I can act, Creed speaks up.

"Stop."

"What?" Kaleb snarls.

"Thank you." Creed mutters

Whatever Kaleb's expecting it isn't that. A wariness enters his gaze, like he's not sure what to do with the information. Honestly I'm kind of shocked too.

"I didn't do it for you," Kaleb mutters, his eyes find mine.

"I know, but that doesn't change things. It seems like you have a grudge against your old man too, so how about you join us, eat pizza, fill me in, and we can come up with a plan together?"

"And why would I do something like that?" Kaleb studies Creed with a guarded look, as if he's expecting some kind of trick.

"Because, we have a common enemy."

"I don't need your help," Kaleb snaps.

"Maybe not, but the more monsters the merrier." Creed drops his mask, and sheds the carefree attitude, fully embracing a twisted smirk that darkens his eyes and promises violence.

I shiver as the temperature feels like it dropped a few degrees with that look alone.

Kaleb's eyes spark with interest, but he's still wary.

"I don't trust you."

Creed merely shrugs.

"You don't have to," he reasons.

They stare at each other for a long time.Too long. The silence was awkward and heavy. It's clear they're having some sort of gorilla chest-beating, male mind-melding party that I didn't get an invite to.

Eventually, Kaleb sighs.

"Okay." Just like that he walks over to the chair against the wall and pulls it towards the cot, still staying a wary distance away, but it's clear some sort of truce has been made.

"Here," Creed says, taking one of the pizzas off me and holding it out in offering.

Kaleb takes it, but doesn't open it.

"I suppose you want to know how you got here?"

"That would be a good start."

"Well, I came across Nyx in the woodlands surrounding the house. *He* was out there, talking shit, making it easy to out manoeuvre him. When I finally found her, she slumped into my arms."

His eyes landed on me, and I remember the moment he saved me. The relief I'd felt knowing I wasn't alone anymore, and I was going to be okay. I flush under his gaze, and try to focus on his voice as he fills Creed in on what came after.

CHAPTER SEVEN

P <u>*reviously*</u>

She's lighter than I thought she'd be. My little kitten, in my arms at last. How I've longed to hold her like this, feel her skin against my own. It feels like my heart has finally started to beat again, after stopping all those years ago. I cradle her to me, breathing in her scent and holding it in my lungs. She shifts in my grip, her face screwing up, a frown marring her previously peaceful expression.

"Creed.' She murmurs.

The fucked up ferret is the only other one on the property other than the pitiful excuse for a human I share blood with. That has to be Creed.

I'll kill him.

She was mine.

"Must . . . Help . . . Creed."

I growl at her mutterings.

No. Let the meerkat be turned into a tea-cosy.

"Please . . ." She whispers a final plea, as her face relaxes again, slipping back into darkness.

Fuck.

I have a choice to make.

I could just spirit her away, right here, right now, like I want to.

Or . . .

Urgh.

I start to retrace my steps taking her away from this place, but I don't get very far.

For years I've tormented myself, wondering if there was anything I could have done, any way I could've helped, maybe if I had stayed she could have gotten away.

Scoff, you'd both be dead, idiot.

I don't want her to know the same torment.

Torment smorement, let's go.

No.

I shake my head trying to clear the voice.

No. I mean it. Not this time.

He doesn't control me.

Besides, if he steps out of line, I can sacrifice him to the demon in my mind.

Yessssss. Why didn't you just say so? Blood, screams, pretty pretty.

He did take her.

He put her in harm's way.

If anyone is ending him, it will be me. With my mind made up, I cradle my prize closer, and creep towards the house. I break out in goosebumps as I feel the ghosts of this forest stroke over my skin. Countless screams that were never heard. Final moments that have gone unwitnessed. How many bones have gone unfound? Was she still here? My mother.

My heart races, even after all these years I expect her to come running through the trees and throw her arms around me as if I were still a boy.

Pathetic.

Shut it.

As I close the distance, the mansion looms over me. Making me feel small.

Vulnerable.

"No," I hiss into the empty air. "Never again."

I'm the monster in the dark. I'm the hunter. I'm the one who will rain down chaos and devastation. I'm the one who will raze his kingdom to the ground around him until it's nothing but ash on the wind. I must grip Nyx a little too tightly as she lets out a whine. I instantly relax my grip, whispering an apology under my breath.

"I'm sorry, Kitten.

"Where are we?"

She's awake.

For a second I hold my breath not saying anything, afraid to frighten her.

> *Girl with the raven hair,*
> *Will you ever see me as anything but a spare.*

Awareness slowly seeps into her expression, sharpening her focus.

"Creed!" She looks at me, with panic in her eyes, "We have to help him, I think he got shot."

"That's the plan, Kitten."

As soon as I place her down, she's off like a rocket, no stealth or caution to her steps at all.

"Kitten!" I hiss under my breath, trying to call her back to me, but she's already disappearing back into the house. I chase after her, my strides eating up the distance. I hear her footsteps hit the ground, drawing my focus, a sound which pushes me forward. The last time I walked these halls my mother held my hand, a bunny clutched in my other. Now I have my Kitten, my reckless, impulsive little Hellcat of Chaos. I smile as I race to catch her.

All too soon the chase ends.

"Creed!" Nyx runs to his side, and checks for a pulse. "He's alive, quick help me with him." She tries to roll him over, to see what the damage is. The red strain on the carpet is slowly growing. I approach them, my steps tentative, honestly I'm not sure if I want him to live or die at this point.

Seeing her hands on him. The little silken touches.

I want to shoot him myself.

Pushing my feelings aside, I kneel beside her, to help her. I lift up Creed's t-shirt, trying to find the source of the bleeding. The bullet has caught his side, but the long jagged wound might look bad, but it's just a nasty graze. It would be a bitch to keep clean but he should survive with some first aid, stitches and maybe fluids.

Fucker's lucky it didn't nick something important or he'd be dead already.

"We need to find something to stop the bleeding, and we need to get the fuck out of here." I know my father wouldn't think to look for Nyx inside the mansion, he thinks all women are weak, pitiful, frightened little things who will bolt and panic until he sinks his teeth in. He's probably already dick deep in some poor little whore, some poor victim who will be lucky if they survive his frustrations. Still, it isn't a smart idea to hang around. He won't leave a mess like this festering for long.

"It was your dad," she whispers, gauging my reaction. If it's a look of surprise she's hoping for, she won't find it. My earliest memories are filled with screams, blood, and my father's laughter.

"I know."

"Wait, how can you know already?" She eyes me with suspicion.

"Not the time, Kitten, not if you want us all to get out of here alive."

I see the way her hands tremble, the adrenaline she's currently feeling won't last. When it runs out she's going to crash hard and there's no way I can get both of them out of here by myself.

"See what you can find in the drawers, see if there's a medkit or something."

She moves over to the desk,

"Why would there be a—?" The question disappears on her lips as a medical kit comes into view. She pulls it out and brings it over, and although it looks like she wants to ask a million questions, she bites her tongue.

Good, because I'm not sure how I'd be able to answer them. It's not like I can tell her my brother's so paranoid and anal retentive, that it's a given that he's got a plan for every fucking letter of the alphabet. He's a Ryker after all. Slippery fuckers the lot of them.

"Is he going to be okay?" she asks, her worry clear to see.

He won't be if you keep looking at him like that.

I clear my throat before answering, but annoyance still creeps into my voice.

"He was lucky."

For now, anyway.

"He won't stay that way if we can't get this wound closed, grab that whiskey." I gesture with my head towards the decanter. Nyx quickly retrieves it, before kneeling on the other side of his body.

"Cover his mouth." She places her tiny hands over his lips, completely trusting me.

I wonder what else we could make her do.

My monster whispers in my mind.

It had never taken interest in a girl before, maybe the Kitten's a tamer of monsters.

I take a swig of whiskey before dumping a generous helping over the open wound on Creed's side. As soon as the alcohol touches his injury he screams and thrashes before the pain knocks him out once more.

"I'm sorry, it's going to be okay," Nyx soothes, brushing his damp hair back from his face.

Don't make promises, I won't be able to keep, Kitten.

"We're getting you out of here."

I go to work on stitching up the wound as best as I can, it isn't going to be easy moving the big lug, it might take time but we can't risk leaving a blood trail. Once I think the stitches will hold well enough to get the fucker out of here, I dress it with some gauze.

"Okay, that will have to do. We've gotta get out of here."

It's only a matter of time before—

The sound of the front door opening and closing, echoes through the still hallways.

Panic flares in Nyx's eyes.

Both of us hold our breath, neither of us wanting to attract attention.

We need to move.

I gesture to the door leading off to the side, praying it isn't going to be some sort of bathroom. It's our only option though. We might not know who has come through the front door, but there was only one logical destination.

This office.

Nyx nods, and starts making her way to the door leaving me to worry about Creed. I'm not a small man, but Creed has a weight advantage that isn't going to make this easy. I get the fucker up over my shoulder in a fireman's carry, and follow after Nyx. Every single step makes the man whimper like a little injured puppy. We're lucky there are no ears in range, or the poor little meerkat would have become a poor little meat shield.

We make our way through the door, and we enter what looks to be a sitting room, of sorts. Floor to ceiling bookcases, just stuffed with various tomes, some old leather bound monstrosities, some more slender and modern looking.

Probably just another way to lord wealth over others.

Look at me, I'm smort, I read the books. I mock silently.

Luckily there's a second exit, which looks like it leads back into the main hallway. Nyx stands against it now, pressing her ear to the wood, listening for movement. It's only moments before the voices drift through the closed door. Two guys, from the sounds of it. Soon they're close enough to pick up on their conversation.

"We always get the shitty jobs," Dipshit whines.

"Shh, don't complain," A gruffer, probably older voice replies.

"Urgh, but clean up? Really?" From the sound of his voice the guy can't be much older than a fucking punk-ass kid.

"Look, Mr Ryker just said to clean up the mess, okay? So that's what we do." The older guy's clearly fed up with the kid's whining.

"But I didn't sign up to be a rich dick's janitor. I wanted excitement, you know; girls, money, all the fun shit."

It takes all my self control not to scoff at his words.

It always sounds good at the beginning, until you end up being cannon fodder and left in an unmarked grave.

"Yeah, yeah, but you have to start somewhere. At least you're not babysitting the whiny brat complaining about cleaning up. It could always be worse." You can almost see the patronising smirk.

The younger one chuckles.

"Fuck you, man. This is the room, right?"

The footsteps stop . . . Right outside the fucking door.

There's nothing to hide behind, even if there was, there wasn't time.

This is it.

I shift the dead weight on my shoulder, getting ready to throw the useless sack of shit at the people on the other side of the door. The shock of having a ten-ton fuckface flying at them, should buy us a couple of minutes to try and get the drop on them.

The doorknob starts to turn almost in slow motion, but it's just the adrenaline coursing through my system. My body coils like a spring, ready to pounce. Nyx reaches out grabbing the doorknob, halting it in its tracks.

"Shit, it must be locked."

"Knobhead, that's the wrong room. It's this one."

The knob returns to its original position, and the guy walks away, entering the room we'd just left.

That was fucking close. Too close.

Nyx presses her ear to the door, listening for voices, but it seems we're in luck and it's just the two of them. She cautiously opens the door a crack, and pokes her head out to check that the coast is clear.

We're lucky the egotistical fuckwit who sired me can't be bothered to explain things to his '*lessers*', otherwise the men would probably notice a missing corpse and would be on the hunt, but as there are no thunderous footsteps it seems like we're in the clear.

As Nyx slips out of the room, my gut clenches with fear. I wait for the shouts, the screams that would follow if she's caught. It's barely a second before she sticks her head back in, but it feels like a lot longer.

"It's clear, let's go," Nyx whispers.

We move as quietly as we can down the hallway, Creed's moans have stopped, causing Nyx to keep throwing worried glances his way. Progress is slow, slower than I'd like. While Nyx's head is turned I poked the fuckwits side, eliciting a groan of pain from him. Knowing he is still alive soothes some of the worry on Nyx's face, not that it was a hardship to cause him pain, it pisses me off how much she cares for the wanker.

A nice guy would be happy she's found a family, with people to care about after Maria was ripped away from her. But I'm not a nice guy.

I want her.

I want to keep her all to myself.

Ever since I saw her curled up on my bed.

She. Is. Mine.

Nyx is retracting our steps, leading us back to the forest. Creed might be stable now, but I doubt we'll be able to walk out of here.

I stop, causing Nyx to look back at me with a frown.

"We need a car." I explain, turning and leading the way towards the garage. My memories of the mansion are patchy at best but I've spent so long watching cars come and go, I'm pretty sure I can find it. I can't let Nyx know who I am, at least not yet. I need her trust to get us all out of here alive.

Walking into the garage is like walking into a show-room. Way too many cars for just two people, from massive presidential style SUVs, to sleek sports cars, luxury sedans, and a couple of muscle cars I would kill to take a closer look at. I doubted Nyx would be up for leaving Creed behind just so I could pick a pretty ride.

Shame.

"Over there." Nyx gestures to a mounted lockbox, which has to contain the keys to the wheeled candy store.

"Which keys?"

The only car I know for sure will be here, and fit us all, is the SUV that dropped them off here. I rip the door off, and pluck the first key that looks like it might fit the bill.

"These will do," I say, tossing the keys to her. She frowns before hitting the unlock button, a happy little chirp sounds in the distance and we head towards it.

Please be something big, please be something big.

Bingo.

It's the SUV.

"Figures," Nyx mutters beside me, and I raise an eyebrow in question.

I can't ask her anything without risking my identity, so I ignore the comment.

She opens the back door, and I get hit with a sense of deja vu as I shove Creed inside. It isn't any easier than shoving the doctor in the boot when I kidnapped him, even with Nyx's help. Creed's heavier, and bulkier. I flip him off my shoulder, *accidentally* hitting him against the door frame.

Oops.

Nyx catches my smile that I fail to hide, and shakes her head. The edges of her lips curl up with amusement. Clearly my antics don't bother her in the slightest.

Beautiful, my cheeky kittycat.

"Here," she says, tossing me the keys. "I've got Creed, you drive." She climbs in the back, lifting Creed's head and putting it on her lap. I grit my teeth and slam the door with a little more force than necessary.

The sound echoes throughout the garage so I hurry into the driver's seat before anyone comes looking, all the while I'm imagining peeling Creed's face off.

Shoving the key into the ignition, I imagine it's his eye socket.

Stepping on the accelerator, I imagine it's his face.

With those comforting thoughts, we drive off into the retreating daylight.

Nyx's eyes meet mine in the rearview mirror and for the first time in a while, I don't feel so alone.

CHAPTER EIGHT

*W*here the fuck are you, Creed?

I don't believe he's dead. He can't be.

This is Creed we're talking about. He's had a few close scrapes but to eat a bullet and just be gone?

No.

Not Creed.

I don't care what my father said, until I see his body with my own eyes, I can't believe he's gone.

I've been checking my phone every few minutes, every chime, every notification, I expect to see his name.

Hell... Right now I'd take a dick pic, and a snarky comment over this... Nothingness.

I push open the safe house door without knocking, only to come face to face with a gun pointed in my face.

"Easy, old man, it's just me."

From the looks of him, it's been a while since the guy took a break. He's sporting some bags under his eyes that could smuggle a couple of bodies, despite the discarded coffee cups all over the place.

Has he even slept?

I step into the room and take a look around.

I had to give it to him, the guy's been busy.

There's no space left on the walls. Print outs, photographs, scraps of paper with strings running from place to place mapping all the different connections, it's crazy.

"Made any progress?" I ask, tentatively.

"What do you think?" he snarls, holstering his gun.

"It's still early days." I don't know if the words are designed to comfort him or myself.

"I just can't . . . I need to . . ." He looks around frantically, searching for something. Some connection that's been missed. I place a hand on his shoulder, drawing his attention to me.

"We will find them," I swear, looking deep into his eyes, praying he'll calm the fuck down long enough to help me.

"I can't lose her too, I can't. Maria would never forgive—" He chokes back a sob.

"We won't. Nyx is a fighter, wherever she is, you know she'll be giving them hell. I will tear this entire world apart until I find the people responsible, and I will destroy whatever scraps my Queen has left behind. We need to keep focused, if we are going to bring her home."

Jason's eyes lose some of their manic edge, and his gaze sharpens.

He's back. Thank fuck for that.

"Did you find the people who cleaned up the office?"

"No, it was a bust. I mean if I just come out and ask my dad, he'd be able to tell me, but that'll also paint a target on Creed's back."

If he's still alive.

The longer he stays out of touch, the harder it is to believe.

And then there's Nyx.

I've tried keeping her away from my father. I tried to keep my distance. I tried to keep her fucking safe. For what? Guilt threatens to swallow me whole, Creed always knew what this world was like, he knew every day could possibly be his last, but Nyx, my feisty Wildcat, hadn't signed up for this. She didn't grow up in this twisted bloody world like we did. If they are both dead, it's because of my decisions, my orders which sent them to the grave.

There is no one else to blame.

It's all my fault.

"Where did your head go just then?" Jason asks, watching me with a concerned expression.

"It's nothing, let's go over what we know again," I suggest.

"Be my guest"—Jason gestures to the walls around us—"it's all right there. Every clue and every dead-fucking-end." He flops down on the sofa, sipping from yet another coffee cup as he eyes the walls.

"There has to be a clue, someone has to know something." I frown, deep in thought

"No one is going to talk while your dad wields his power over everyone, like a gun to their head," Jason snarks.

"We need to know what the officer from the other day knows." I think out loud, my gut tells me there's more there. Something I'm missing.

"We've read the file a million times, what more do you want to know?" Jason sighs, exasperated

"Who the fuck put him up to it, of course," I snarl.

I never did anything to this guy, so there had to be more there, there just had to be.

"But he swears up and down it was you, that there was no one else," Jason reasons.

"Well he's fucking wrong," I snap.

"He doesn't seem to think he is. Even if he is hiding something, there's no getting to him. He's been moved into witness protection after the stunt he pulled. Only the Captain has access to those files and he's not going to hand them over to you. Last time you spoke it wasn't like you were making friendship bracelets and braiding each other's hair."

"The Captain doesn't have hair," I argue, eliciting an eye roll from the detective.

"Fucking braid his pubes then, who the fuck cares? Are you going somewhere with this?" he snaps back.

I smirk at the detective.

"How long have you been with the force?" I ask as casually as possible, but it doesn't stop Jason's eyes from narrowing in suspicion.

"It's all I've ever known, why do you ask?"

"Well if only a Captain can get results—" I don't need to spell it out for him, the change in his body language is enough to tell me he's following. He knows what I'm insinuating.

"No, fuck off with that line of thinking. I'm a detective, not a Captain," he says in a tone which leaves little room for arguing.

Like that's ever stopped me in the past.

"Look, the way I see it, going after the Captain restricts my fathers powerbase. If he doesn't have the BPD in his pocket he'll have to be a lot more careful. It automatically makes Nyx and Creed safer, and gives us breathing room. Just think about how many eyes the BPD has . . ."

He still doesn't seem convinced, but I don't know how I can get through to him. His concern for Nyx was both making him reckless, and way too cautious. This is only a fucking promotion after all.

"Think of it as community service, Collins doesn't deserve to be in power. He's a corrupt sack of shit who should have been ousted years ago. You saw what he was like, he didn't care about me going to jail. All he was interested in was what I could give him. Not what I've done, what I could do. He doesn't care how much blood I have on my hands, or if I was innocent."

"Okay, okay, I get it," he snaps, but there's no real heat in his words. More just reluctant resignation, and frustration. He's one step closer to accepting my proposal. Taking stock of all the leads on the walls, it wasn't like we had a lot of options.

I let him turn my words over for a little while. He'll come to see it's the only choice. We need to liberate Blight from my fathers grip. We just have to hope it isn't too little, too late.

I reach over to take the coffee cup from his hand, but it looks like some weird tar, hardly what I would call coffee. I sniff it and recoil.

"Urgh, what the fuck is that supposed to be?" I asks, handing it back

"Coffee," he grunts in reply.

"That doesn't count as coffee." I screw my nose up, whatever is in that cup cannot be counted as drinkable, even if it is caffeinated.

"Oh, I'm terribly sorry, rich boy, not up to your standard?" he teases.

"When all this is over, I'm going to show you what coffee is actually meant to be like." The words escape my mouth before I even realise what I'm saying, but it's too late to take them back, and if I'm completely honest. I don't hate the idea.

Jason chuckles beside me.

"You know what? I think I might actually like that," he admits.

Chapter Nine

*M*yself as Captain?

The idea is absurd, but I can see the potential in it. I'm not stupid enough to think this whole thing would be as straightforward as Kaiden makes out. Doing this we will be actively making moves against Mr Ryker. There's no way in hell he's just going to stand by and let us do what we want.

"Are you sure you've thought this through?" I ask, cautiously.

"It's the only move we have right now. Either we'll be helping Nyx and Creed, or . . ."

"We will be avenging them," I finish for him.

Silence reigns between us as we each fight to leash our emotions. As much as we try to remain optimistic, it's tough. Mr Ryker isn't someone to take lightly. This plan . . . There's no way to know for sure if I'll succeed, let alone if it'll cripple him enough that he won't just be able to openly slaughter us.

"Can I ask you a question?" The dynamic between us has changed, it's almost comfortable at this point, despite everything. When Kaiden doesn't reply I think 'fuck it' and ask anyway.

"Why are you doing all this? I mean, give it a few years and you'll have the keys to the kingdom. Why risk everything?" I study his reaction closely, I need to know what he's thinking, if I'm going to do this.

"You know why."

"Spell it out for me."

"It needs doing," he says with a shrug.

"It has needed doing for years if half of this stuff is true." I gesture to the pieces of paper surrounding us, every little thing Kaiden knows about his father's operation is plastered on these walls.

"I wasn't ready," he mutters.

Not good enough.

"And now you are?" I ask, pushing him.

He's down his right hand man, and at this point his chest is just as open and raw as mine, if we're going to do this I need to hear the words.

"No," he snaps.

Here we go.

"I can plan for years, decades, I could wait forever for the perfect moment and still nothing will be guaranteed, but the fact Nyx is out there—" he pauses briefly, regaining his composure, "I can't wait any longer."

"I get it, I do, but you can't do this half-cocked?" I reason.

"Half-cocked?" His tone has turned deadly, his eyes lost some of their hauntedness. The Kaiden in front of me now is every bit the lethal crime prince he's rumoured to be. A killer.

I pushed too far.

Shit

"You don't think I've thought this through? You don't think I've tormented myself with every single fucking scenerio?" he spits.

"I'm not saying that—"

"I've planned for years. Every lesson my father tried to carve into my brain, every time he flayed my soul open for his own amusement. My plan was systematic, careful, minimal risk, just the way I like it. But then Nyx came in, like a wrecking ball to everything. She broke through my icy facade, my carefully constructed armour, like it was nothing. She made me into a fucking human being. Do you have any idea how hard it is to be a human around my father? How even being in his presence makes me feel dirty. I feel sick to my stomach, but if I so much as twitch he will kill me. If he does, who's left? Who will take him down? You?" He laughs cruelly, "So no, I am not half-cocked. I'm not rushing. I'm taking action because I can't fucking stand it anymore. I want to carve his blood out of my veins. I want to cut him into pieces so small the wind carries him away. I want to erase him from this fucking planet."

He glares at me, his resolve burning in his eyes.

He's all in, there's no doubt about it.

"Okay. So you want to go after the Captain? It's going to take time, and there's no guarantee I'll be the one to take his place. I mean they could transfer someone in from a different precinct."

"Oh, Jason, it's cute how innocent you are sometimes." He smirks, that stupid fucking playboy smile. The one that makes it very hard for his teeth to not spontaneously come out of the back of his head.

"Watch it, boy," I snap.

"What I mean is, your promotion is guaranteed with my backing." He says it in that fucking *'isn't it obvious'* tone of his. But he's a branch on the crazy family tree if he thinks I'll just be another puppet.

"I won't be corrupt," I insist.

"I'm not asking you to be."

"But you said—"

"I know what I said. We both understand the need for the good and the bad, and I reckon us working together will be a good thing. We might be able to fix this town, just a little bit. You'd do your boys in blue shit, and I'd keep a grip on the shadows."

That doesn't sound too bad, I mean, this town is like a tower of cards. Both sides need each other or the entire thing collapses. The police make people feel safe, and the Rykers handle the bigger sharks, ones second rate police departments are ill equipped to handle.

"But you know we'll clash at some point," I reason, it's inevitable.

"Then we clash, or we at least go through the motions. I know you've realised it's not black and white here. This town is way past the saving point, too many hungry predators circling, waiting to move in and pounce. Haven proves that."

"Better the devil you know," I mumble.

"What was that?" Kaiden asks.

"Something Maria used to say," I reply, a small smile forming on my lips.

"She was a good one," he replies, mirroring my sad smile.

"Was she?" I ask. I feel guilty as soon as the words leave my mouth, but I can't help but feel like I didn't know her at all.

"Yeah, she had her secrets, clearly, but she wasn't malicious. She could never be evil. She had to have her reasons."

I scoff.

"Sure, let's just ask her all about those shall we? Oh wait. We can't," I snap, instantly regretting saying them when Kaiden's cold mask slips into place.

"You done?" he hisses.

What the fuck am I doing? This isn't the time. I should be focusing on Nyx not moping like a bellend.

"Yeah," I sigh.

There will be time to address all this shit later, for now we need to focus on the task at hand.

"So what are you thinking?" I cautiously ask, I'm not sure what he's going to suggest. Ever since that phone call he's been on edge. Almost like he's fraying, unravelling . . . He's lost without her.

Kaiden gets up and walks to the wall to pin four photographs, well three and a name, the king and his generals so to speak. The four men responsible for so much heartbreak.

"We leave my father for last, he deserves to watch his empire crumble, he deserves to know we're coming for him. The Butcher's the enforcer, he's the bogeyman, the hammer my father uses to keep people in line. He doesn't need money, and doesn't have any loyalty to anyone but himself. He's paid in skin, innocent and guilty victims alike, for his sick and twisted experiments. As long as he has people to pickle, he's manageable."

"Wait, you let someone like that near Nyx? What the fuck? Why would you—?"

Kaiden chuckles.

"What's so fucking funny?" I snarl.

"You sound like Creed right now, you know?"

"Fuck. Off."

"Seriously, he said the exact same thing. But what's done is done. Moving on . . ."

I grumble an affirmation, we are going to come back to this at some point, if he wants to be in Nyx's life we're going to need some ground rules, like not getting examinations from people who want to cut her up.

"We know someone took Ellis, we just don't know where he ended up. Whoever is trying to frame me obviously got their hands on him, but as I said, the doctor is easily swayed, just give him experiment fodder and he'll be as loyal as someone like that can be. I think it's premature to discount him just yet, but until he shows his face it's a dead end."

"Well, he's officially listed as a missing person after the car crash, so when he does show his face again we should hear about it. Captain gave me that case, so any updates will come to me," I explain.

"Good, speaking of our Captain, I think he's the logical mark out of these two. The other guy is someone I was always told to call "Uncle". He's the closest thing my father has to a friend, and he's smart as a whip. He's always been in charge of imports, exports, contracts, all the tedious stuff my father couldn't be arsed with. He's got a mind for business and likes his numbers. He's always turned a blind eye to the more unsavoury aspects of a criminal empire, but he's not naive. He's fucking careful, and paranoid as shit."

"He doesn't sound so bad."

"Don't get me wrong, his paranoia makes him lethal. If he thinks you're going to fuck with him, he will have a blade to your throat before you can blink. He doesn't care about evidence, or innocence. The only reason he doesn't have a body count to rival the butcher is because my father usually stills his hand. For some reason, even in the deepest depths of paranoia, he's never once doubted my Father. Not once."

"Sounds charming. So we have a mad scientist; a paranoid, kill happy accountant; a psycho with a God complex; and a slimy corrupt police captain. When you put it like that, yeah I have to agree the Captain does seem like the easiest mark. How did someone like that even end up as one of your dad's cronies? I mean, I wouldn't trust him to change a lightbulb without help."

"He's simple, pliable, and when he gets told to jump, he jumps. He doesn't have any real power, not like the others, but he is a means to an end. I mean, it doesn't take a brain surgeon to destroy evidence and lose paperwork." Kaiden shrugs.

"And if there was hard evidence that your dad wanted destroying—"

"He'd be the one to do it."

"Creed and Nyx?" I ask, hopeful.

"It's a long shot, I'm not going to lie. But it's the only one we have," Kaiden replies, but there's a steel in his voice, a resolve. He believes in this plan, and even if it is risky as fuck, the time for playing it safe has passed.

"Okay, I'm in, we just need to get him fired right?"

Kaiden laughs, "No, we will need to do more than that."

"What do you mean, more?"

"You saw the shit he pulled in the interrogation room. If he could be fired, he would have been years ago."

"But no one has spoken against him, no one's reported him. If we just—"

"Just what? Tell his mummy? Get him to say how sorry he is? Make him promise he will be a good little boy?"

"I didn't mean—"

"Good, because you can't be so fucking stupid to think that would actually work? You think everyone is blind to him? That no one else but you, the almighty detective, sees what a disgusting pig he is?"

"I wasn't saying that—"

"Good, because we are doing this my way."

"What a bullet in the head?"

"If I have to."

"How does that make you any different to the people we're trying to stop?"

"You just don't get it," he hisses.

"Fuck you, I do get it. I know it needs to be done, but there are other ways. Better ways." I try to be the logical one.

"Fine, you think you can do better. Let's hear it."

"Get him to incriminate himself, get undeniable proof. Your dad's power can only go so far, there's got to be a tipping point. A point where he has to walk away, right?"

"Maybe, but don't kid yourself. We are not the heroes in this story."

"Maybe, but we don't have to be the villains either," I reply.

Chapter Ten

The impromptu pizza party was nice, all things considered, but as the evening drew on, it seemed like whatever cease fire Kaleb and Creed had reached wasn't going to last.

"You need a fucking plan," shouts Creed, "killing people does not count as a plan."

"Well, it's my plan," Kaleb shouts back.

Back to Creed

"That barely counts as half a plan."

Back to Kaleb

"Plan: Kill Keith. Dad equals dead, me equals happy."

It was like a fucking tennis match.

"Wow, psycho school one-oh-one. Did they also teach you your ABC's? Apple, Banana and Cutting-a-bitch?"

Kaleb growls before stomping away. Probably to go hunt for something to hit that isn't Creed.

Not that I'd blame him right now if he chose to re-arrange Creed's face.

"What the fuck are you playing at?" I hiss at Creed, "Can you stop provoking him for two fucking seconds?"

"That was hardly my fault." His green eyes shining mischievously..

Fucking shit-stirrer.

"You have got to be kidding me, ABC's? Really? What are you, a two-year old?"

"He started it, if he had something resembling a solid plan—" Creed tries to argue with me.

"Are you even listening to yourself right now? He start-ed it? Really?" I cross my arms over my chest and glare at him.

"Well, it's true," he pouts.

"Grow the fuck up, Creed, or I swear to God . . ."

"You'll do what, Princess? Tell me what you want to do to me. Pretty please? Me on top?" He smirks, and I see red.

"You can't take anything fucking seriously, can you? Everything is just some fucking joke. Do you even know the danger we are in right now? He will not stop until we are both dead. It's just a matter of fucking time. He killed my entire family, just for shits and giggles. He didn't need to set those monsters on my sisters at Haven, but he did. Why? Because he's a fucking psycho. We have one fucking ally right now and you are determined to keep poking him. Pushing him over the edge."

"You feel sorry for him, don't you, Princess? The poor, pitiful lost soul. You can't save everyone you know."

Creed's angry, well good for him. This is something he should be angry about. Glad he's finally getting with the fucking program.

"No, I don't feel sorry for him. He doesn't need or want my pity. He's beyond that, he's tethered to his demons, he wields them as a weapon. He fucking saved us you ungrateful prick, or don't you realise that?"

"I said thank you," he snaps.

"Big fucking whoop. How about you just stop being a critical asshole and actually share your own ideas?" I snap back.

"You can't be seriously calling his destructo suicide mission a plan?" he argues.

"I don't care. There is only one thing I care about right now." My voice turns glacial, a voice Kaiden would be proud of.

Time to bring the manchild to heel.

"Oh yeah, and I'm sure you're going to tell me all about it, right, Princess?" he sneers.

"Kaiden. He's what I care about. You know, your brother, your best friend, who probably thinks we're dead right now."

Creed scoffs and rolls his eyes.

"He knows it would take more than that to take me out."

He can't fucking believe that can he?

Just how big is his fucking ego?

"Oh really? Just how long do you think he's going to hold shit together once he sees the blood coating his office? Once his dad spits whatever poison, spins whatever tale he wants. You're what? Just hoping that Kaiden thinks you're invincible?"

"Jason won't let him do anything rash. He's a cop." Creed sounds confident, and maybe if any cop can stop Kaiden, it'd be Jason. But he underestimates Jason's bloodlust, I've seen it. Back in the hospital, when he swore to me that the people responsible would pay. He wasn't talking about arresting them.

"You think anyone can stop Kaiden if he really wants something?" I ask, eyebrow cocked.

We sit in silence for a moment, just staring.

"Shit," Creed mutters, defeated.

"Yeah, shit. Now you can sit there, and figure out how to be a fucking adult for longer than thirty seconds, and I will convince Kaleb to not beat your ass."

"Oh don't make any promises, I'm not sure I want you to keep, Princess." he teases.

I merely roll my eyes at him, but can't hide the small smile.

Fucker is going to get himself killed.

I pad down the hallway, listening for movement, for any clue to point me in the direction Kaleb went. I check rooms as I go, before I hear a soft thump followed by another, gaining in tempo. I follow the noise to a closed door. I gently knock but don't get a response. I knock again but the sound just continues.

Thud

Thud.

I gently push the door open and I can barely believe my eyes.

Kaleb has his back to me, wailing on a boxing bag as if it had personally offended him.

Probably imagining it's Creed's face.

He wears earphones which are turned up to the maximum, blasting music. I can hear it from the doorway.

No wonder he never heard me.

Clothed, you would struggle to find much difference between the brothers, but shirtless is a completely different story. Kaleb's back is criss-crossed with so many scars that they're clearly visible from this side of the room. Marks on top of marks mar his skin. His flesh must have been ripped open over and over again. Clean slices, jagged tears, deep intricate marks caused by various horrific tools. I feel my own skin tighten in protest just looking at them.

The pain, it . . . I can't even begin to imagine.

It must have been immense.

My feet carry me across the room without conscious thought.

Each step shows more horrors. More pain. My heart breaks for him.

Not out of pity, but as one human to another.

No one deserves this.

Not a single person.

I stop mere inches away from his back. I can feel the heat from his skin, his skin pebbles as my breath teases his shoulders.

"It's rude to sneak up on people, Kitten."

He makes no attempt to remove his headphones, so I don't reply with words. I reach out, pressing a palm against his shoulder blade. He flinches at my touch as if I've burned him, hissing in a breath through his teeth. I try to remove my hand but it has a mind of its own, as if the heat of his skin has fused us together and every nerve ending on my palm lights up. He rips his earphones out, storming away, putting distance between us.

"I'm sorry," I whisper, not sure the words carry across the chasm I feel has opened between us.

"I don't need your pity," he spits, putting his t-shirt back on.

"I didn't mean to just barge in, I knocked but—"

"So you thought you'd just come in anyway," he scoffs.

"I came to find you."

"Well I wasn't exactly hiding, what do you want? A cookie?" he snaps.

"Watch your tone," I snarl back.

"I'm sorry, Kitten, your pets might roll over and let you stroke their bellies, but you touch me again, tell me what to do . . ." he laughs cruelly, "What am I saying? You'd like it, wouldn't you, Kitten? You want to play with my monster, feel my sharp teeth against your neck, my claws raking against your skin."

I swallow, my skin heating as the images assault my mind.

How can two brothers, twins, be such complete opposites? Kaiden is rules incarnate, he controls, he dominates. Kaleb is fire, destruction, and unpredictability. Both are dangerous men, and both have the power to ruin me completely.

"I'm with Kaiden." The words fly out of my mouth. We may not have discussed things, but I was not the kind of girl to play around like that.

"Of course, the golden twin." Kaleb chuckles cruelly, "well let's see how fucking golden he is when he's rotting in a tiny prison cell."

"How did you—?" I start, confused.

How could he know about the arrest warrant, unless he had something to do with it?

"What did you do?" I snap.

"The joys of having a twin that no one knows about, you do shit, they take the blame. Even Kaiden himself doesn't know he has a twin. It was the one good idea my dickhead dad did right. The only people who knew about my existence were my parents and whatever people they brought in to torment me. To train me, to make me stronger. The only exception was Maria, she was allowed to tend to my wounds sometimes, it would've been bad form to let me die of an infection or some shit after all."

"Why would you do something like that?"

"To get him out of the way. I might be a monster, but I'm not going to kill my twin. I might need him for spare parts one day." He smirks.

"You are underestimating Kaiden," I warn him.

"Even he won't be able to talk his way out of a police officer kidnapping, not when there's a witness. He was practically feral when I let the little douchecanoe go sailing down the river. He was practically foaming at the mouth."

"There's something very wrong with you."

"Oh, Kitten, there's not a lot right with me." He chuckles. "But at least we'll be able to use it to our benefit."

"Great," I mutter, sarcastically, "because what I really need is even more psycho to add to the giant clusterfuck that is becoming my life."

"Just embrace the Chaos, Kitten. It makes things a shit ton easier."

"I'll keep that in mind but for now we need to talk."

"I thought that was what we were doing." He smiles at me, an awkward half smile that looks a little bit alien on his face.

"All of us."

"No," he replies, his expression closing off once more.

"Come on, he's not that bad," I encourage him.

"I said, no."

"Please." I'm not above begging at this point. We need a solid, genuine plan. We need to force Mr Ryker to go on the defensive.

"You saw what it was like."

"This time will be different," I plead.

"Yeah, this time I won't walk away, I will pound him so hard he'll look like roadkill."

I snigger, maybe I've been spending too much time with Creed after all.

"Might not want to mention about pounding Creed, he might like it."

The look on Kaleb's face is a mix of horror and repulsion. I couldn't contain it. I started to laugh.

Clearly, Creed isn't his type.

"Come on," I reach out, grabbing his hand and pulling him towards the door, "I'll protect you." I tease, leading him in Creed's direction.

CHAPTER ELEVEN

Sitting in my office feels surreal, but if Kaiden's plan works out I suppose it won't be my office for much longer. I'd managed to convince him to give me twenty four hours to attempt a plan which doesn't end in a body bag. That's a line I don't want to cross, not yet, not for someone like the Captain. He's pretty much all bark and no bite, not a good person, he deserves to pay for his crimes. To be humiliated and reduced to nothing but the disgusting worm he is. A much more fitting punishment than a bullet to the head.

I checked out a wire from the armoury. Well I say 'checked out' but it was more of a walk in there and just take it while the guard was taking a leak.

If I can just prove what he's like. Some undeniable proof, something unrecoverable, then we can get him removed without bloodshed.

At least that's the idea.

Once I've attached the wire, and popped the receiver in my desk drawer I go in search of the captain. It doesn't take long before I find the slimy excuse for a human hanging out near the holding pens. I overhear him shamelessly propositioning a couple of the streetwalkers. The women were clearly uncomfortable, but no one was going to interfere with the Captain.

Well, no one but me.

"Captain, a word if you will," I call over to him. His beady eyes snap up, seeking out the interruption, but any reprimand dies on his tongue when he sees who it is. He whispers something to the ladies, who screw their noses up in disgust and huddle closer together, before he starts to walk towards me. I want nothing more than to wipe the toothy grin off his stupid face. He walks with a swagger to his step as if he owns the whole fucking world. He pisses me off.

"This better be good, Wyatt, I was in the middle of something." He turns and leers at the girls, giving them a little wave. They cringe and retreat further into their cell.

"Let's talk somewhere more private," I suggest.

Getting him to incriminate himself isn't the problem, getting him to incriminate himself without dragging other people down the river with him, well, that's an entirely different story.

"My office," he grunts, leading the way. "What's all this about?"

"Oh I just want your expertise on the latest case."

"A case? Wyatt, you are my best detective, surely you're capable of handling this yourself, if you're not then what the fuck am I paying you for?" He waves me off, already his mind is focused on the poor women back in lock up.

"Oh, okay, then I'll just take my questions straight to the Rykers' then, shall I?" I smirk at his back, as his posture goes rigid at the mere name.

Seems like Kaiden really did a number on our dear captain.

"I'm sure there's no need for that, come, come. We can sort it out," he replies.

"I thought so," I mutter under my breath.

The guy is so sickeningly predictable. Forever taking the most spineless option.

I close the door behind him and take a seat opposite the pompous prick, who spreads out in his chair like a gelatinous blob. It'd clearly been a while since he'd even entertained the idea of physical activity.

Maybe when you're so slimy on the inside, it eventually shows on the outside.

I chuckle at my own thoughts, causing the Captain to frown at me.

"So this case?" he prompts, annoyed with me. He always has this way of talking down to people, as if everyone's wasting his time, and it really makes me want to high five his face with a chair.

Deep breath, Wyatt. Remember the plan.

"Remind me again why I can't bring my questions to the Ryker's directly? I mean there was that car fire near their property. Procedure dictates I canvas, gather evidence, I'm sure a wealthy family like that would have CCTV cameras."

"Hahaha, the Rykers' are much too busy to be bothered like that."

"But procedure—" I insist, pushing him towards some sort of confession.

I need more.

"Procedure is whatever I say it is, Wyatt," he snaps.

Better.

"Oh, so you just want me to throw out the rule book? Just like that? Because you said so?" I challenge him.

"I am your Captain," he splutters, turning an interesting colour.

Maybe this will end in a body bag, if the fucker has a heart attack.

"Exactly, you are the one who is meant to encourage us to do our jobs, instead you keep wanting me to do mine with a hand tied behind my back."

Collins sighs.

"Look, I know it's frustrating, you're a good cop, but there are certain lines we can't cross.," he tries to placate me. "At the end of the day, it's for your own good."

"What's that meant to mean? Is that a threat?" I snarl.

"Watch it, Wyatt. No one is threatening you. If anything, I'm looking out for your righteous ass."

I scoff, I can't help it.

Collins narrows his eyes, clearly getting tired of my shit.

"Listen and listen good you ungrateful prick. You wanna play white knight? Be my fucking guest. Be the perfect poster boy, tick every box, wank over a job well done every night. I don't care. But stay away from the Rykers. That's my only fucking rule. You cause them problems and you will be causing me problems. Cause me problems and I will have your badge, and if that's the only thing that happens, consider yourself fucking lucky. Keep pushing, keep poking and you will end up in the morgue. I don't care if you're investigating them for teabagging the Queen of fucking Sheba, they are not involved in anything, they certainly didn't see anything regarding a stupid car fire."

Bingo. Probably not enough dirt on Mr Ryker, but should be enough for Collins to kiss his career goodbye.

"You were the one who said to investigate the fire," I argue.

"Yeah, on fucking paper. It's nothing more than a vandalism case, close it as such and move on," he snaps, talking to me as if I'm an idiot.

"But there's a missing person."

Despite everything, he can't be this blasé about that, surely?

"Has anyone actually reported him missing?" Collins reasons.

"Well no—"

"So he's not missing."

"But there was blood at the scene and—" I argue back.

Afterall, not everyone has someone to report them, and the doctor has no family.

"He's . . . Not . . . Missing . . . Unless someone reports it, he's probably just recovering in some cushy little hideaway. Got it?"

"But—"

"Wyatt," he snarls in warning. "Close it."

"Fine," I spit, knocking over my chair as I walk out.

It isn't the first time I've butted heads with the Captain so no one looks up as I hurry through the bullpen. No one stops me on the way to my office, and as the door finally closes behind me I take a deep breath to calm my anger.

It was meant to all be an act but I can't help it, the man gets under my skin.

Fucking parasite.

The sooner he's gone, the sooner there might be a chance to whip this precinct into some semblance of competency.

I lock the door behind me, using one of those removable devices to stop anyone from just barging in. I would have installed a lock, but that would make it seem like I have things to hide, and for most people around here the temptation would prove too much.

No, it's better this way. Less likely to raise suspicions.

I slip the metal box out of my trouser pocket, and remove the two connecting wires. It's already getting a bit on the toasty side, stupid piece of shit. I bundle it up and chuck it in my top drawer, making a mental note to return it later.

Not that anyone would even notice it missing.

I open the bottom drawer where the receiver is and quickly move the recording to a USB stick.

Fingers crossed this will be enough.

I have a contact I can trust, I've given him the inside scoop a couple of times, someone who I'd almost call a friend. The plan is to give it to him, and he'll make it public. It'll probably make the front page first thing in the morning, all without involving my name at all. Seems like a solid plan.

I send a quick text message to my guy. I've already briefed him when I thought this whole thing up, so he should be expecting my message, but I still feel relieved when Paul replies straight away. Now it's just a matter of handing the USB to him and letting him work his magic. *Front page news, here we come.*

Things are going smoothly, but there's a niggling feeling in the back of my head that maybe it's going a little too smoothly.

Chapter Twelve

I thought Jason was finally seeing things my way.

I thought he was prepared to do anything.

Who was I fucking kidding?

If you want something done you have to do it yourself.

Jason had texted saying he had it all under control, but he's clearly delusional if he thinks his plan is going to work. He can't seriously believe no one has complained about him before. Sometimes the easiest way to deal with a problem is the most direct way. A bullet. None of this nam-bee pam-bee bambi doe-eyed shit. He's nothing but an old fool if he thinks this will work, that my father's reach only goes so far. But sometimes we need to make our own mistakes, before we can see the truth.

Luckily I'm not restrained by the same ideals of right and wrong. I've already made the mistakes, learned from my lessons. I need my family back together, and there is nothing going to stop me from reaching my goal. I will protect my family, no matter the cost.

Jason comes strutting out of the precinct, with a confident stride that makes him look like a smug prick. Clearly he thinks everything's coming up roses, and I'm happy to let him keep believing so, it keeps him out of my way. I've got an appointment with the Captain and I don't want to miss it.

I head around to the back of the station, not the part where every Tom, Dick and Harry of the police force parks . . . No . . . I'm after a different target, and it doesn't take me long before I spot it. There's one car, parked illegally, partially blocking the fire escape.

Three fucking guesses who owns that ride.

It's flashy. In your face, and it screams midlife crisis.

A shiny, red BMW, who-gives-a-fuck what model. It's straight out of 'the how to overcompensate for your tiny dick' handbook.

Only an egotistical fuck would park in such a place, no cameras and his bloated sense of self entitlement makes him an easy mark. You'd think the Captain of the police department would know better, but years of living under my fathers protection has made him sloppy. Honestly, I'm surprised my dad tolerates him, but when you look at the potential replacements, no one else has Collins' cruel streak. My father spent a considerable amount of effort feeding that streak, so there was no possible way Collins would ever grow something pesky, like a conscience. A new captain would be a risk, and it's probably the only reason why Collins has lasted this long, regardless of him being such a fucking liability.

My father does not like change.

I hop up onto the bonnet of the shiny red car, delighting in the sound the metal makes as it takes my weight. The way it bends and shifts under every step as I make my way onto the roof, is music to my ears. I bounce on the roof, laughing as the car rocks under me. I can almost see his face now, that delightful purple shade which makes it look like his head is going to explode.

One day.

Just because I act cool and calm doesn't mean to say I'm incapable of getting the job done. The darkness I inherited calls to me, encouraging cruelty. It flames the desire in me to see my enemies bleed. . . Despite everything I hate about my father, half of the blood running in my veins is his.

The car alarm is being stubborn, even Collins isn't too egotistical not to lock his car, surely? I hop back down onto the bonnet leaving a dent which won't be coming out anytime soon, and I'm finally greeted with the sound I'm after.

The alarm is going to make that sorry excuse of a man deliver himself straight to me. He has to know the car is his, the sound is too close to the station for it to be anyone else's. I jump from the bonnet, my feet finding solid ground once more. I straighten my cufflinks and collar as I stroll over to the fire door, I underestimated the speed the rounded man can travel, as the door swings outwards towards me. I pull back narrowly avoiding being hit in the face. My shoe however isn't so lucky, the corner of the door runs over the sleek black polish, scuffing their perfection.

I growl, menacingly. It's the first thing Collins hears as the car alarm switches off with a merry little chirp.

How fucking dare he.

Collins' eyes widen in fright as he sees me.

"What are—?"

Before he can finish his sentence I have him pinned by his throat against the brickwork, he claws at my hand with his bloated fingers, but he's no match for me. Spending his days behind a desk has made him fat, lazy, and spoiled. He's lived life to excess with no regards to his own wellbeing, or the wellbeing of those around him.

His face turns purple as his eyes begin to roll back into his head. The fight leaves him as his flailing slows.

I let go of his throat and he crumples to the floor, gasping for breath.

"I'm sorry, I'm sorry," he mutters, between inhales.

"Fix it," I snarl.

I need the order, I need the control. Without Nyx—
Too much has been taken.

"I said, fix it," I snap.

He looks up at me in panic, completely clueless.

I kick him swiftly in the stomach. My shoe is already ruined so I don't bother to hold back. He coughs and sputters as he fights the pain. He starts to heave, clutching his gut.

"You throw up on me and I swear you'll become very fucking friendly with your insides," I warn, my voice deadly. "Unless you want to wear your large intestine like a scarf?"

He shakes his head, as a small whimper escapes his lips.

"Good," I coo, as he kneels before me, trying to pull himself together. I bring my foot up to his chest and pin him against the wall under my heel.. As I lean down, his eyes pinch with pain as my weight rests against his breast bone. For a moment I imagine my foot just crushing his rib cage completely. Imagining the snap of ribs, the screams of agony. The very bones that were meant to protect him, turning on him. Riddling his soft organs with holes. The sounds he'd make as he slowly drowns, as his blood pools in his lungs.

Collins lets out another whimper of pain and I lay off just a little.

"Fix . . . It." I say, emotionless. Cold. Tapping my foot against his chest.

Realisation dawns in his eyes. He frantically starts to rub at my shoe with his sleeve, in a fruitless attempt to remove the scuff mark. Of course without the right tools he doesn't have a hope in hell, but just seeing the imperfection is enough to bring me dangerously close to the edge. I need this outlet, need his terror and panic. I can't break, so I break others. Ever since my Wildcat started to thaw my frozen walls, it's been harder to keep myself together. I'd started to feel again, and feelings were messy. Unpredictable. I smiled. Everything about that woman was unpredictable. Her moods, her temper, hell even our initial meeting was all unpredictable. I mean throwing herself at me like some naked savage. *Crazy woman.* There is only one thing I can predict, the way she comes apart under my touch, the blushes when her mind inevitably turns dirty, her sweet surrender. Her submission. She was made to be mine.

I get lost in my thoughts, slowly regaining some of my calm as I think about the delightful ways I'm going to punish that sweet little body of hers. How she will beg for my marks, take my punishments like a good girl. She'll take some of the pain she inflicted on me when she left. She will make it better. She will put me back together again.

Collins brings my attention back to him, as he makes some sort of animalistic noise almost as if he is going to . . .

How dare he.

I snatch my foot out of his grasp and punch him in the throat.

"You dare spit at me?" I snarl as he writhes below me gasping for air like a fish out of water. "You think a disgusting wretch like you has the right to even lick the ground I fucking walk on?" He shakes it head furiously, pointing to my shoes.

"Just . . . trying to—" he huffs out between gasps.

"Fix them?" I finish, and he nods frantically.

"Oh, Collins, poor little Collins. Once I'm done with you, I'll turn your hide into a buffering cloth. So you will get the scuff marks out, all in good time. It'll probably be the only useful thing you've done in your whole pathetic life."

"Please. Spare me," he pleads.

"Keys," I snap, holding out my hand.

He gives them up without a fight. I grab him by the scruff of his neck, pulling him over to the boot of the car. I open it using a button on the keyfob.

"In," I order.

He freezes, sensing the danger. Some people might flee, some people might fight. All responses would be ad-

BLOOD TIES

mirable, instinctual. But there's also a third one. Freeze, and that's what Collins does.

Good old spineless Collins. Even faced with death he can't stand up for himself.

I coax him into the boot. Well, when I say coax, what I really mean is kick his legs out from under him, and I push him face first into the dark space. He tumbles in with an *oof* which brings a small smile to my lips. That small sound of pain, so sweet and musical.

I can't wait to hear his screams. I just know he's going to be a screamer. He's too much of a little bitch to be anything else.

I slam the boot closed, sparing little thought to his fingers. Unfortunately the guy is smart enough to keep all limbs inside the vehicle. No almost severed fingers poking out of the boot, waving to the people behind us as I drive down the road.

Shame.

I head to the driver's seat and get in, adjusting the seat to make space for my longer legs. And then I'm off, burning rubber, and taking corners with a speed that creates a 'thunk' as Collins rolls about in the boot. Every sharp turn is music to my ears, calming me somewhat. Cars are simple. Machines do what you expect, turn when you tell them to turn, speed when you press your foot down. It's logical, calculated and controlled. Driving like this is the closest I've felt to being calm since I saw the blood stains in my office.

Unfortunately all good things come to an end, as I pull up in front of the nondescript building me and Creed always referred to as our playground. This is where we take people we want to hear scream, this is our safe space, way out on the edge of town. Each room has been carefully built, tools carefully selected and outfitted, and yet with a single flick of a switch the entire room can be engulfed in cleansing fire, destroying all evidence. It's part dungeon, part crematorium, but it's all ours. A place for our demons to be let out, a place we can embrace our darkest selves, judgement free. No limits, no restraint. Just the promise of violence on the air.

A promise I am going to fulfil.

CHAPTER THIRTEEN

The following morning, I'm already up and pacing by the time today's paper hits the welcome mat. I rush over, snatch it from the ground and scan the front page.

Nothing.

No Corrupt Captain, no big black and white letters painting Collins' shame for all the whole world to see. No, just another fluff piece, another vanity project, I flick through hoping for something, but with every page I turn, my feeling of dread grows.

Where the fuck is it?

The story should be here, Paul said it would be. He showed me the story, we worked on it together yesterday, all it needed was to be submitted to the editor. A task Paul insisted he could do by himself.

I phone Paul.

Please pick up.

Come on.

I snarl at the phone as it goes to voicemail. I hang up to try again

It was a late night, he could just be sleeping.

I try to convince myself it's true, but my thoughts sound hollow.

"Come on, come on," I mutter as I pace my small living room.

Still nothing.

I try to ring Kaiden next.

This has his fathers fingerprints all over it. I just know it. I can feel a target lodged on my back. My time is ticking. I don't care about being in the crosshairs, it's not the first time I've pissed someone off and it certainly won't be the last, but something feels different about this.

I need help.

I hate to admit it, but I need Kaiden's help.

The phone rings.

Damn it.

No answer.

If this is just some sick power play . . .

I throw the phone onto the sofa and run my fingers through my hair, gripping it at the roots.

Think, Wyatt, think.

You've been in worse situations.

I laugh at my own hysteria.

You don't even know if something's happened. He could have just missed the printing deadline and it'll be front page news tomorrow instead.

"That's right, the first step is to check the facts." I grab my car keys and coat, before rushing out of the door.

If Paul's just sleeping, it's nothing a good old rousing knock won't solve.

I drive across town, stopping for nothing. I need to know he's okay. Guilt starts to claw at my insides making the coffee I had earlier start to turn on me. I fight to keep it down as I pull up outside of his apartment. He shares his space with some other journalists, always joking about not needing his own space as he never gets to spend much time there anyway. The three of them had pooled their resources to get a pretty nice apartment in one of the nicer areas of town, which was logical. Journalists are not always known for their friend making skills in Blight, which made living in the rougher areas more dangerous.

I stride up to the apartment door with a confidence I'm not feeling, and press the buzzer.

Nothing

No response.

No rustling.

No 'are you going to get that?'

Nothing but silence.

My sense of dread increases as I knock on the door, just in case the bell is broken.

Wishful thinking, Wyatt.

My gut's been screaming at me that something was wrong since the moment I woke up this morning. Those same instincts have kept me alive all these years. I take a look around me, there aren't a lot of people around at this time of the morning, and if they're awake, they're face down in caffeine, too much in a hurry to worry about little old me. It doesn't take much to force the lock, and within a few minutes I'm closing the door behind me.

When something dies, it leaves an aura. It's not a smell per se, after all, decomposition takes a while before odours are noticeable. It's not your sight which tells you you're in the presence of the dead. It's something more than that. Something which makes your hair stand on end, and goosebumps break out over your skin. It's as if ghostly fingers are trying to turn you away, protecting the victims dignity, or protecting the poor soul who stumbles over them. I've never been able to tell which it is. But standing there in the hallway, I know what I'm going to find. My skin prickles, death and violence lingers in the air. You can almost hear the whispered screams still echoing, or maybe it's just my guilt, as I take that first step into a fresh Hell.

"Hello? Police, I'm coming in," I announce loudly. My voice echoes back to me almost mockingly.

"Paul? Are you here, buddy?" I ask the silence, straining to hear anything, the slightest creak of a floorboard, the rustle of clothing, even a pained moan signalling life.

Nothing.

I make my way up the stairs, gun drawn. I'm pretty sure whoever was here is long gone, but you can never be too careful.

I'm already mentally prepared to walk into a murder scene, but I still fight the urge to hurl when I see them. Sitting side by side they would have looked like friends just enjoying a show on the television. But the illusion is shattered as I look at their faces, faces contorted into masks of pain. I can't even remember the names of Paul's flatmates, but I force myself to look at them, so I'll never forget their tortured expressions.

It's all your fault . . .

If you'd just listened to Kaiden . . .

You just had to push . . .

They're dead because of you.

It's my fault, that's undeniable. I brought a monster to their door all under the premise of doing the right thing. I might as well have slit their throats myself.

It would've been fucking kinder.

The one with the dark hair, has had his ears cut off. His eyes are frozen with terror, his jaw hanging open on a silent, never-ending scream. His hands are bound behind him, like the others. Nails through their feet to hold them all in the perfect position. The other flatmate had his eyes removed. Maria's empty eyes flash through my mind as I try to battle my emotions. Finally my eyes rest on Paul.

Good old Paul, who just wanted to help.

Paul's jaw is hanging open at an odd angle. There's nothing but a congealed blood pool which had settled behind his teeth.His tongue is missing.

Hear no evil.

See no evil.

Speak no evil.

It's a message if I ever did see one.

Fucking Keith Ryker.

It had to be him.

If he thinks he can get me to back down, he has another thing coming. But he's made me realise something very important. I was the only one concerned with rules, with what's right and wrong. It's time for me to throw the fucking rule book away. If he wants to play dirty, I have to do the same. An eye for an eye, an ear for an ear, and a tongue for a tongue. Every drop of blood he's spilled, I'll carve it from his flesh until his victims are satisfied. He will regret doing this. I'll make sure of it. I might be a dead man walking at this point, there's no way he doesn't know of my involvement, it was just a matter of time. But being a dead man has its advantages, a walking corpse has nothing left to lose. I'll take down as many people as fucking possible, clearing a path for Kaiden.

Hopefully, a path to Nyx.

My heart stutters thinking of her. Fate was a cruel mistress, giving me a taste of fatherhood, a glimpse of what life could've been like, and now I won't be there. I won't be able to protect her.

If she's even alive.

If she's dead, at least she won't be lonely for long. If she's alive, Kaiden won't stop, he'll protect her with his life.

Even if I don't actually like the kid.

Who was I kidding? As long as he dropped the father-in-law shit, he's just about tolerable.

All I want is her happiness.

First things first, I need to get to the station. I have a bullet with Collins' name on it. Paul and his friends are dead, all to protect that slimy fuckweed. But nothing will protect him from me.

I holster my weapon and have a quick look around the apartment for the recording or any trace of the story we'd been planning, but whoever did this hit was thorough. There isn't a trace left.

With a final whispered farewell to Paul, and a quick prayer that Maria watch over his soul, I leave the apartment, closing the door behind me.

I place an anonymous call to the station, reporting the bodies, before I slide back behind the wheel of my car, and pull into the rapidly growing traffic.

CHAPTER FOURTEEN

It's taken a bit of convincing but we've managed to get on the same page. We need to work with Kaiden and Jason, the five of us together, to take down Keith. If we don't know what they're doing, it's possible we could get in the way of each other, and the slimy sack of shit Keith Ryker is, could just slip through the cracks. Plus, leaving Kaiden and Jason in the dark about what happened is wrong, they have just as much of a right to justice as we do, and without knowing we're okay I fear they'll do something unpredictable, and reckless.

The Detective might seem level headed, but I've seen it. The darkness. I mean, there's no love loss between him and Creed, but he's my father. It has to count for something. I imagine he's looking for me, if only for Maria's sake.

So the plan is to go to the safe house Creed's told us about, where Kaiden should be expecting us, and use it as an information drop off. Fill him in with what we've learned and leave some proof of life.

"I want to come too," I whine.

"No way, Princess, we don't know what we could be walking into," Creed tries to reason.

"You were shot, at this point I'm probably more useful than you, or are you forgetting who helped drag your unconscious ass here?" I argue

"You were fucking lucky, and you know it," he snaps

"So were you. You egotistical fuckwit."

There's no way I can let him out of my sight. The gunshot still haunts me, the sound echoes every time I close my eyes.

"If anything happens to you I—" Creed murmurs, and for a split second a haunted look passes over his eyes before it disappears just as quick.

"You'd what?" I snap, pushing him.

"I'd . . . I mean Kaiden would kill me."

Kaiden this, Kaiden that.

"Kaiden's not fucking here, so stop hiding behind that as an excuse. I'm not a quiet little doll you can just pop back in the box when it suits. I'm just as much a part of this as you are."

"I can't even deal with you, do you not understand the danger we're in?" he snaps, like a parent losing his temper with a child.

My blood turns to ice in my veins.

"How fucking dare you? Of course I fucking do," I snarl.

"So why—?"

"Because I have to."

"Bollocks, you don't need to play the hero, Princess."

Is that what he thinks? That I have some sort of weird hero complex?

"I can't just stay here, waiting. I can't just sit on my hands and let you guys go into danger. I can't just do nothing."

"You can guard the house."

Guard the house?

Guard the fucking . . .

He didn't just . . .

Fuck. Him.

"DON'T FUCKING CODDLE ME!" I scream, my hand curling into a fist, my nails digging into my palm. "I can't be useless while people I care about are in danger, I'd rather die than be the only one left again. I can't . . . I can't do it. I won't."

"Nothing's going to—" Creed tries to reason but Kaleb cuts him off.

"Enough." That one word carries weight. Our attention snaps to the previously silent shadow in the corner.

The fire in his eyes was capable of burning the world to ash. My heart's already pounding but that look changes my rage into something 'other'. It calls to my bloodlust, but calms me. I'm still angry, but it curls around me like a snake, waiting, but still hungry, ready to strike. It makes me feel powerful, in control.

Kaleb tilts his head at me, assessing my stance, his eyes trail down my body, before resting on my hands. He pushes off of the wall, where he'd been leaning and stalks over to me, bringing my clenched hand up between us. Gently he prises my nails from my palm, and I wince a little at the sharp sting. I hadn't even realised how hard I was squeezing.

Kaleb runs his thumb over the broken skin, smearing the small amount of blood away. He slowly brings his thumb to his lips, and runs his tongue over the evidence, erasing the last traces of blood, all while keeping eye contact. Heat flushes through my body, one swipe of his tongue is enough to summon all sorts of images in my head. The type of scenes you only find in the most delicious of books.

I snatch my hand away as Creed mutters something behind me.

"She's coming with us," Kaleb orders, no reasoning, no explanations.

"What? You can't be serious?" Creed starts to argue as I turn to face him, a smug look plastered on my face.

"Two to one asshole, I'm coming." But it's too early for any real victory.

"On two conditions," Kaleb adds.

Oh shit.

I turn back to look at him, ready to argue my case.

"If you want to come, Kitten, you have to take orders."

I nod. I need to be a part of this so badly, I'm willing to do practically anything, including as I was told.

Within reason.

"Two," he continues, holding up two fingers. "You need to learn how to look after yourself."

I scoff.

"I can look after myself just fine." Now it was Creed's turn to scoff, so I whip my eyes to him and level him with a glare.

"Well you'll have no problems proving it then, will you?" he challenges, drawing my attention back to him. He sports a mischievous glint in his eye which spells trouble.

When Kaiden gets that glint it means danger, and I have a funny feeling whatever Kaleb has planned is going to hurt.

Oh shit.

I looked back at Creed, but he's wearing a smug look.

"Should've been careful what you wished for, Princess," he replies, before he follows Kaleb out of the room.

Me and my big fucking mouth.

It doesn't matter what they have planned, I'll do it. I'll prove myself. There's no other option. I have to go with them.

I follow them, somewhat reluctantly, back to the room I'd previously found Kaleb in the last time he stormed off. There was a lot more in here than I remember.

I mean, give a girl a break, I was a little distracted last time.

Along with the punching bag, there are various mats leaning against the walls, and a weight rack. Various bars and other gym equipment. It stinks of testosterone, and male anger. It's time for this so-called 'Kitten' to sharpen her claws.

"So, what do you want to see?" I say cockily, striding over to the weights and sizing them up.

They looked a lot smaller from across the room, up close they look like weapons of mass destruction. I wrap a hand around the smallest one, hoping that carrying drinks in the club had made me stronger than I thought.

Surprise surprise, I'm not.

Creed's chuckle pisses me right off as I wrap both of my hands around the weight in question.

Stupid fucking thing.

"No, Kitten," Kaleb puts his hand over mine, encouraging me to give up the weight. The relief I feel is immediate, the fear of embarrassing myself ebbs away. "You won't have to fight many of those off."

"Wait, what?" *What the hell did that mean?*

A sinister smirk twists his lips, Creed chuckles as he starts throwing mats to the floor.

"Simple, you have to fight us off," Kaleb states, replacing the weight back on the rack.

"Us? You mean both of you?" I spin around waiting for Creed to let me in on the joke.

They can't be serious.

"Well we ain't going to a tea party, Princess. I doubt they'll line up politely if they're going to attack you," Creed teases.

"That's not fair," I start to argue.

"Suck it up, buttercup, if life was fair we wouldn't even be in this position in the first place," Creed replies.

"I think I liked it better when you two didn't agree on anything," I mutter under my breath.

"Heard that," Creed chirps, throwing the last mat down on the floor.

"It's okay, Kitten," Kaleb's breath tickles my ear, "I know you can take it."

I whip around at his words, goosebumps breaking out over my skin. His smirk proves he knows just where my head went with those words.

I shake my head, reminding myself why I'm doing this. *Kaiden.*

He's in danger.

He needs to know we're safe, well maybe not safe, but alive at least.

I need to warn him about his dad.

I'm doing this for Kaiden.

I glare at Kaleb, knowing the game he's playing, but there's no way in hell. He might look like Kaiden but that's where the similarities end.

"So how is this going to work, are you just going to attack me or . . .?" I ask, kind of curious about what they have planned.

I'd taken a few womens lessons as part of the whole 'reclaiming your power' thing we had going on at Haven, but it was more dancerise than anything remotely fucking useful.

Kaleb lets out a low growl and his eyes harden.

"Oi, Kaleb. How about we give the Princess a demonstration first?" Creed challenges, a hint of malice in his eyes. A slow sinister smirk twists Kaleb's face into something frightening.

"Oh, meerkat, you have no idea how much of a bad idea that is."

"Come on, I promise to take it easy on you," Creed teases.

Fuck.

Someone is going to die.

"You have no idea how many times you've almost become roadkill, do you?" Kaleb warns.

"Kill, smill . . . We doing this or not?" Creed crosses his arms, looking bored.

131

"Look, I'm with Kaleb, I don't think this is a good idea, Creed."

"Kitten, I never said it wasn't a good idea, I just need him to know what he's signing up for. I don't need him bitching when his lady friends won't go near him after I rearrange his face."

Creed chuckles.

"There's nothing you can do to me that will keep the ladies away."

"Sure about that? I'm pretty sure the smell of your rotting corpse would have them fleeing," Kaleb snarls, curling his fingers to make a fist.

"If you have a chance with the ladies, then I'm sure smell isn't a problem." Creed jibbed back.

Children, a bunch of fucking children.

Kaleb launches himself at Creed and I stand back to watch my 'lesson'. Maybe after Creed has the snot beaten out of him it will temper some of his ridiculous ego. I have no idea what the hell he's been playing at but if this is what he needs to do . . .

I cringe as Kaleb's fist connects with Creed's jaw, which causes him to laugh. Creed is actually loving this, he isn't angry, or anything else logical. He just has this manic desperation about him as he throws a punch back. Kaleb grins, looking just as deranged with a bloody smile. They're not holding back at all.

I can't watch.

There's no lesson here, there's nothing but senseless violence.

They grapple with each other, each trying to seek the upper hand. The only thing that seems willing to give in, is the seams of their t-shirts as they claw at each other, pulling, pushing, doing anything to try and get the upper hand. Sizewise, Creed has the advantage, although Kaleb is strong and has raw power by the bucket load, Creed is just bigger. He is taller and built like a brick shit-house, he is fucking massive.

Both men are sporting bloody faces from busted lips, but most of the blows they're trading are aimed at the main body. Seems like apart from the first anger fueled punch, an almost gentleman's agreement has been reached. But it's still too much, we're meant to all be on the same side.

"Stop," I scream, "this isn't helping anyone."

Kaleb's attention snaps to me for a brief second, Creed takes the opening, snaking his foot behind his, causing Kaleb to topple with a crash. Creed instantly leaps on him and starts to rain punches down, all Kaleb can do is try to buck him off as he defends his face.

"Creed, what the fuck? Stop!" I demand, but it seems like he's already lost to me, it's like he's somewhere else entirely. Kaleb manages to get a sneaky shot to Creed's injured side, before bringing a foot up, and rolling them over.

"Give. Up," he snaps in Creed's face, but he still isn't listening.

It's almost like he's gone feral. Kaleb pins his arms under his knees but still he keeps trying to struggle on.

"No, keep going," Creed hisses through clenched teeth.

"No, you've lost," Kaleb replies, coolly.

"It's not over."

"Do you want to die? Is that it?" Kaleb studies him closely,

"No, I—"

"You what?"

"It's nothing man, just let me up."

"Not happening. You. What?" Kaleb challenges, repeating his question.

"Fuck you, man, I don't have to tell you shit."

"You're right, but you owe her an explation for whatever the fuck that was about," Kaleb replies, nodding towards me.

I didn't realise but my cheeks are wet, as Creed's eyes meet mine. I hastily wipe them away. I don't even know why I'm crying, but seeing the pain Creed's carrying, it feels familiar. It's the same manic desperation I felt when I first woke up and realised everything had been taken from me.

"Oh, Princess, I'm sorry," Creed sighs. "Let me up, let me go to her."

Kaleb's grip tightens on Creed as his eyes search mine. I have no idea what he sees but he releases him, before stalking over to the bag and wailing on it.

Creed gets up off the floor, and brushes the non-existent dirt off his knees before making his way over to me. He briefly looks over towards Kaleb before sliding his arms around me, pressing a kiss to my forehead.

"I'm really sorry, I never want to make you cry."

"I'm okay," I reassure him. "I just . . . what was all that about?"

Creed sighs, squeezing me tightly.

"Honestly?"

I nod.

"I don't really know, just thinking about the mansion, and Keith, and how things could have gone so much differently . . . I just feel like I could've done more, like I should've done more . . . I could've lost you, I mean, anything happens to you and Kaiden wouldn't be the same again. I've seen it, you are perfect for him, I saw it from the moment you came crashing into our lives. You woke up parts of him, made him feel again, he's turning into the brother I remember more and more every day. You have no idea just how much you saved him. He's never going to forgive me. I let him down, I let you down . . ."

I put a hand over his mouth, cutting him off entirely as his eyes widen with surprise for a moment.

"Stop. I know you've always played the fool, but I didn't realise just how much of an idiot you truly are. You haven't let anyone down . . ."

"Mhmmm," Creed tries to argue into my hand.

"No, you're going to shut up, and fucking listen to me," I snap.

I feel Creed smile against my hand, his eyes sparkling. I wait for just a moment, waiting for more interruptions. When he remains silent, I continue.

"You have not let anyone down. If not for you, I wouldn't have left that room alive. I don't doubt you've always had Kaiden's back. Just seeing you face danger for him, I mean you ran into a building with unknown armed people, just because Kaiden was in there. When you care about someone, you fight for them, you protect them. People might see you as some blunt force, or just a meathead. But I see you, Creed. You haven't let anyone down, you'd die before you do. It's just who you are, you're a protector, a guardian, someone I can rely on without question. But . . . And you better be fucking listening to me, Creed . . . If you ever pull some shit like that again, where you decide to argue with a fucking bullet, death will be the least of your worries. You hear me?"

He slowly nods against my hand, and I move it away. I've finished saying what I needed to say, I just hope he's truly heard me.

"Good."

I step out of Creed's embrace and notice the blood on his shirt.

"Your stitches," I exclaim, lifting his ruined shirt for a better look. At my cry Kaleb stops hammering on the bag and walks back over.

"What have you done now, idiot?" Kaleb snaps, moving me to one side and taking a look at them.

"Well if someone didn't throw a cheap shot, it would have been fine," Creed snarls back.

"Kitten, go get the supplies from the basement so we can put humpty dumpty back together again will you?" Kaleb asks.

"Sure." I reply and run out of the room, to go find them.

On my return I hear murmured voices so I stop, curious as to what they talk about when I'm not there. Honestly, I'm surprised they can actually be civil with each other for the couple of minutes it took for me to go on a supply run.

"If you ever make her cry again . . ." Kaleb threatens.

"Trust me, if you don't dismember me, I'll do it myself. I never wanted to upset her," Creed replies.

"You'd have more than dismemberment to worry about," Kaleb grumbles.

Seems they have a unique version of civil, maybe death threats are their love language.

I chuckle at my own musings, meaning I'm also busted.

"Took you long enough, Princess. Kaleb was just telling me how we should get matching best friend necklaces, and . . . OW! What the fuck man?"

"Oops, finger slipped," Kaleb replies, wiping the blood from his hand onto his ruined t-shirt.

"Slipped? Sure, it did. Just as you clearly want to slip into ah—" Creed's sentence was cut off as Kaleb's hand fastens around his throat.

"Necklace, you say, yes, very pretty. Maybe it's a little bit too loose though. Easily fixable," Kaleb growls deep and low.

I rest my hand on his arm to separate them both.

"Here, the supplies," I offer.

Kaleb grunts, but takes the supplies off me, before rummaging through to find what he needs to fix up Creed.

"I've been thinking," I hesitantly say, "You two need a babysitter, as much as you want to keep me at home, if I stay here only one of you will be coming back. You guys need me."

"No idea what you mean, Princess, we're grown adults, we can play nice when it counts," Creed replies, trying to shut me down again.

"For some reason I don't believe you, I'm coming whether you like it or not." I'm not going to give up and just sit pretty, it's not the type of person I am.

"You can't even shoot," Creed challenges. "You can't watch our backs, you'll just distract us. I know you mean well but—"

"So teach me then." I demand.

"You can't just become an expert overnight," Creed argues.

"Maybe not, but I'm not trying to be the best marksman. If someone is coming at me I doubt even a toddler can miss at point blank range." I cross my arms, there's no changing my mind.

"I'll teach you to shoot," Kaleb agrees, much to Creed's annoyance. "You're right, without a constant reminder to not kill him, the temptation would probably be too great. Fuck knows how you've survived this long." Kaleb aims the last bit to Creed.

In response Creed just blows him a kiss.

"Love you too, baby boy." Creed smirks.

Kaleb growls, his hands forming a fist.

"Okay, let's go." I quickly put myself between them, putting my hand over Kalebs fist to try and curb his anger.

One of these days Creed is going to piss off the wrong person. He just can't leave anything alone, can he?

CHAPTER FIFTEEN

I stroll into the mansion, my shirt itchy against my skin.

Dried blood does that.

The shirt's completely ruined, but working out some of my issues has made me feel more grounded. I'm still fraying at the edges, but the blood sacrifice has made the day more tolerable. I'd been right, Collins is a screamer, I haven't even asked him any questions yet . . . I just tenderised him. Soon I will find out what happened to Nyx and Creed, but I need to get a grip on my anger first. I'll never get answers if I kill him but there's something about him that just pisses me off.

My main priority right now is to get Jason with the programme. I thought with Nyx being missing he'd be more . . . Ruthless. I know he has it in him, I've seen his anger, the twisted hunger for revenge eating away at him. He knows what's at stake. But yet he still clings to his ideals like some naive wretch. It's pathetic, and we don't have time for it. He needs to get with the fucking program, we need action, but I know if I push him too hard it'll backfire. I need him to willingly come to me, embrace the path that we need to walk, in order to win.

I gave him twenty four hours, time we can't really afford to waste, because I need time to think, I need to regain my composure a little bit. I can't have Jason doubting me, not now. I've realised what needs to happen. I've always known I'll be the one to kill my father, but if I don't take out the people who support him first, there'll be too much resistance during my takeover. The rivers will run red overnight, it'll be a civil war on the streets, and there are too many powerful forces waiting for such a weakness. Forces which won't hesitate to swoop in and claim Blight for their own.

As I head to grab a shower I pass my fathers study.

"Son," he calls out to me. One word and my skin crawls. The constant reminder of our shared blood makes me sick. I pause to take a deep breath, trying to compose myself and hide the disdain on my face.

"Yes, Father?" I call out, sticking my head into his office.

He has the phone pressed to his ear, clearly in the middle of something. He slowly looks me up and down, noticing the way I'm perfectly dressed, the impeccable image he demands from me. His eyes settle on the red stain across my chest, the rise of an eyebrow is the closest thing he shows to emotion.

"One second," he says into the mouthpiece before pressing the mute button, "Oh, pray tell, who was unfortunate enough to get on your bad side," he asks, his eyes sparkling with excitement.

"Someone who thought he was untouchable, he now knows otherwise." I shrug, hoping my vagueness isn't noticeable.

"Tut tut, my boy. You mean to tell me they're still alive? I thought I taught you better than that."

Oh you taught me plenty alright.

"I haven't finished and sometimes you just can't rush these things."

"Mhmm" Keith Ryker replies, his eyes glazing over with memory. "My apologies, son, you are right sometimes it is a good thing to take your time." He smirks, as if we are sharing a private joke and it makes me want to rip his face off.

Of course he'd think it's a girl.

I fight to keep the disgust off my face, instead I try to imagine all the things I want to do to Collins. All the different ways I can make him squeal for mercy. Mercy he wouldn't be getting.

"They make the prettiest screams, but I doubt they'd be able to handle you, Father."

It's true, Collins squeals are oh so satisfying.

I let my mask fall away, my emotions showing on my face, the cruelness, the hate, the enjoyment I felt as his cries echoed around the small space.

"Hmm, you are probably right. Your street trash is just that, disgusting cretins. I suppose I should just be thankful you clear it up. Makes the real prizes easier to spot. Talking of prizes, that Nyx girl . . ."

My body tenses at the mention of her name, and I feel his eyes on me like a sniper's scope.

"I believe you called her Creed's whore?" I try to keep my voice steady, emotionless, but it trembles ever so slightly mentioning my brother's name.

"Yes, shame really. Well, it appears she's a wild one, keep your eyes open for her, will you?"

"Of course, Father."

"The things I will do to her." He smiles cruelly, daydreaming of things I dread to think, "If she survives, I know a few people interested in such a commodity. People with deep pockets."

"You plan to sell her? To whom?"

His eyes narrow on me, and I instantly know I have fucked up.

"Are you questioning me, boy?" His tone sounds almost reasonable but that was when he's the most deadly.

"No, Father, I'm sorry, Father," I reply, trying to look meek and unthreatening. It's almost impossible when my body is coiled tighter than a rattlesnake ready to strike.

"Sit." He gestures to the chair opposite him, as he sits lording behind his desk. He picks his phone and unmutes it, bringing it back to his ear.

I sink into the chair, trying to avoid eye contact so I don't antagonise him further, but I can feel his eyes boring a hole on the side of my face.

"Sorry about that, kids." he says with a chuckle.

I have no idea who's on the other end of the line.

"You said it was done? Jolly good . . . Three of them? Huh, that was more than we discussed, but as long as the story dies, what's a couple more?" He pauses listening to the response before he laughs loudly, "that is genius. The three monkeys, hahaha. Hear, see, and speak . . . No, yeah I get it," he pauses again, his previous amusement disappearing as quickly as it came. "I said, I got it," he snaps, "I will wire you the rest of the amount, as agreed. Don't leave town yet. I might have another job for you."

The last words are said for my benefit. I don't have to look up to know that if I don't impress him soon, the next job he'll give them would involve me. I can't afford any mistakes right now. Nyx is alive, my father confirmed it.

I just need to find her, before he can get his greedy paws on her.

I'll figure the rest out later.

My attention is drawn back to my father as he puts the phone down on the table.

"So, where were we? Oh yes. I believe you had questions?" He raises an eyebrow at me.

"No, Father, no questions. You lead, I follow," I repeat the words he'd carved into the inside of my skull.

"That's right. But I've noticed lately you've been forgetting that. It's almost like you've been having ideas. Now why would you go and do something so dangerous?" If you didn't know any better you would think he's just being a concerned parent. The way he's rolling up his shirt sleeves told an entirely different story. Less fairytale, more nightmare. I know there's no winning when he's like this, any answer I give him will be the wrong one so I opt for silence.

He prowls around the desk before coming to stand before me, leaning back, his arms crossed over his chest. *The perfect position to look down on me.*

I fight the urge to stand up, I'm not a boy anymore, I'm a fully grown man. I matched his height, so he only gets these chances while I'm sitting. I don't need to look down on him though, I already know I'm better. More than he could hope to be. I despise him from the very depths of my soul. It doesn't stop me from flinching when my father raises his hand.

He reaches for the intercom, and as the line connects, I scold myself for my weakness.

"Sebastian, bring in our guests, please."

My head snaps up at the word guests, and my eyes meet his smug self-satisfied smirk. He saw my flinch, my weakness, and I fucking hate myself.

"You fuck this up, boy, and you will not be leaving this room alive, I don't give a shit who you are. Understood?" he hisses, his eyes going to the door.

Now I'm just fucking confused. Here I am in a blood soaked shirt, and my father deems this is a good time for guests. He genuinely seems worried. I don't think I've ever seen him worried before. Who could possibly have this effect on him? My curiosity is piqued.

Just who is it?

The door opens inwards and in steps a very regal looking gentleman. I automatically feel defensive. No matter how gentlemanly he might look, there is no way anyone who is visiting my father can be considered good.

The playing board just got a little bit more complicated.

"Deus Jula, I'm so glad you could make it." My father practically fawns over him. My skin crawls, my father doesn't fawn over anyone.

Just what the fuck had he gotten us into this time?

The man in question just grunts, and shakes my father off like an unwanted gnat. He casts his eyes around the room, an obvious look of disgust on his face. Eventually his eyes settled on me. I'm held captive in his gaze, this is a true predator. For the first time in my life I didn't feel like the big fish in the little pond, and I don't fucking like it.

"This him?" he asks my father, as if I wasn't even in the room.

"Yes, yes. Stand up boy, make the gentleman feel welcome." It's like my father has undergone a complete personality transplant, "Yes, Deus, this is my first born son. Strong, ruthless, and . . ." He chuckles, "no stranger to getting his hands dirty, as you can see. Kaiden is a fine boy, my pride and joy."

Has hell frozen over?

Was this one of the signs of the apocalypse?

Maybe I was just having some sort of hallucinating stroke, is that a thing? I feel like it could be a thing.

I spot a dainty little thing, hidden almost entirely by the Deus's shadow. This is a fucking meat auction and I'm the poor sod on the chopping block.

"He doesn't look like much," the Deus states, his eyes roaming over me like a pig at the market.

My eyes snap back to his, I can't disguise the anger in my gaze, but I hold myself back from saying anything, barely. I can't afford to mess this up, I just have to get out of here as quickly as humanly possible. Nyx needs me.

"Maybe I was wrong," the Deus chuckles, "he's smarter than he looks. What do you think, my dove?"

The woman steps out from behind him and I finally manage to take a good look at her. Dove was an apt nickname for her, bright blue eyes, white blond hair, pale skin, she looked almost statuesque. Fragile, breakable. She peeks shyly up at me, studying me through her long lashes. I see the corner of her lips curl into a twisted, predatory smirk, before she quickly resumes her meek demeanour.

"Whatever you wish for, Father. If this is the future of the Jula clan, then it is my duty as first born to see that your wishes are fulfilled," she replies. Her voice was almost musical, a whisper of gentle soothing tones.

No fucking way!

"Was this the one you wanted, or not?" he snaps at her. "Women," he adds under his breath, looking at my father.

"He is," the strange woman replies.

Fuck. No.

She walks towards me, and her mask drops with every step. This woman is a fucking snake, prone to strangling men in their sleep. At least if my Wildcat strangles me there'd be some fun punishments we'd both enjoy, but there'd be none of that with this viper.

"Hello," she says, in that innocent tone of hers. It's completely at odds with the twisted, cruel smile she wears. "I've heard so many things. Your coldness, your . . ." she rests her hand on my abdomen, "appetites." She gives me a flirty smile, "and of course, your brutality." Her fingers run over the dried blood. I want to push her away, but I can't, not without angering her father.

"Yes, I've thought about you a lot." She leans towards me, as our fathers talk, getting uncomfortably close. "I can't wait to impale myself on your cock and drain you for all your worth," she whispers in my ear, before pulling away. Her hands are still dancing over my abs.

Her hand starts to reach lower and there's nothing I can do. If I spurn her I might as well just kill myself, as there'd be no getting out of this room alive. Who'd save Nyx then? No. I need to stay calm.

Nyx. Nyx. Nyx.

I repeat her name as a mantra in my head, picturing her smiling, teasing face. Her beautiful eyes, so full of warmth and life. The way her hair felt in my fingers.

"Nice to meet you, too," the woman murmurs, eyes focusing on my tightening trousers. If she thinks my reaction has anything to do with her, she's fucking delusional. As her hand travels further, I look towards our fathers for some sort of help. It's not like they're going to let her just fuck me right here, right?

Please, no.

"Dovey, that's enough my sweet," her father coos, "you haven't even told him your name."

"Sorry, Daddy, you know what they say about early birds getting the worms." She giggles, and it takes all my effort not to be sick.

This cannot be happening.

"Enough, Dove. You are a lady," the Deus shouts, causing my dad, and the woman in front of me, to flinch.

"Yes, Daddy, I'm sorry, Daddy." Her weak demeanour is back, her eyes firmly glued to the floor. She walks off to rejoin her father, in the same position I first saw her. I try to breathe a sigh of relief but the toxic plume of fragrance she's left in her wake is suffocating.

"It seems we have a deal, Keith." the Deus says.

All I can do is stand there in horror as I watch the shutters slam down on my life.

"The replacement men make up part of the dowry as agreed. If these ones all end up dead like the last, then there won't be any more. A leader knows when to sacrifice his men. How you managed to lose all of them in one hit on a club is embarrassing. As for the shipment we discussed, nine o'clock Friday, and everything better go smoothly. Think of it as an exercise to prove to me you are in fact as resourceful as you say you are." He sticks his hand out towards my father, who wipes his hand on his trousers before shaking the Deus's hand with both of his.

What.

The.

Fuck!

The club? Haven?

He was behind it?

He killed Maria?

Why?

Why would he organise a hit on our own club?

"Yes, sir, of course. You are so generous, Deus, we will not let you down."

"See to it that you don't. You know what happens to people who disappoint me."

My father lets out a squeak of pain as the Deus squeezes his fingers.

"Kaiden, wasn't it?" he asks, his attention turning back to me.

"Yes, sir," I reply, trying to keep my voice strong.

"You hurt my daughter, and there will not be any part of your skin not screaming in agony, no bone in your body unbroken, and yet you will be kept alive. And that will just be the start of it. Consider yourself warned."

My blood turns cold,

He means every single fucking word.

I am so fucked.

Without so much as a backward glance he leaves, taking his *precious* daughter with him.

Precious, my ass, she's more like a psychotic gremlin. Which fucker fed her after midnight?

"Well that was intense," My father says cheerfully, rubbing his hands together in glee, before taking a seat at his desk.

I just sit back in the seat opposite, saying nothing.

What could I say?

"Seems you're good for something after all," my father drones on, oblivious to my seething. Too lost in his latest victory to pay attention to me.

Just think about Nyx.

I have to find Nyx.

"Was that all you needed me for, father?" I ask, hesitantly.

"Actually," my father replies, grinning like the Cheshire cat, "there is one more thing I need you to do. That detective . . . The one who bailed you out."

"Detective Wyatt?"

"That's the one, well it seems he's been causing waves. I need you to see to it that those waves stop. He's clearly vying for the Captain's spot and that would cause me nothing but headaches."

"What do you want me to do?"

"Urgh, I have to think for you now, do I? Useless. I don't care what you do, as long as the breath leaves his body, and he can't be a nuisance to me any longer."

"You want him dead?"

Keith smiles a cruel smile.

"Now I never said that, did I?"

Yeah, he never actually gives me orders to kill, not when he doesn't trust me, but I know what he means.

"No, Father. I shall remove the problem."

I'm already thinking of ways I can convince him to hide, I mean he's already spending a lot of time at the safe house. It won't hurt for him to move in and quit his job to–

"I can see the cogs turning in that head of yours, boy. I know the detective was nice to you, he might have even helped you, but he is a tool. They are all tools. Nothing more."

"Of course, Father."

"Glad you see things my way, I don't need you going soft on me."

His face lights up with an idea, as he claps his hands together dramatically.

This wasn't going to be good.

"You can take your wedding gift with you, the men the Deus was kind enough to give us. Let them get a feel for how we operate, I've been assured of their bloodlust and cruelty, but you can never be too sure."

Fuck, babysitters.

I remember seeing the autopsy pictures of the thugs from Haven, at least now I know where they came from, and I finally know who was behind the hit. The only thing I don't know is why. It makes no sense why my father would do it. It makes us look weak, vulnerable.

So why? And who killed them all? It clearly wasn't my dad. He didn't want to upset whoever the fuck that was, the guy clearly wasn't pleased to find out his men had all perished.

"Actually, bring him to me alive."

"Alive?"

"Yes, what better way to prove our power over the newcomers than a hazing of blood? The *incorruptible detective*," he sneers, "he's the perfect warning for those who don't do as they are told." The last words are a hidden threat. One I hear loud and clear.

With my head swimming with questions I couldn't voice, I give my father an obedient head nod, and with a wave of his hand he dismisses me. How am I going to begin to untangle the mutant pretzel that's become my life?

One problem at a time. Firstly, how am I going to save the Detective? I can't let Nyx lose him when they only just found each other. The problem is, there doesn't seem to be a path to take where all of us will make it out of this alive. Nyx is Jason's priority, mine too. We'dl both give our lives for her. The big question was . . . Will we have to?

Chapter Sixteen

I storm into the station, the door slamming against the wall in my haste.

I don't care.

All I can see are the faces of Paul and his flatmates.

Why did they have to die?

Officers and detectives alike, jump out of my path. It isn't the first time I've been this angry, but this is the first time I truly have nothing left to lose. Maybe in the same way you can feel ghosts at a crime scene, you can also sense a dead man walking. No one meets my eyes, and the ones who accidentally catch my gaze wither and slink away.

With every step towards the Captain's office, my heart thuds louder and louder in my ears. I'd spent years always trying to do the right thing and look where it's gotten me. Why do the scum, the despicable lowlifes, the rotting infection strangling humanity, why do they all get to live? Why do they get to draw breath after oblivious breath? Why do they get to continue to pollute this town, and strangle it with their thorny vines? Why do they get to spread their corruption, their greed, and malice? Yet people, genuine people, the best of humanity, people like Maria who was an angel in human form, people like Paul who just wanted to tell the truth, they die.

They try to break them. They get up.

They see the darkness. They don't succumb.

They want to do the right thing despite the odds.

They are the people who deserve to live.

People like Keith Ryker, the Captain, the men behind the horrendous acts plastering the walls of the safe house. They don't deserve to be called human anymore, the self serving, corrupt, toxic scum.

It's only a matter of time before I'll be joining my love. I can feel it.

The tick-tock of my life running out with every beat of my heart.

But I'm not going down alone.

I kick the Captain's door in, drawing my gun.

This is for Paul.

This is for his flatmates.

This is for every innocent life that's been shattered to protect his ass.

I still my hand, mid draw.

Where is he?

The office is completely empty.

I look down to check my watch. It's late morning, even Collins would have dragged his ass here by now.

"Anyone seen Collins?" I call out into the bullpen.

A chorus of 'nopes', and 'not todays' reach me.

"Not one of you knows where he might have gone?" I ask, annoyed.

How fucking lucky can one piece of shit be?

"Saw him run out of here, keys in hand. Looked like he was in a rush," one of the uniformed officers chirps up.

Finally, at least someone has a set of fucking eyes around here.

"Any idea where he went?"

"I don't know, sir. Sorry." With a final shrug the officer walks off to resume his duties.

I let out an exaggerated sigh, there isn't really much I can do just hanging around in his office like this. The police station is one of the safest places for me, at least for now, so I decide I can give Kaiden another hour to get in touch before I go in search of the Captain myself. I'll spend the time in my office, compiling as many of my findings as possible and getting my affairs in order. You never know, someone, somewhere might be able to take my notes and finish what I've started.

I look up at the clock in my office.

One hour.

Sitting behind my desk I look around the small space. This office had been the one thing I used to be weirdly proud of. We don't have a Sergeant in this precinct. The last one had been shot and killed over eight years ago and never replaced, which meant I made the office my own. No one had complained when I just moved in.

I'd gotten sick to death of the other Detectives in the bullpen, all of their joking, lacklustre performances; they all lacked ambition, hell most of them were missing basic fucking empathy. They'd probably cheered when I left them to their own devices. Without me there, they were free to do as they wished without me constantly looking over their shoulder.

I sigh.

I just hope whoever follows in my footsteps, will try and make this town just a little bit better. That'll be enough for me.

I opened my top drawer to start putting my things in order, but instead of my normal supplies, resting on top of them was a small box. No bigger than the palm of my hand.

Bomb?

I hold my breath for a moment, waiting for a telltale click, or something to warn me the trap has been triggered, but as I sit there staring at the box . . . nothing happens.

What the hell?

I study it, refusing to pick it up at first. I can't see any obvious signs of booby traps, still, it seems way too suspicious to let down my guard.

Maybe it's Nyx reaching out, sending a message, the gift box idea would have probably been something Creed would do to fuck with me. I half expect his laughter behind me, as he teases me for being a paranoid old man.

Gingerly, I pick up the box, it's light, probably no more than a couple of hundred grams, which isn't surprising given its size.

I untie the red ribbon, and let it fall to the floor.

Slowly I open the lid. What I see inside horrifies me.

Shutting my eyes does nothing to erase the image from my mind.

A set of bloody, sawn off ears.

A set of milky, lifeless eyes.

And a hunk of meat I can only presume was once Paul's tongue.

Once I control the bile trying to squeeze its way up my throat I spring into action.

He was here.

"Guys," I bellow at the top of my lungs, "Get in here quick."

My words are met with a stampede of feet. The uniformed officer I spoke to before is the first through the door.

"Lock down the station, no one in or out. I want my office and this box dusted for prints, the ribbon too. I want DNA tests run on the contents of the box, and I want it all done yesterday," I shout, placing the box down carefully on my desk.

Why do they always seem one fucking step ahead of me?

If I just came straight here this morning I might have been able to catch them in the act.

The fact they sent me the parts means they're done being subtle. The threat is clear. I'm next, and there's no place, in Blight or outside it, I'll be safe.

The station comes alive around me, responding to my orders. Even if they're completely useless and lazy, the idea of their home being infiltrated infuriates them, just as much as it does me. How can the power of the badge fuel their inflated egos, and sense of self importance, if someone can just walk in, and shit all over the station?

I walk outside to go phone Kaiden. I have to at least tell him what's going on, even if there's no saving me. My death is going to mean something, even if I have to make a deal with the son of the devil.

This time he actually picks up.

"Detective, you must be in some serious trouble to be calling me."

"You could say that," I reply, not entirely sure what to say next, "look, I messed up, okay? I don't need you to gloat, but I could do with your help."

"Say no more, what are friends for, meet at the safe house?"

"I'll be there in about thirty minutes, I just need to deal with the situation here first."

"Perfect," Kaiden replies, before hanging up.

I stare at the phone for a little while.

That was . . . Odd.

No gloating?

No questions?

It was very unlike Kaiden.

I don't know him well, but my gut twists. Something isn't right. We aren't close, but since the arrest warrant, I was under the impression things between us had changed. At least a little bit. That phone call was systematic, methodical. It's the Kaiden who stood in his kitchen, his back turned to the lowly peasant who wasn't worth his time.

Something has happened.

I'm not sure what it is, but I feel like he's trying to warn me of something. We aren't friends. For him to call me a friend . . . Well, it's weird. It's the last thing he'd ever admit to. Still I have nowhere else to go, nowhere to run to, I'm going to head to the safe house. If I'm going to die today, I'll go down swinging.

Chapter Seventeen

Adrenaline courses through my veins as I watch him.

Kaiden is pacing outside of the safehouse Creed had told us about, but something isn't right. Massive thugs surround the building like buzzing flies. I know Kaiden has people at his beck and call, all sorts of unsavoury types, but Creed doesn't recognise any of the faces, and as his right hand man, he knows everyone. These guys are certainly not the type to be here selling cookies.

Just what are you up to?

I want to run up to him and throw my arms around him. The loneliness which surrounds him breaks my heart. Every sound causes his gaze to whip up, eyes narrowed. He's suspicious of everyone around him, totally on edge.

Even from here I can tell he hasn't been sleeping well, his hair is a little bit more raggedy than normal, that unkempt look you only get when you've run your hands through it more times than you should.

It's seeing him like this, without Creed, that makes me realise just how much they need each other. I study Creed, who's crouched next to me as Kaleb scouts the perimeter, any sign of his usual easy going smile is gone, his jaw is tense, and his forehead is wrinkled with worry.

"I should have reached out to him sooner," he whispers, "I thought he'd be okay."

Guilt floods his expression, and my heart breaks for him.

"He loves you like a brother, idiot, what did you expect?"

My question hangs between us, both of us knowing it needs no answer.

It doesn't matter. We'll be reunited soon enough. But one thing is clear, that whole one man army is a ruse. Kaiden feels deeper than anyone gives him credit for.

Lost in our thoughts, we don't hear the footsteps behind us until a hand falls on my shoulder. My entire body tenses, ready to let out a scream.

"It's okay, Kitten, it's just me."

I sigh in relief, spinning round to meet Kaleb's gaze.

"So?" Creed asks, skipping all small talk.

"There's five of them lurking around the outside, I can't get close enough to see how many are inside, but I saw movement. If I didn't know any better, I'd say it's an ambush."

"No, no way," Creed argues, "that's not how Kaiden plays, and there's no way he would bring so many men. None of this makes sense."

"It does if it was Keith's idea," I suggest.

"Kitten makes a good point, if, and that's a big if, Kaiden is actually working against our father like you claim. He could be getting suspicious after the incident at the house. If he knows you are alive, he knows his secrets are not going to be buried for long," Kaleb aims his words towards Creed.

"Well, what are we going to do?" I ask.

If he's ambushing someone it isn't like we can just walk up there. We have to play it smart.

"We go home. We are not prepared for this, we have no idea what kind of training those men have, and there's only the three of us. It's too risky," Kaleb answers.

I look at Creed, waiting for him to argue, make some sort of outburst, but he just watches Kaiden walk into the house.

"We can't just leave—" I start.

"We don't have a choice," Creed argues, "running in there now helps no one. Especially not Kaiden, we have to be smart about this. Covert."

"Covert? How can you say that? He needs to know we're okay, and if Kaleb is right about Keith fucking Ryker, he's in danger. We need to help him."

"How will it help him when he sees us mowed down in front of him, eh, Princess?"

"We could sneak up and surprise them, or—"

"Kitten, you are not listening to us." Kaleb tries to calm me down, but we are so fucking close.

He's right there . . .

"But we can't just leave." Even as I say the words the fight has left my voice. I know deep down they're right, but the idea of leaving him . . . I just can't do it.

"He'd understand, Princess. He wouldn't want you to be hurt."

"Okay," I mutter, defeated.

As Creed starts to pull me away, the sound of an engine comes hurtling down the street, faster than most would drive. My eyes are drawn to the vehicle as it gets closer.

A car I recognise.

A car I'd travelled in.

Jason's car.

No.

Not him.

Kaiden wouldn't . . .

I freeze.

Kaleb is the first to notice something is wrong.

"Shit," he mutters, looking at me with conflicted eyes.

"What's going— oh." Creed's eyes open wide with recognition.

"No. No. This isn't . . . He wouldn't . . ." I start to blubber.

It makes no sense, even if he was ordered to. He's . . . he's my dad. Kaiden, he . . . No. I just can't believe it. Kaiden wouldn't ambush my father.

"The extra man power makes sense now. This is Keith's doing. A power play."

"You're so sure, aren't you, so fucking sure the golden boy isn't a chip off the old block?" Kaleb sneers, disagreeing with Creed.

"Fuck you, he's like a brother to me," Creed snaps back.

Kaleb just laughs.

"Brother's don't mean shit," he replies, dismissively.

"You don't know him," I speak up.

"Oh, Kitten, and you think you do, after just a few days? Give me a break. You see what he wants you to see. He's a Ryker."

"Yeah? Well last time I checked, so are you, so how about you shut the fuck up?" I snap.

Kaleb just growls, low and menacing, clearly pissed off. *Yeah, well, get over it.*

"Whatever you think about Kaiden, we can't let Jason walk into a trap. He's my dad." The words sound alien on my tongue, but despite the awkwardness between us, I can't just stand by and watch him get hurt.

"If my twin is such a good guy, he probably has a plan, right?" Kaleb asks.

Me and Creed share a look, Kaiden was always a planner, but I really don't like the odds he's up against.

"Usually yes, but I don't know," Creed murmurs.

"You never liked Jason anyway," I snap, venom dripping from my words. Creed doesn't really deserve my anger, I'm just scared and really fucking sick to death of feeling so damn powerless all the time.

"That's not true, Princess. We had our differences sure, but–"

"Yeah yeah, that's great and everything. How about we work on his eulogy later, and figure this shit out now, yeah?" Kaleb points towards where Jason is getting out of the car.

I look back and forth between Kaleb and Creed, waiting, praying one of them will say something. Do something. Anything. Anytime now.

But they don't.

They sit there.

Waiting.

Watching

Every step Jason takes up that path, my heart thunders in my chest.

Every step draws him closer and closer to the trap.

No.

No.

I nudge Creed, but he doesn't break his gaze from Jason.

I turn to Kaleb, my eyes wide with panic.

Please.

I beg him.

Please.

He slowly shakes his head.

No.

"No," I whisper. "Not again."

Jason is at the door.

Hand raised, about to knock.

It's now or never.

Fine. If they won't do anything, I'll have to do it myself.

I push against Creed and Kaleb, sending them stumbling to regain their balance as they crouched.

"Kitten!"

"Princess!"

Their hissed words carry to me, the worry and panic in their tones might have caused me to hesitate once upon a time, but they had their chance, and they were just going to sit there. I have no idea what I'm going to do, no plan, no real reason for running into danger like this. I mean, I barely know the man, but I know in my heart of hearts I can't just sit back and watch. If anything happened . . . I'd never forgive myself.

As his knuckles come in contact with the door, his eyes are drawn to my movement. As his gaze snaps to mine it's like everything goes into slow motion. The pain in his eyes is so visceral, but the relief at seeing me, the way his lips strain to form a smile. The smile of a father welcoming me home ... Me ... A nobody ... But for just a second, I can tell, I'm his whole world, his family. My name is written on his heart just as surely as his name is on mine.

"Dad!" I call out, arms reaching, but I'm still too far away.

I wish for my words to carry to him, to let him know no matter what I'm here, that he is my family, that I don't care about the past, the secrets. We have a second chance, and I'm done wallowing in self pity. I'm done with the lies, it's time to start over.

The door swings inwards, more arms than humanly possible reach out, grabbing his arms, legs, anything that they can get a hold of.

No. Please, no.

I beg as I will my legs to run faster.

Please just let me make it.

Jason's smile never falters as he's pulled into the house, the door slamming shut behind him. The sound is so final, it causes a tear to fall down my cheek.

Hands wrap round my waist from behind.

A weight far greater than my own, tackles me to the floor.

I kick out, clawing at the hands holding me.

"We've got to stop meeting like this, Kitten."

"Let . . . Me . . . Go . . ." I huff out between breaths.

"Are you trying to get yourself killed?" he hisses in my ear, pulling me back towards our hiding place as if I weigh nothing at all.

"I have to—"

"You have to do what? Run in, force Kaiden to put a bullet in you? Or worse? What do you think those men would do to you? Remember Haven," he snaps.

The colour drains out of my face, and I lose my fight.

Haven.

The girls.

The sounds.

I instantly feel sick remembering the cries of my sisters, the sound of flesh against flesh, the whimpers of pain, and the sick laughter of delight at their terror.

"Yeah, I thought so," Kaleb mutters, depositing me into Creed's arms.

"I'm sorry," Creed murmurs against my hair. I don't need to look at him to know he's shooting daggers at Kaleb. "What he means to say is that we can't afford to lose you, we need to play this carefully."

"You mean you're going to help me?" I ask, wiping the moisture from my eyes, and looking up at him.

Creed smiles down at me, not his jokester playboy one, but a genuine smile. One that reassures me, reminds me I'm safe. That he'll protect me.

"For you, Princess, anything."

"And you?" I ask, levelling a glare at Kaleb.

"I might be a bloodthirsty monster, Kitten, but you hold my leash. All you ever need to do is ask," he replies with a shrug.

Chapter Eighteen

I have no plan.

No way out.

All I can do is watch Jason struggle as the men force him into the chair in the middle of the room. He looks around, taking note of our investigation, which now lies in tatters on the floor.

I expect to see betrayal in his eyes, some sort of accusation that I'm exactly what he always expected me to be, but instead he looks at me with an expression I can't place. His eyes keep trailing to the door.

If he's expecting freedom it's something I can't afford to give.

"I wish it didn't have to be this way." The words are out of my mouth before I can stop them. This wasn't the time for wishes, or empty platitudes.

This is it. The hard line. If I cross this, I know there will be no saving me, no redemption. Nyx could never forgive me.

Is it worth it?

"I don't care what happens to me, all I ask is for one thing," his voice carries an inner strength I'm not surprised to hear, even surrounded by thugs. It's in this situation, against the odds, I can see the family resemblance between him and Nyx.

Maybe they both have problems accepting the inevitable, or maybe they both just refuse to give in to fear.

"Ha, I don't think you are in a position to bargain, old man." One of the thugs laughs, back handing him across the face.

Jason spits out the blood from his mouth, but still the hatred I expect to see never enters his eyes.

"If I wanted to talk to a gorilla, I would have gone to see Creed, not some two-bit nobody with a face even a mother can't love." Jason chuckles, the darkness I'm all too familiar with flickering in his eyes.

"Why you—" the gorilla in question starts to round on Jason but he never flinches.

The sound of a gun cocking echoes around the room, and the gorilla freezes before slowly turning to face down the barrel of the gun I have pointed at him.

"Now, I can't remember giving the order to play with our guest. Does anyone want to correct me?" My voice is cold as ice, threatening, deadly. Just the way I fucking like it.

The silence is deafening. It's like the entire room is collectively holding its breath.

"No one has anything to say?"

I look at each of them, forcing every single one of them to shy away from my gaze.

Pathetic.

"Not one, single person? Huh. Weird. So why on Earth did you, a brainless hunk of meat, act on your own? Is that how the Jula family operates?"

"No sir, sorry sir," the gorilla replies.

He probably has a name, but he doesn't deserve for me to fucking learn it. He wasn't going to be staying long.

"Oh no, you don't get to call me sir. Sir is solely for my subordinates. It's a title of respect, which you clearly don't have."

"I'm sorry, sir, please, I'll do anything."

"Glad to hear it. You can die."

His eyes widen in horror as I squeeze the trigger.

For the first time, I see Jason flinch, as the contents of the gorilla's head spray over him. He scowls at me as if I did it on purpose, like I wasn't trying to save him from a beating or anything. He was acting as if I'd just woken up one day and thought red would suit him better.

He did say he didn't want to get his hands dirty, and now look at him.

"I believe you had one wish?" I say, trying to get us back on track. I have to keep the power in the room, I have no idea what kind of loyalty might be between the men.

"Well, now I want a fucking shower," he grumbles, unable to wipe the blood from his face.

"You disrespectful little . . . he was my brother."

Oh, here we go.

I can't hold back my eye roll as I turn to face him.

"Does stupid run in your family?" I ask, my tone leaving very little room for arguments. Not that he even tries, instead he charges me like an angry bull. I fire a warning shot into the floor in front of him, halting his progress as he glares at the gun in my hand.

If looks could kill, buddy, you might have stood a chance.

"Tut tut tut. You know, I'm very disappointed with you lot. Such attitude, such ego. You've not proven yourself enough to take such liberties with me. All of you on your knees. NOW!" I bark.

Reluctantly they fall to their knees one by one, but by the looks in their eyes their submission is a long way off. I have officially kicked the hornet's nest.

Fuck.

"I will give you one chance. Well not him." I level a glare at Mister he-was-my-brother, "you had a chance and set fire to it, along with the only fuck I may have actually given." I pull my attention from him and go back to addressing the room. "Rules are simple. No weapons, whoever brings me his heart gets a favour."

Might thin their numbers a little, while I have a chance to think.

"How do we know you'll keep your word?" one of the thugs pipes up. Once upon a time I would have admired his bravery, now I'm pretty sure it's just misplaced stupidity and he isn't in fact courageous at all. Wherever the Jula dragged these guys from, it must have involved the bottom of the rejects barrel and then some. Clearly they thought fucking little of us, if these are considered a *'gift'*.

I raise my eyebrow, and cross my arms, staring him down.

Three, two.

"Nevermind, sorry boss," he apologises, avoiding my gaze.

I didn't even get time to finish my countdown

"You have ten minutes, time starts now." I stand back and watch the chaos unfold for a moment, positioning myself as a shield in front of Jason. He might have seen the aftermath of violence, but he didn't need to see this level of cruelty.

After I'm sure they're all fully distracted, and making sufficient noise and won't overhear anything, I talk to Jason over my shoulder, never taking my eyes off the Jula men.

"I know you don't believe me, but I really didn't have a choice. I'm sorry. I'm working on a plan, I swear it, I—"

"That's not important. Nyx is outside."

I turn towards him.

"Really?" I couldn't believe it. All this time searching and she just turns up? "She was here? That mean's Creed has to be alive too . . ."

"Maybe, I mean I only saw her, but . . ." Jason replies.

An almighty crash sounds as the door is kicked in, a familiar silhouette framed in the doorway.

No fucking way.

Maybe all I needed to do was say his name three times to summon the dickhead.

The curved blades of his sparkly rainbow karambit knives catch the light as he dives into the fray, slicing up limbs and flesh alike with a maniacal laughter. The sound is contagious and I soon find myself laughing along with him. It doesn't take long for the mountain of meat to realise they have a traitor in their midst, and they turn away from their initial target. Soon a panting Creed is standing by my side, clutching his side with one hand, his remaining blade in the other.

The men seem to rally around one of the bigger ones, he has a slash across one eye, but it doesn't seem to bother him much as the blood runs down his face.

This guy's a fucking monster.

"Missing something?" He chuckles, twirling Creed's missing karambit in his hand.

"I don't think glitter suits you," Creed teases, causing the man to growl his frustration. He doesn't seem like he's the type to be challenged so openly.

"How about I sink it into your fucking eye and then the colour won't fucking matter."

"Or," Creed sounds as if he doesn't have a care in the world. I swear I watch as the big guy develops a complex on the spot, "You can hand Gertie back, before Bertie gets annoyed and seeks revenge."

"Who?" The big guy's clearly puzzled.

I half expect him to scratch his head like some sort of primate.

"Bertie," Creed says slowly pointing to the knife in his hand. "Gertie." He slowly moves his finger to point to the other blade. "They are a couple in love, and they really hate to be parted, you should have seen the wedding," Creed continues, talking his normal brand of nonsense, giving me time to think. "Stabbifer officiated. It was beautiful. I cried like a baby. Do you cry at weddings, big boy? I bet you do."

"ENOUGH!" the guy bellows, seething in anger, but Creed completely ignores him.

"Talking of Stabbifer, that old man better not have touched my bike," Creed threatens, it seems he doesn't have a problem getting shot but mess around with his bike and it's a completely different ballgame.

Guy has some fucked up priorities.

"It's safe," I assure him, "I had it moved, even if you were dead, like my father claimed, I knew you wouldn't want him touching your abomination."

"Aww, she's grown on you, hasn't she? Just admit it." Creed smirks.

"Fuck no, there was no body to burn so I was going to set fire to that instead." I smirk back, watching his eyes widen in horror.

"You would never," Creed hisses in outrage at the thought.

"Who knows? Probably best to let me know you're alive next time." I can't hold back the bitterness which laces my tone. There would be time to get the full story, but it wasn't now.

"As touching as this all is," the big guy sneers, "we fighting or what?"

What kind of leader asks for permission from his enemies, it's laughable.

The men around him are getting restless. We're blatantly disrespecting their nominated leader without so much as a single repercussion. It's subtle, but they've all started to slowly drift away from him.

It seems loyalty's a foreign concept to them.

The shift hasn't gone unnoticed by the big guy, the slightly panicked gleam in his eye is a dead giveaway.

Where has all that bravado gone now, fuckface?

"Oi, psycho, are you going to get your ass in here or are you going to let me have all the fun? I mean if you want me to wrap one up for you so he can't fight back then—" Creed shouts.

I have no idea who he's talking to, but if it gets us out of this situation I'm all for it.

Creed's new friend runs in through the broken door wearing a hood pulled over his head, making him look like the reaper himself has come to the party. At the arrival of the stranger the tedious stalemate breaks and chaos ensues.

CHAPTER NINETEEN

I live for the chaos, the feel of the knife through flesh, my knuckles scraping against teeth as I cave their faces in. A dark chuckle escapes my lips as red taints my vision. I weave in and out, hacking at flesh left right and centre, soon the meerkat hops back into the fray and I have to mind my blade.

Fighting alongside someone is weird, I'm not used to holding back, and being careful. Usually I can just let loose, give into the madness and bloodlust. These shackles, this restraint, it causes me to be sloppy. Having to be mindful of another slows me down, and I catch a fist to the stomach, robbing me of wind.

Shit.

Pain is my friend, and I push through it, but like sharks scenting blood in the water, my weakness hasn't gone unnoticed. As I gasp, forcing air into my lungs, one of the men turns on me. I'm too slow, my body refuses to cooperate as I struggle for air.

Fuck.

As I brace myself for the inevitable hit, a gunshot rings out and his face disappears.

"Pop goes the weasel!" I chuckle, my body unfreezing.

"You alright there, psycho? Need a nap break?" Creed quips.

"Fuck you," I hiss, my knife sinking into another hunk of meat, moving onto the next. I'm not sure how many people are left. I have to give it to the fuckers, they're stubborn.

"In your dreams," Creed teases, blowing me a kiss.

Fucking weirdo.

Both of us are drenched in blood, a manic gleam in our eyes. I don't need to look at Kaiden to know he's probably spotless.

Prick.

Someone tackles me from behind, and Creed just laughs as I fall on my face. Throwing my elbow backwards, I'm rewarded by the crunch of a nose breaking.

Bullseye.

I wriggle out of the thugs grip as he howls in pain, Creed boots him in the face, ceasing his cries.

"I had that," I mutter, eyeing up the unconscious lump. Creed just shrugs, and smirks at me.

I roll my eyes, and get back on my feet, my hood falling backwards.

Shit.

I spin round to meet Kaiden's gaze as his eyes widen with shock. He still has the gun in his hand and he raises it, pointing it at me.

"You," he hisses.

I shrug as I stare at him. If he expects me to throw myself at his mercy or roll over and show him my belly, he has another thing coming.

"I guess you're to blame for the arrest warrant."

"Maybe," I reply. I can see the edge of madness in his eyes, and I know I have to handle this carefully, and it isn't exactly a strength of mine.

Kill him.

Yay. My inner monster, with the ever so helpful suggestions.

Great, where were you when we were playing slice and dice? You want to show up now of all times.

We should kill him.

Spare. Parts, I mentally hiss back.

My monster huffs it's annoyance, but remains quiet. *Thank fuck.*

"Erm, I hate to interrupt you ladies and your fucking tea party, but could someone please untie me?" Jason snaps, drawing everyone's attention.

"Oh yeah." Kaiden turns away, holstering his weapon, so he can work on the knots binding Jason to the chair. It's now, while we are distracted, the guy Creed had kicked unconscious decides to take his last stand.

Clearly Creed didn't kick him hard enough as he bounced back fucking quick, and he's managed to pull himself away to a safe distance while we were distracted. *Sneaky fuck.*

Our blades wouldn't reach that far, and aren't made for throwing. We'd be just as likely to hit Jason or Kaiden if we even try.

"K!" Creed shouts, not that it will do much when Kaiden doesn't have his gun in his hand. I feel myself taking a step forward, not really knowing why. It will be no skin off my nose if something happens to him, the only reason I'm here in the first place is because she asked me.

We can do nothing as the guy closes the distance, some kind of switchblade or something glints in his hand. Kaiden has turned to face his attacker, and I'm finally going to see the fucker get dirty. There is no panic on his face which surprises me a little. I presumed he's the golden child, the spoiled one, but he has a hardness and resilience in his eyes you only get when you've seen things.

Interesting.

A gunshot rings out, and the thug crumples. We all stand confused as the body hits the floor.

"Wildcat?" Kaiden's voice trembles.

"You were meant to stay outside, Princess," Creed scolds.

I look back to the body, a perfect headshot. Impressive considering she's never used a gun before today.

She flings the gun to the side causing us all to flinch.

Pretty sure she didn't put the safety on.

She runs to Jason first, surprising us all. She throws herself at him ignoring the blood and who knows what. She hugs him tightly, as if she's afraid he'll disappear the moment she lets go. But I don't think anyone is as surprised as Jason is. After the initial shock passes, he brings his one freed hand up to return the hug.

"I'm okay, I'm okay," he coos in her ear, soothing her.

He's touching her.

Ours.

The monster whispers, but my mind is elsewhere.

Remembering that final hug, the crushing embrace where she tried to cram all of her emotions into one. My mother.

Looking carefully around the room, I can see the familiar masks of loss painted on all of their faces. Not one of us dares to speak, no one wants to break such a fragile moment. Even my monster gets the message and shuts up.

"I thought I lost you," Nyx whispers, pulling away and working on the last knot to free him. As soon as his hands are released, he stands up and pulls her into another hug.

"I'm not going anywhere, Spitfire, you're stuck with me." He smiles as he tucks her head under his chin. She wriggles out of his grip to look up at him,

"Good, I'm going to hold you to that." She smiles.

"By the way, did I hear what I thought I heard earlier?" he asks, a slight mischievous glint to his eye.

"No," Nyx snaps. The delightful way the blood rushes to her cheeks tells us that the little kitten is clearly telling porkies.

"Oh, and just what might that have been?" Creed teases, ever the curious meerkat that one.

I heard it. I know her secret. She called him Dad.

"Nothing, just shut up Creed," she hisses.

"It doesn't sound like nothing," he replies.

"Maybe Jason just got knocked around the head a few too many times?" Nyx tries to deflect.

"He's old, but not hard of hearing just yet, Princess. Come on . . . What did you say?" Creed whines like a toddler. A sound that goes straight through me. My skin starts to itch, all this . . . Urgh. This whole happy family thing, it doesn't sit right, it makes me feel uncomfortable.

This happiness, it's nothing but a distraction. A tease, a slight taste of something I could never have.

"We should leave," I snap.

I can't stay here.

Not for another minute.

"He's right," Kaiden replies, which comes as a shock. I mean, I'm right, but the fact he's admitting it is surprising.

"Of course I'm right. We go back to the safe house." I don't leave room for arguing as I quickly exit the house. Creed knows where it is, but I can't stand to be with them for a minute more. I know my brother will want answers, but I need to get my head on straight.

"Wait."

The one voice that could instantly stop me in my tracks. Of course she couldn't just let me go.

Nyx runs to catch up to me, trying to catch her breath. "Thanks for helping me."

Didn't she realise, she never has to thank me?

Doesn't she know I'd gladly do anything for her?

Jason, Creed and Kaiden gather in the doorway of the house to watch us. I suppose I wouldn't trust me with her either if the situations were reversed. But I've seen their bonds, I know none of them pose a threat to her, and they're just as hopelessly devoted to her as I am, even if they don't admit it. I hate it with every fibre of my being, but I know she needs them, maybe not forever, but she does for now. We have a war to win and the more meat shields she has, the better.

"I'll meet you back at the safe house." I try to put distance between us, hoping that it'll make things a little less painful. There'll be a time for us, but now isn't it. I'm too broken, too damaged, too wrong. I don't fit.

"Are you going to be okay?" she asks, looking up at me with those big brown eyes of hers. The genuine concern there stuns me. I know she has a big heart, but how can she care for someone like me? It's only a matter of time before she discovers what I've done. Would she still be able to look at me like that, afterwards?

"Of course, Kitten. I'm always okay."

"Liar."

"Maybe, but it doesn't change my answer."

I can see our spectators getting restless, it isn't going to be long before they're going to storm over to save her.

Not that she needs saving.

Not from me.

"Go. I'll see you soon," I encourage her. She frowns, clearly not liking the idea. It did strike me as odd that she finally has all her pets in one place and she's still standing with me.

Greedy little thing.

"Nyx," Jason calls out.

"Coming," she calls back, without turning around.

Because of course she would go to them, no one ever wants to stay.

The monster almost sounds . . . sad.

That's a new one, and it brings a small smile to my lips.

"Straight to the safe house, you hear me?" Her stern voice is laughable, and the way she crosses her arms over her chest is . . . distracting.

"Kitten, don't take that tone with me," I warn, it's a tone that would lead to trouble, and it's something she isn't ready for just yet.

Something must have shown in my eyes as she quickly changes tactics.

"Please?" she pouts.

Fuck.

"Kitten, the way you say please like that . . . It gives me ideas," I growl, closing the distance. The smell of blood clings to her skin, mixing with her own uniqueness. Violence and defiance.

Abyss help me, she couldn't be more perfect.

"Run away, Kitten. If you think our audience would stop me from taking you right here, you're mistaken."

I watch the flush creep up her neck, and turn her cheeks a delicious shade of pink.

Interesting.

I make a note of her reaction for later, it seems that my Kitten does have some surprises for me after all.

"See you at the safe house," she manages to squeak out, turning away and running to safety.

I watch her all the way until she's safely within their grasp.

Soon, my Kitten.

You will feel my claws.

You will feel my bite.

And you will love every second of it.

We will rule the chaos together as we were always meant to.

CHAPTER TWENTY

Letting Kaleb go off by himself doesn't sit right with me. I can't put my finger on it but I feel like he's just as much a part of this as the rest of us. His reluctance to join us—this weird dysfunctional family, bonded by pain and revenge—well, I can understand his hesitation. Who knows what the future holds, why open yourself to a pain so deep it rips the air from your lungs. Losing my family, Ma, my sisters, it cut deep. Every morning when I wake up I miss them terribly. For someone who has been alone as long as he has, this weirdness would feel alien. Kaiden didn't exactly give him a warm welcome either, so I can hardly blame him for his confusion.

Still . . .

I look back towards where Kaleb had disappeared, I have to hope he's going to keep his word. I don't know why, but the thought of him disappearing leaves a bad taste in my mouth. Maybe Creed's right. Maybe I do have a complex and need to save everyone.

"Wildcat?" Kaiden's voice makes me smile, it feels like it's been way too long since I've heard my nickname on his lips. "I should thank you."

"What for?" I ask, I mean Creed and Kaleb did the work, I just . . .

For a moment I remember the feel of the gun going off in my hand, and the way such a powerful opponent crumpled. I wait for the realisation to hit me, my first kill. I actually took a life. Someone is dead because of me. But no matter how I try, no matter how I think about it, the sense of guilt, the self loathing, the horror at what I did, it never arrives.

And it horrifies me more than anything else.

Am I a monster?

Am I losing myself?

For a moment I picture Ma's face, what she would say. She'd be horrified, disgusted maybe. But then again, who the fuck really knows. It's not like she was ever honest with me in the first place. She had this whole entire secret life she never told me about, who knows what actually lay under all those masks she wore. Did I ever know her?

"You killed a man to protect me, to protect us." He pulls me into a hug and I feel my anger melt away as his arms hold me. Surrounded by Kaiden's strength I feel more in control of my emotions than I have done in what feels like forever. It's only been a few days since he handed me that box and told me he'd be right back, yet so much has happened.

Did he still mean the words he'd said to me? When he called me his?

Did I still want him to?

I look past him to Creed. When I thought I'd lost him . . . And then there's the whole Kaleb issue, which I'm not even going to start unboxing.

I breathe deep, pushing the thoughts away. I focus on the slow, steady beat of Kaiden's heart under my palm, the way he holds me close, the way the heat from his body infuses into mine.

This is what I need.

This is what I want.

Kaiden's hand reaches down to cup my cheek, forcing my eyes to his. There's something off about his gaze. His normal look has a tinge of madness to it.

"My Wildcat," the words lack his normal authority, his possessiveness. It's almost like he's asking if I'm real. His touch is tentative, unsure.

"I'm not going anywhere, Kaiden. Never," I repeat the words he whispered to me mere days ago. I hope they reassure him as much as they did me. He smiles at me, remembering our time together and it seems to banish some of the haunted look in his eyes.

"Let's get out of here," he says, pressing a kiss to my forehead, "I imagine we have a lot to talk about."

"That's a fucking understatement," Jason mutters, but he says nothing more as we make our way back to where we had hidden the car.

"Nice headshot by the way, Nyx," Creed teases, making small talk on the way back.

"I was aiming for his leg," I mutter, causing him to let out a small chuckle.

"Of course you were, Princess, always trying to save the monsters," he teases me.

"Yeah, well I saved your ass, didn't I?" I snap back.

"And the world thanks you, I mean what a fine ass it is, there'd be a day of national mourning if anything happened to it," he jokes.

I know what he's doing, he's trying to keep us out of our heads, to focus on the here and now, and the fact we're all together. But the truth is, war lurks just around the corner, and we have no idea who will win. We were lucky today, it's a miracle we walked away with no serious injuries.

"Creed," Kaiden lets out a warning growl, as we approach our ride. "Care to explain what *that* is doing here?" He points to the car we stole from his garage.

It isn't the most inconspicuous thing, but we were hard pushed for time and it had enough space for us all.

"Don't look at me, boss, your girlfriend and your psycho twin were the ones who stole it."

"Maybe if someone hadn't gotten themselves shot, we wouldn't have needed to steal a car," I snap back, I am not taking the blame for this.

"I see." Kaiden's voice is cold.

"We didn't have a choice, it was the one that made sense, and you have so many cars, I thought it would be okay, I mean I thought it was you stealing your own car, well not stealing, because you can't steal from yourself, what I mean is Creed was shot and we needed to get out of there and it just seemed like the logical option. I mean you have others, right? It's not like you have had to walk everywhere. I mean how many cars does one person need? I even stopped Kaleb from setting it on fire after we escaped."

"When we get back, Wildcat, we are going to talk. About all of it. For now get in the car. Creed, you know where we're going, you drive. Jason in the back with us. You're still a wanted man." No one argues with Kaiden's orders as we get into our seats.

"Pull up 'round the front," Kaiden orders, I feel like we're losing him somehow, like he's building up a wall between us all, brick by brick. He removes a bottle of whiskey from the hidden minibar, because of course this thing has a fucking minibar. He hands a bottle to Jason and pulls out one for himself.

"Our fingerprints will be all over that place," he offers in a way of explanation. Apparently that's enough for Jason, as he pops the top and soaks a rag that Kaiden passes over to him, before stuffing it in the top.

"Are you sure about this?" Jason asks, frowning at the bottle.

"Still trying to play the good guy?" Kaiden questions, eyebrow raised.

"Just checking," Jason mutters.

"Wait, what?" I ask, "You're not serious, you can't just set the place on fire."

No one seems to acknowledge my words as Creed pulls up outside.

"Want help, K?" Creed asks, turning in his seat.

"No, we have this. Right, Jason?" He aims the last bit at the detective.

"You can't do this, what about your job?" I ask. He looks at me and gives me a sad smile. "Let Creed do it, we all know he likes setting fires," I suggest, giving him an out.

"It's true." Creed grins mischievously from the front seat.

"No. We have this. Right, Jason?" Kaiden repeats, this time a bit firmer. A certain level of acceptance enters Jason's eyes.

"Back off," I snap.

"Excuse me?" he hisses, his tone deadly.

"You heard me. Don't make him do something he doesn't want to do. He's not one of your soldiers."

"Nyx, stop. It's okay." Jason tries to placate my rising anger.

How fucking dare Kaiden act this way. After everything . . .

I haven't forgotten how he set a trap for my father, and we'd be having words about that later. He could have fucking died, and now he's making him set fire to his career. Literally.

"Yes, we have this," Jason replies, looking Kaiden in the eye, and taking the lighter from his hand.

"After you." Kaiden gestures to the door, and Jason slips out. Kaiden follows after him. I feel completely powerless as they light the rags on fire before throwing the ignited bottles through the windows of the building. It doesn't take long before the building is engulfed in flames. The bodies and any evidence against us burning with it. I can't help but feel this fight, this mission of revenge is slowly changing us all. Tainting us, pushing us to do things we shouldn't.

Just how many times can we push the line? Dance backwards and forwards along it before we inevitably slip? Is it even worth doing all of this if we lose ourselves in the process?

My mind slips to Kaleb, to the haunted look on his eyes, he's been fighting this war longer than any of us, has seen things a young boy should never have to see.

Is that what we're all going to end up like?

Broken?

So focused on revenge we can't stop to acknowledge anything good, anything pure.

I remember how he flinched from my touch, how his smiles looked forced, maniacal even. How every part of him screams to leave him alone, like a wounded animal not letting anyone close.

Is that what we all are now?

Nothing but wounded animals with nothing left to lose?

No. I won't let us go that far.

We might be dysfunctional on a good day, and we're clearly not good people. But that doesn't mean we can't do good.

As I watch the flames reach higher, curling out of the windows, reaching for freedom, I realise something. Sometimes fire is needed, you have to burn away the bad, you have to cleanse the rot from the forest to allow the chance for new growth. A whole new generation could grow up experiencing sunlight, the freedom of a clear sky. They'd be able to hope without limits.

Once Kaiden and Jason are back in the car, Creed drives off, back to the safe house. I try to relax, to breathe easy, but I'm surrounded by an impending sense of doom.

Tonight will be a night to heal, to rest.

In the morning, we go to war.

CHAPTER TWENTY ONE

T he drive was silent, each of us lost to our own thoughts. Even Creed stays abnormally quiet, just focusing on driving. I knew I had a brother, but how could I not know I had a twin? I suppose now it made sense that my father kept us apart, but I was still confused as to why? Was it just some sick experiment? Some kind of sick ploy to see which one would turn out 'right'?

My brother.

I didn't need to ask about my mother, I can see it in his eyes. The fact he doesn't care if he lives or dies, the haunted look in his eyes when Nyx hugged Jason. She is dead. The why doesn't matter. I've spent years hating a dead woman, hating myself for not being good enough, hating the brother she clearly loved the most. One day I would hear the full story but right now, I just can't do it. I look at my reflection in the tinted glass, what can I even say to him? Did he even want me to say anything at all? I sigh, but it doesn't go by unnoticed. Her long fingers slide in between my own, holding my hand. She gives it a reassuring squeeze and says nothing. I should have known that, even when she's pissed at me, even when she's distracted, focused on her own problems, she's still selfless. Always mindful of others around her.

As long as I have her, it will be okay.

But I'd be an idiot not to notice the way the others look at her. The way my twin stands a little bit too close, the way Creed hovers around her, afraid she might break a nail. She's mesmerised all of them, but there's no way I can give her up. Not now. I've tried walking away a hundred times, and now I know what it feels like to lose her, I can't bear the thought of it ever happening again.

I look towards her, tracing my eyes over her body, memorising every line and drinking her in as if she might disappear at any moment. The words she repeated back to me echo in my head, she'll never leave me. She promised.

My eyes catch hers in the glass, the reflection doing nothing to dampen the change in her eyes. Gone is the scared bunny. Somehow, she's become a Queen without me, there's an edge to her which wasn't there before, a danger. She's always been a fighter, always a feisty one, but now there's something more. Maybe it's the fact she drew blood, maybe the way she killed a man protecting me, but she's something more now. An equal. The most amazing woman I could ever hope for.

"I love you," The words come out whispered, but in the silence of the car they bounce around, seeming to grow louder. It's probably all in my imagination, but there's no stopping the words the moment they leave my lips.

"About time," laughs Creed from the front seat.

Jason just chuckles, which I suppose is as close to approval as he is going to give. But there is really only one reaction which matters.

Her eyes widen in the reflection, I hope with shock and not horror, but I need her words.

"Wildcat?" I ask, hesitantly. I never meant to just blurt it out like this in front of everyone. Honestly my timing probably couldn't be worse, or less romantic, but that doesn't make my words any less true. I do love her. I never intended to fall for her, I didn't even think it was possible for someone like me to love. But she had done the impossible.

"Really?" she asks, turning to face me.

Out of all the reactions, I wasn't expecting that one. She almost looks . . . Hurt?

"Of course," I reply, "I'm not in the business of saying things I don't mean."

"I know, it's not you . . ."

"Then what? What is it?" I don't mean for my words to come out sounding so harsh.

"Don't get mad at me," she snaps.

"I'm not mad."

"You sound mad."

"Look, I'm not mad, this is just not how I imagined this going." I sigh.

Not that I even gave it much thought, if I had maybe I wouldn't be making such a fucking fool of myself right now.

"I'm sorry," she starts apologising, making me feel even more like shit.

My eye's meet Creed's in the rearview mirror, I can see the tell tale crinkle in the corner of his eye as he fights back laughter.

Fucker.

I bet Jason is eating this up too, I don't dare look at him, choosing to look out of the window instead.

"Kaiden," her voice pleads, but I don't want to turn and look at her. I can't take the rejection. Not now. "I do, you know," she mutters, the words so quiet I can barely hear her.

"You what?" I need to hear her words, I need to know for sure that she feels the same.

"You know what." She blushes a delightful shade of pink, which causes me to chuckle.

"Wildcat," I coo, "What did I say about using your words?" I smirk as her mind automatically goes exactly where I wanted it to. She's remembering when I had her pressed against me, on this very seat. Moaning under my touch, squirming under my torment.

"I love you," she grumbles. My heart leaps at her words, but it still wasn't enough.

"Sorry, I don't think I caught that," I tease. "Louder, Wildcat, it's not like you to be bashful."

I looked up at Creed, knowing he'd be first to join the teasing. He never missed a chance to wind her up. When my eyes meet his, instead of the mischief I'm expecting, he almost looks . . . tortured. He quickly looks away,

"It's ok, you don't have to say it." I give her an out, not wanting to torture the man I call my brother. We couldn't fall out over a girl, but it's clear we are going to have to talk.

"You are such an insufferable prick. You know that? You are a big headed, egotistical, pain in my ass. You are so entitled it's actually unreal. You think you own everything, and every-fucking-person you meet. You are infuriating, and so fucking stubborn." She takes a deep breath, her eyes softening as she looks at me. "But, de-spite all of that, and ignoring the fact I want to punch you in the face just as much as I want to kiss you, I do love you . . . Somehow. It's probably a shocker to us all."

I couldn't help it. I laugh.

Even a declaration of love, she had to do it in her own unique, unapologetic style. There's just no winning with this woman, but that's just the way I like it. I'll take her fire along with her passion, I'll take her strong will anyday. I just want her. In all her unrefined, defiant, perfection.

My Wildcat.

Creed pulls up and switches off the engine.

"We're here. Welcome to Casa Psycho."

I look out the window and am surprised. I know this building. As kids we used to dare each other to come here, even now people think it's haunted and stay away. It's the perfect safe house, the ghosts the perfect security system. If anyone hears any screaming it'll just be written off as kid's playing pranks or the wind. No one wants to be the crazy person ranting about ghosts in the street.

We all file out of the car, and walk up to the house.

On the doorstep is a small stack of pizzas, but no sign of where they'd come from.

"What's with him and pizza?" Creed mutters.

"Shut up, who doesn't love pizza," Nyx replies, picking up the stack.

"We are not eating doorstep food, who knows if any-ones tampered with it." I look at the boxes suspiciously.

"Don't be a baby, they're fine. Kaleb wouldn't poison me."

"I don't think it's you, he's worried about," Jason mutters.

Glad someone is on the same side as me.

"Are you forgetting that he just helped save your asses?" Nyx chirps up, blinking up at me with those big innocent as fuck eyes.

"I was trying to," I mutter.

As we make our way in and divide up the pizzas there's no sign of my elusive twin. He must have just ordered the pizzas and had them delivered. At least Nyx had the forethought to keep one of the pizzas aside for him. Last thing we need is a hangry psycho.

Jason takes his pizza, and mentions something about finding a shower, and a bed. Creed takes his leave shortly after, saying he needs to check on his stitches. That leaves just the two of us. For the first time since the car, we are alone.

"We need to talk." I hesitantly break the awkwardness growing between us.

"I know." She sighs.

How can she know? How can she know that her mistaking him for me hurt? I need to know what's happened, where we stand.

"This is about the car, right? I never meant to steal from you—"

It's not about the car. It's about my . . . twin." The word feels weird on my tongue, betrayal gripping my heart. The lies just seem to keep stacking up.

"Kaleb? I promise, if it wasn't an emergency—"

"Wildcat, let me finish, okay."

She nods and lets me continue.

"You said you thought he was me . . . Did he . . .?" I leave the question unspoken but she manages to fill in the blanks.

"Oh god, no. I . . . No . . . I swear we never, he never made a move on me like that. Not once he knew we were together. We may have had a little bit of a moment, but I nipped it in the bud. I wouldn't do that to you. I . . . love you." Hearing the words coming out of her lips once more, unprompted, went a little way to settling the ache in my chest.

"Still hesitating, I see." I feign a look of disappointment, watching her eyes widen a little bit in panic.

Watching her emotions morph so freely, so unrestrained and unfiltered really did make winding her up fun. I pull her towards me, eliciting a small gasp from her lips.

"I'll just have to make it so every part of your body craves my touch, engrave my name on every single part of your heart and soul. Make it so no one can make you feel the way I do. I will own you with every brush of my tongue, every trace of my fingers. I will make it so every step you take you'll feel the echo of me inside you, owning every single part of you. You are mine, and by the time I'm through with you, you and everyone else will know the truth of my words. Everyone will know just who you belong to when you're screaming my name."

Her eyes narrow in defiance, submission is never an easy thing for my Wildcat, but it makes it all the more sweeter when she does give in.

"Cocky much?" She can deny it all she wants, but the flush of her cheeks tells me all I need to know. She wants this. She wants us.

"Cocky would be this," I grab her by the hair holding her close to me as I run my nose down her neck. Goosebumps pebble in my wake, and I smile against her skin. "Still going to deny me? Pretend you aren't as desperate for me as I am to get a single taste of you?"

"I thought we had to talk," she mutters.

"Oh we do, but I think it can wait. Don't you?"

She lets out a small whimper of need, her defences crumbling as I press a kiss to her throat.

"I need your words, Wildcat. I need to hear that you want me, just as badly as I want you. Or all of this stops here." She says nothing, caught between her pride and the urge to submit to me.

I start to slowly pull away, giving her a chance to stop me. I look her in the eye, her lips are so close, it's so fucking tempting to just take her. I watch the war in her eyes, as her hand creeps up to fist my shirt, stopping me from moving any further away from her.

"Yes?" I raise an eyebrow at her. She has to say it. There needs to be no chance of regret or misunderstanding. She has to give herself to me fully, anything less is unacceptable.

She already has all of me. There's nothing I won't do for her, even if that something is walking away right now.

"Oh, you stubborn prick, will you just fucking kiss me already?" she growls, her frustration clear as day.

"Kiss you where?" I smirk.

"Here?" I press a small kiss to her temple.

"Here?" I press another to the top of her ear.

"Here?" I pepper kisses along her jaw working my way to her lips.

"More," she whispers, her breath mixing with mine as I hover just out of reach.

"Tell me what you want, tell me what you need. You know I'm more than happy to give it to you, come on, Wildcat. Use your words." I rub my nose against hers, I just need her skin against mine, no matter how small it might be.

"I want you, fuck. Kaiden, I need you. Please. I want to feel your skin against mine, I want you to own every inch of my body until all I can think about is you, I want to fall apart, and know that you will always put me back together again. Over and over. I want to see you come undone, I want you. Every fucking inch of you." Her words are filled with desperation and longing.

I growl, the urge to take her here on the table is fucking overwhelming.

"Good girl." I finally close the distance taking the kiss I crave. Her moan against my lips, as she finally gets what she wants, gives me the access I need to turn the kiss into a claiming. Her tongue eagerly meets mine and I get lost in the sensation of her.

My hands snake round her, lifting her ass and settling her on the table as I move in between her legs, never breaking our kiss. Her nails scrape against my chest, as the other hand curls in my hair, there's no escape, no retreat.

"Show me your bedroom," I manage to force out as we both gasp for air. She giggles, the most sexy little sound. A sound which makes me want to pin her under me and see what other noises I can ring out of her sexy little body.

All in good time.

This has been a long time coming, and I'm not usually a patient man, but with her I want to take my time, I want to make her body addicted to my touch, ruin her for all but me. She is mine.

She pushes against my chest, and I take a step back. She hops off the table, with a twinkle of mischief in her eye.

Fuck, she's going to be the death of me.

She goes up on tiptoes, her hand snakes around my neck pulling me down to meet her.

"Wildcat," I growl in warning. "I will take you over this table."

She giggles, and shakes her head.

"Catch me," she whispers against my lips.

Her words catch me off guard as she runs from me. Pausing in the doorway she looks over her shoulder, smirking.

"What's with the blank look? When have I ever made your life easy?" she teases, starting the chase.

"You're going to pay for that," I call after her, only to be met with more giggles.

I slowly stalk after her, letting the sound of her footsteps guide me. She isn't trying to get anyway, and if it were anyone else I'd be suspicious they are luring me into a trap. But Nyx's giggles and her joy are contagious, I find myself hurrying despite myself. The glimpse I catch of her ass as she turns the corner, begs for my marks.

Fuck.

Just you fucking wait.

I watch her disappear into her bedroom, shutting the door behind her. I imagine her on the other side, panting slightly, lips parted. Is she holding her breath at the sound of my approaching footsteps? Is she trembling in anticipation, aching for me? Will she try to hide, prolonging both of our suffering?

As I close the distance to her door, I tap on the wall with every step. I can almost hear her heartbeat quickening, it takes every bit of self control I have to keep my footsteps slow, stalking. If she wants to play a game, it's a game I will win.

I reach for the handle, slowly turning it. I can feel her gaze watching the steady rotation, the anticipation in the air is almost tangible. As the door swings open, there the cheeky minx stands wearing nothing but a smirk.

Holy fuck!

"Cat got your tongue?" she teases.

"Oh you'll have my tongue alright, you'll be coming all over it very soon."

"Promises, promises," she purrs, running her fingers down her body. I watch entranced before snapping my eyes back to hers.

"You should know by now, I don't make promises I don't intend to keep. Now on the bed, sweetheart. Show me how wet you are for me." She slowly walks over to the bed, adding an extra sway to her hips, my own hypnotising siren call.

"Fuck, you're perfect." The words are out without conscious thought, this woman makes me lose all control. I don't have any defences against her at all.

She lays back on the bed, a slight blush spreading on her cheeks. Suddenly she looks vulnerable, almost unsure. It isn't the first time I've seen her naked, but surrendering herself, exposing herself is a difficult line to cross. I can see the slight hesitation there.

We can't have that.

I walk over to her, losing my tie as I go. She watches my fingers closely as I undo each button of my shirt, slowly teasing her with more skin. Every part that's revealed to her, she drinks in hungrily. I kick my shoes off by the side of the bed, leaving only my trousers on. I toy with my belt buckle, watching her as she runs her tongue over her lip hungrily.

Shit.

Thoughts of sliding into that sassy little mouth of hers, have me straining the seams. But now isn't the time. I want to erase all of her doubts, I want her to know that she's it for me. She's ruined me for all others with her attitude, her resolve, every brilliant part of her.

I lay down next to her, taking her hand and putting it on my chest.

"You feel that?" I ask.

She nods.

"Yes," she whispers.

"As long as my heart still beats, it's yours. I will protect you with my very life, Nyx. You have nothing to fear with me."

"I know, it's not that."

"Then what is this uncertainty I see in your eyes?"

"I worry that this is all a dream, I just have a hard time believing you'd want a nobody like me. I'm not rich, I'm not civilised, and I can't make people piss themselves with a look, like you can. I'm not special, and I'm just scared you'll figure all that out."

"Nyx, listen to me, and listen closely. I don't care if you're rich, I have money for both of us. I don't care about you being civilised, I actually prefer your honesty, your openness. It's beautiful, refreshing, and so totally you. I wouldn't change a thing. You don't need to intimidate anyone, you have a whole group of people ready to go to bat for you, sweetheart. All you need to do is be yourself. As for you not being special, that's just a straight up lie."

"But—"

"No buts. You have done what no one else could, you've turned me from a shell of a man into someone who feels. You've given me a reason to fight, something to defend. You have made me the strongest I have ever been. You are special, and I will get on my knees and worship you every single fucking day, until you agree."

She smiles up at me, her uncertainty absent from her gaze. All I can see is adoration.

"I love you, Kaiden."

No hesitation.

No doubt.

Just love.

"I love you, too. I do believe I gave you an order though."

"Did you?" she says innocently, but the mischief sparkling in her eyes makes her look anything but innocent.

"Yes, I told you to spread your legs and let me see how wet you are for me."

"And if I say no?"

"Choice is yours, sweetheart, we can do this the easy way, where you spread your legs like a good girl and get the rewards that come with it . . . or you can be a brat, and I'll have to show you how to behave. Either way this ends with me getting what I want from you."

"Make. Me." She smirks.

Oh, Wildcat, it's on.

I pin her under my body, entwining our legs, everywhere her skin touches mine feels amazing. It's like the ice is melting away, every brush of her lips against mine breathes life into me. I snake my knees in between hers while she's distracted by the way my tongue dominates hers, owning, tasting, swallowing every gasp and moan, as she writhes under me. I undo my belt buckle, the sound of the clasp coming undone causes her to squirm more in anticipation.

I sit back on my knees, her legs either side of me. I drink in the sight of her. Her lust filled eyes, her kissed lips, the way she's quivering in need under me.

Hands on her knees, I force her legs wide, baring her to my gaze.

"That wasn't so hard now, was it?" I watch as defiance flashes in her eyes.

Ever the feisty one.

"Yeah yeah, are you going to make good on your promise now?" She smirks, knowing I'm a man of my word.

I chuckle.

"Of course. Look at you spread out so invitingly, like my own personal feast. How can I resist?" I run my fingers down her stomach, tracing over her hips and along the outside of her thighs. I follow one of her legs, all the way down, throwing an ankle over my shoulder. As I pepper kisses from her ankle up her calf, I track my fingers ever so lightly over her other leg, the sensation causes her to let out little gasps and moans at my barely there touches.

"More, please," she pleads, her voice barely more than a whisper as she squirms under my touch. I chuckle darkly against her skin.

"That's it, pretty girl, beg for me," I murmur against her skin.

"Please, Kaiden, I need it. I need you. Your tongue. Please."

"Mmmm, such a good girl. How can I refuse your pretty cries?"

I dive into her like a starving man, the contrast to my light kisses is shocking, and she arches her back in pleasure as I spear her with my tongue.

"Yes, Kaiden, yes," she cries.

I pull slowly back, giving her long slow licks, and then flicking her clit. The sudden change of sensations is too much as she starts to buck under me, her hands in my hair as she starts to ride my face, taking her pleasure.

This wasn't part of the plan, I was going to punish her, keep her on the edge, but I find myself just as lost to the sensations as she is.

Punishment can wait.

I growl against her.

Fuck, she tastes good.

"Come all over my face, Wildcat, mark me as yours. I want to smell your sweet pussy on me all fucking day." I look up at her, meeting her gaze as she pulls me back against her.

Who fucking needs air anyway?

That's it, my pretty girl, use me, fucking own me.

I slide two fingers deep inside her, stretching her as she squirms under me.

"More," she begs.

I add another, forcing her to take the third as I feast.

Her nails dig into my skull, almost to the point of pain, but it just fuels me further.

She tenses around my fingers, back arching off the bed in pleasure as she grinds against my face. It isn't long before she crests the wave of her pleasure, coming all over my tongue just as I promised. My name on her lips is the sweetest reward as her eyes glaze over with ecstasy.

"I told you, I keep my word," I tease.

"Mhmm," she murmurs, her eyes closing as she embraces her relaxed state.

"Remember what else I told you?"

"Mhmm"

"Good girls get rewards, brats get taught how to behave."

"Mhmm". She's clearly not listening, maybe she needs a reminder just who she's dealing with.

I put my hand around her throat, forcing her to open her eyes and look at me. As her gaze meets mine, I smirk.

"You should have taken my warning, Wildcat. Your safeword is . . ." I pondered for a moment, trying to think of a good one for her, something we'd both easily remember.

"Bagel. That can be the safeword," she answers, I frown at her odd choice.

"Bagel?"

"Yeah, from that first breakfast. I'm pretty sure that was the first time I saw the real you." She blushes. I would have never guessed something so simple meant so much to her. I make a vow to pay closer attention in future.

"Bagel, it is then. Now do you know what happens to brats who don't do as they're told?"

"They get orgasm's, apparently," she teases.

"Oh, sweetheart, that was a freebie, now . . . The real fun begins."

CHAPTER TWENTY TWO

O *h, holy shitballs!*

The intensity in his eyes, the promises they hold. They say you should be careful what you wish for, and I imagine I'm going to fully understand what they mean by it.

"Hands above your head," he demands.

He's done asking, he's done playing nice.

My pride is at war with my curiosity as he slides his belt free from his trousers.

"Now, Wildcat. I won't ask again."

My arms start moving before the words even fully register in my bliss-hazed brain. He curls my hands around the bar at the top of the bed.

"Stay," he commands. The urge to rebel at the order is strong, I'm not some obedient dog. My defiance must have shown on my face as he raises his eyebrow questioningly. When I don't say anything further, choosing to bide my time, he smiles. "Good girl, you're learning."

He wraps the belt around my wrists, binding me to the headboard. I automatically pull against the restraints, testing them, but they offer no give.

"You're mine now, sweetheart, and you're playing by my rules."

He kisses me in a way that offers no escape, his tongue invades, taking what he wants from me. He's in total control now, and there's nothing I can do. Pinned under his hard body, his touches are too much, and not enough. I can feel him everywhere, but still I need more.

"Kaiden, please," I plead, needing more. Needing him. Fuck, if I don't get him inside me . . .

He chuckles that dark, sinister chuckle of his and it goes straight to my core, making me desperate for him.

"Maybe next time you'll be a good girl from the beginning, but now it's time for your punishment."

"No, I can't," I beg.

"You can, and you will." He leaves me no room for argument, this is going to happen. I briefly think of the safeword, but it's a last resort. I trust him completely. If he says I can, I have no doubt in my mind.

"Three. One for making me chase you, one for answering back, and one for not believing how fucking incredible you are. I think that's fair, don't you?" he asks.

"Three what?"

"Four."

"Wait, I never—"

"Five, and you will address me as Sir. Still want to argue?"

I consider it for a moment, five might be a little, or it might be a lot, but am I really going to risk more?

"No . . ." He gives me that questioning look again, the one that promises more punishment if I want to play this game. "Sir." The word feels heavy on my tongue, submission has never come easily to me. I'm a natural fighter through and through. I've always had to be.

"Good girl." Those two words.

Fuck!

On anyone else's lips they'd sound condescending, but on his . . . they sound positively sinful. Every feminist bone in my body withers, needing to hear those words on his lips once more.

He crawls off me, and I instantly miss his weight on me. A whimper of need passes my lips and I'm helpless to hold it back. He smirks, standing beside the bed, his fingers tracing the waistband of his trousers.

"Was that a complaint, sweetheart?"

I shake my head, keeping my gaze fixed on his fingers.

"Use your words."

"No, no, sir. No complaints."

"Good," he smirks. "Now you're getting it." I watch eagerly as he undoes the button, the sound of the zip being lowered makes me squirm.

Fuck! I don't think I've ever been so desperate, never needed something as badly as I need him.

He pushes his trousers down, along with his boxers, before standing upright and giving me my first glimpse of his naked body.

And what a fucking body.

I want to map every inch of his skin with my tongue, trace every single hard ridge. I want to have this powerful man under me, I need to make him crumble, make him mine. I drink in the sight of him greedily, his fuck me arms, his toned body, the V of his hips that leads to a cock which makes my mouth water.

He stands there, letting me stare, lazily stroking himself as his eyes bore into me.

"Legs spread, Wildcat, show me where you want me."

My knees drop to the side without hesitation, I love his eyes on me. The way his eyes fill with lust, the slight dangerous spark in his eyes, the predatory hunger. I'd never be able to get enough of this man. I try to close my legs, needing friction, needing something.

"I didn't tell you to close them, did I?" he growls menacingly.

"Sorry, sir," I reply hastily, the words come easier now. I let my legs fall open once more. His eyes are like a physical caress with the intensity of his gaze, but it's still not enough.

"Do not hide what's mine. If I tell you to spread your legs, you keep them there until I tell you otherwise. If I want to look at that pretty pussy of yours for hours, you will lay there trussed up like my own plaything, dripping wet and aching for me. Only then might I give you what you want. Understand?"

"Yes, sir."

Hours? He'd never.

"You are so fucking beautiful," his words are spoken with such intensity I actually believe him. Somehow, even though I'm naked and spread out here, at his mercy, I feel so fucking powerful. So desired. He reaches for his trouser pocket and pulls out a foiled wrapper.

I freeze up a little at seeing him so prepared, protection hadn't even crossed my mind, yet there he is. Prepared like a fucking boy scout.

Just how many women did he sleep with?

"Tell me what you're thinking, Wildcat? Where did your mind just go?"

"It's nothing," I reply, pushing my insecurities aside, it isn't important. Instead, I focus on him.

"No, sweetheart, that's not how this works. Unless you use your safeword, you answer my questions," he orders.

I don't want to seem like that type of girl, all insecure and jealous.

"I'm just surprised you're so well prepared, that's all," I mutter, blushing. I can't meet his eyes. I didn't want to be the crazy girl.

"I am always prepared, because I've never met a woman I could trust, until you. I could never be sure a woman wouldn't sabotage any form of protection, so I always carried my own," he explains calmly, and patiently. I feel stupid even mentioning it. "But since you, Wildcat, from the time I saw a photo of your face, you were all I could think about. There's only ever been you since the moment you came into my life."

"If you didn't trust them, then why did you even sleep with them?"

"Nyx, I'm not a saint, I never claimed to be."

"I'm sorry, I don't mean to be like this."

"You have nothing to be sorry about. We don't have to go any further tonight, if you want to stop."

"No, I want to. I really fucking want to," I explain, running my eyes down his body.

"Thank fuck," he grins.

"You know, if you trust me . . ." I pause, struggling to get my words out, "I have the implant, and the hospital tested me, I'm clean . . . You know, if you wanted to . . . er. . ."

Fuck, why is saying this so fucking awkward. I'm never this awkward.

"I'm clean, and I do trust you, Wildcat. More than I've ever trusted anyone. If you're sure . . .?" Even now he's being considerate, putting my wants and needs before his own.

I want nothing between us, I want to feel the full power of this man, I want him to carve his name inside of me, and paint me as his.

"Fuck me, sir," I say, stretching my legs wide for him.

He rewards me with the most predatory smile which instantly turns me into a desperate mess, aching for him. He crawls up the bed, trapping me once again under his body, the condom discarded without a second thought. He teases me, rubbing his hard cock against me, torturing us both.

"I've waited so long for this, sweetheart. Each moment you were missing, every thought was consumed by you. Needing you, wanting you. You make me feel like I'm going out of my mind." He slowly eases into me, stretching me as he fills me. "Fuck, you feel like coming home, sweetheart, better than I could have ever imagined." He holds himself inside of me, fully rooted before taking my breath away with an all consuming kiss.

Having his cock inside me, the taste of him against my tongue, his possessive growl as he finally claims his prize

... Me. Every single sense is dominated by this man. He is taking no prisoners.

He slowly pulls back before thrusting hard, forcing a gasp from my lips as I wrap my legs around his hips, holding him close, meeting his every thrust. It doesn't take long before I feel that blissful crest start to rise as he works my body like his own personal instrument.

So close ...

The intensity in his gaze, the almost feral gleam to his eyes fuels me further. I already know he's ruined me for all others, he knows just how to play me. When I need it deep, when I need it fast, the moans in my ear make me feral in turn. The kisses he presses to my neck. The way he pinches my nipples before soothing them with his tongue. It's all too much, every touch, every kiss, it feels like he's everywhere.

My body tenses, ready for that blissful release, but it never comes. Kaiden stills inside me, his gaze turning wicked.

"One," he says with a smirk.

Oh no.

Oh. Hell. No!

"Four more to go, Wildcat," he teases.

Fuck.

Sadistic prick.

I'm tempted to say something, but I know it'll only add to my torture. As soon as he thrusts again, any arguments

I may have die on my lips. Being denied, it makes every-thing so much more intense, it doesn't take long before I can feel my orgasm just out of reach, and just like last time, he stops.

"Two."

I growl in frustration at being denied again.

Every time he builds me higher, I feel like I'm going to explode. I'm wound up tighter than a coiled spring. I need release.

"Please," I beg shamelessly, "I need to come."

I buck wantonly against him, mindless with desire.

"Sweetheart, I know what you need, and you will come all over my hard cock when I tell you to and not a second sooner," he orders.

I whimper. It's only been two times, I can't imagine five.

"Please—" He silences my pleading with a trust of his cock, forcing a gasp from my lips. Again and again, he builds me up, refusing to give me the release I need. I try gripping him with my thighs, pushing him to finish me, to end my suffering, but every time, he stills. Every time I try to grind against him, he pins my hips. Three. Four. Five. Numbers lose all meaning as I can do nothing but surrender to him. Take his relentless pounding, his bruising kisses, and his hands all over me, claiming me, carving his name into my very soul.

Finally as I crest that wave once more, I know I'm ruined.

"Come for me, sweetheart. Come now, with my name on your lips," he whispers in my ear, and I'm gone. Stars swim in my eyes as I come with an intensity I'd never known, wave after wave of built up pleasure, slam into me.

A couple more thrusts and he joins me, the feeling of him coming deep inside me pushes me even higher.

Too much.

I cling to him, afraid to let go. I don't want it to end, but at the same time I'm overwhelmed. He presses kisses to my cheek as a tear falls.

"You did so good, sweetheart. I knew you would. You are perfect, my love." He slowly slides from me and I whimper at the loss. "It's okay, I'm not going anywhere." He pulls me to him, allowing me to curl up on his chest. I never knew things could be this way, so intense and so overwhelming.

"Do you need anything?" he asks.

I shake my head, knowing soon I will need to clean up, and actually drink something, but right now it feels like his arms around me are the only thing holding me together.

I must have drifted off for a moment, as the next thing I remember Kaiden is there, his trousers back on, clutching a glass of water.

"I need you to drink up for me, Wildcat, and then you can sleep." The concern in his eyes warms my heart, and

I greedily drink the water. I didn't realise just how thirsty I was, but as soon as the liquid hits my tongue I can't stop until the glass is empty.

After getting up to clean up in the ensuite, I come back to find Kaiden in my bed. He pats the bed beside him.

"Get in here," he orders in a tone that sends a shiver of longing through me.

I remind my lady parts that I do in fact need to walk tomorrow and to shut the fuck up, but I'm not sure if they're is listening, as I look at him all relaxed, and completely at home in my bed. So much has changed in these last few days for both of us. I just wish we could stay like this for longer, but I know deep down this brief moment of peace isn't going to last, it can't.

I curl up in Kaiden's arms, the sense of impending doom easing as he holds me. Listening to the strong, steady beast of his heart, it doesn't take long before I fall into a deep, dreamless sleep.

CHAPTER TWENTY THREE

It's early morning when Kaiden joins me in the kitchen. It's the first time I've seen him looking less than perfect, but I'd take his anal retentiveness over the dreamy as fuck smile he currently wears.

"I swear, if you hurt her . . ." I growl threateningly. He can fill in the blanks, he's a smart man.

"I won't. I love her." He simply shrugs, unapologetic and brash. I kind of admire the way he can just own his feelings in a way I never could. The serenity I see there makes the remaining arguments die on my tongue. War is coming, and he will do everything in his power to keep her safe. I just hope it's going to be enough.

"Good," I grunt out, keeping the rest to myself.

"Look at you embracing your fatherly duties," Kaiden teases, making my skin crawl.

"Of course, even before I knew it I battled with a sense of duty to protect her that went way beyond what would have been considered right. I just wrote it off as grief, that I didn't want to see anyone else lost. I should have known. I should have been there," Once I started, the words came tumbling out, I couldn't stop them. Kaiden understands though. She's changed us all, slowly but surely.

Kaiden pats my shoulder in an awkward show of support, before moving away to grab himself a cup of coffee.

"About Haven," Kaiden starts, hesitantly, turning around to look at me, teaspoon in hand. It'd almost be comical, but for the dread curling in my gut at the seriousness in his expression.

"What about it?" I ask.

"It was my father who did it." He looks ashamed, and unsure. So unlike the man I've come to know. "I understand if that means you don't want anything to do with me, but I'm not my father—"

"I know."

" —I'd never hurt Nyx, or treat her . . . Wait. What do you mean, you know?" He looks shocked.

"You're not your father, if you were . . . you think I'd have let you anywhere near Nyx? I'd have killed you first." I'd already had my suspicions about his father, especially seeing the men at the safe house. I'm not an idiot.

Kaiden nods, and goes back to preparing his coffee just the way he likes it.

"You guys wedding planning yet? Detective isn't getting any younger?" Creed walks in, as joyful as fucking ever.

"Fuck you, Creed, and I think we can lose the 'Detective' now, don't you?"

"Awww was the ickle wickle detective naughty?"

"I was going to kill him, you know? I can't even blame you guys. It was all on me," I confess.

"Kill who?" Creed asks, a frown clouding his usually carefree expression.

"Captain Collins, I burst into his office, gun in hand, ready to squeeze the trigger, but he wasn't there."

"Ahh, I might have had something to do with that," Kaiden interjects.

"What did you do?" I snap.

"Whoa man, you literally just said you were going to kill him, why do you care?" Creed asks.

"Because he needs to pay for what he did. They were all killed to protect him. How many more people have been thrown into the meat grinder while he just lounged about that office of his. Taking bribes and corrupting everything I swore to stand for?"

"So you were just going to shoot him in a police station?" Creed raises a condescending eyebrow.

"Yeah, I know it was ridiculous, but you didn't see the bodies. Paul and his flatmates . . . It was all a message, I was a dead man walking. What did it matter?"

"Who's Paul?" Creed asks.

"Not now," Kaiden cuts him off. He turns to me, "He's still alive, Collins, I mean. I am sorry about your friends, and I won't tell you I told you so. You've already guessed my father wants you dead, but he wants to kill you himself. Nyx slipped away from him, and he's obsessed with finding her. He's not going to give up, and he knows about your connection."

"We can't let him get his hands on her," Creed interrupts.

"He's right, if it comes to a choice, it's not even a choice. You save her, every time." I look them both in the eye, forcing them to see my sincerity.

"She won't like it," Kaiden murmurs.

I smile, yeah he's right, she wouldn't. She'd kick and scream, and probably run off to face down armies no matter how much of a long shot it was.

"All of us would lay down our lives for her." Creed cups his side, his eyes gaining a haunted look about them. We haven't asked what happened, but it was a close call. His eyes say as much. "We can't let anything happen to her, she's everything," he murmurs, but we all hear him.

Kaiden's eyes narrow suspiciously, as he studies Creed closely. Realisation dawns on Creed's face and he laughs.

"I mean, she's the one person on the planet who can help remove the stick from K's ass. She's a miracle worker." His laugh sounds forced even to me, but no one comments. I look at Creed in a new light, it's clear he has feelings for her, I presumed it is more like a little sister or he was doing it for Kaiden's sake, but something had changed over the last few days. One day we were going to have to talk about it, but right now we have other things to focus on.

"Am I to presume that was what yesterday's little ambush was all about? Your father's orders?" I ask, trying to keep us on topic.

"Yes, and you saw my babysitters. I hate to say it, but without Creed and . . . Kaleb, it would have gone down a lot differently." Kaiden almost looks ashamed. "I was trying to find a way out, I swear—"

"I know." I smile at him, "You did what you had to do, and I would have done the same in your position. No hard feelings."

"I don't think it's your hard feelings he's worried about. Have you told Nyx about this yet?" Creed asks.

"Told me what?" Nyx appears in the doorway, rubbing the sleep from her eyes

We all freeze as if we're kids caught up to no good.

"I'm guessing from your reaction it's not good. Just tell me already." she says with a sigh.

"It's about yesterday," Kaiden starts.

S. F. RAE

"You mean when you ambushed my dad and almost got him killed?" she replies, eyebrows raised.

Kaiden looks at a loss for words as he squirms uncomfortably.

"Don't blame him, Spitfire," I interject.

"I wasn't," she snaps. "I was blaming the monster who's responsible for all of this. The fucking monster who chased me around a forest, shot Creed, and killed my mother. Who gloated in my fucking face," she snarls.

"Holy shit, Princess," Creed stares at her in awe, I think we all are.

"I'm not going to blame you, for something you had no control over. You are just as much a victim as everyone else. He is the problem, he is the one who's going to pay for it."

Violence and malice soaks her words, feeding us all. I feel her calling to my bloodlust, the need for revenge is a fire which blazes hot. Not just for Maria, not anymore. It's more than that. It's for Paul, for his flatmates, for every single person who's felt fear at the hands of this monster.

I can see the darkness swirling around Creed and Kaiden as surely as it's swirling around me, the call to slay the beast is strong. Blood soaked justice is sometimes the only justice possible, I see that now. To be the good guy, you sometimes need to be the bad guy.

Clap. Clap. Clap.

We turn to the sound of the noise, as Kaleb steps into the room.

"Bravo, bravo," he says with a smirk. "Rousing speech, Kitten, and just how are you going to kill our psychotic old man?"

"Well, I—"

"Mhmm. Thought so," he sneers.

"Back off," Kaiden snaps, pulling Nyx towards him.

"Oh, I'm terribly sorry, brother dear," Kaleb sneers, "I thought she might want to have an actual plan before she goes skipping off to slay the big bad dragon."

Nyx pushes away from Kaiden, storming up to Kaleb without any fear or concern. I'm not sure if it's recklessness or bravery at this point. You can tell by looking at the guy something's off about him.

"Yes, we need a plan. We were just getting to that part. What about you? Scaring kids and kicking puppies? Or were you just skulking about in the shadows like a fucking creep?"

All of us around the kitchen table are coiled, waiting for his reaction. Ready to swoop in and intervene if needed.

"Oh, Kitten, you don't want to play that game with me. They might roll over and let you pet their bellies, and act like good little neutered mutts. But that's not me, I bite."

"Yeah, well so do I," she snaps, not sensing the danger in his words.

I start to doubt it's bravery, but rather just plain insanity.

Kaleb just chuckles.

"Promises, promises, Kitten."

"I didn't mean—" she looks alarmed, her eyes finding Kaiden, but his gaze never leaves his twin.

"Nyx, can you come here please," Kaiden asks, his cold, icy tone firmly back in place. She walks towards him and he pulls her down onto his lap. As soon as she's back in his arms, he relaxes somewhat, but his eyes remain on his brother.

"As swell as this cock measuring contest is, can we maybe save it for a time when we aren't in peril? I mean I'm pretty sure Kaiden's absence has been noted by now, either we're presumed dead, or dead men walking. I'd rather be proactive before he shows up at our door." I try to get us back on track.

"We are safe here," Kaleb pipes up.

"For now maybe, but it's only a matter of time. We need a plan, ideas, people?" I open it to the room.

"Kill him, simple," Kaleb says matter of factly. "Car bomb, sniper rifle, a poisoned birthday cake, anything. He just needs to die."

"And as I already told you, that doesn't count as a plan, psycho," Creed snaps back.

"Here we go again," Nyx sighs.

Kaleb and Creed continue to throw insults at each other while the rest of us actually try to think.

"Quiet!" Nyx shouts, bringing them both straight to heel. "He will die, he deserves to, but we need to be smart about it."

"It won't be enough just to kill him, we need to erase his entire influence, make it like he never existed," I add.

"Our plan needs to have four stages," Kaiden explains, taking control of the situation. "Firstly we need to cut him off from his power. The Butcher. He's the attack dog, the hammer to his threats. We get rid of him, that will loosen his power considerably. We have to find him first, though."

"Done. Next," Kaleb replies, smug as fuck, languishing on the kitchen chair as if it's a throne.

"What do you mean, done?" Kaiden snaps. Kaleb rolls his eyes and sighs before answering.

"I mean, The Butcher isn't butchering any longer. His head is in a jar in the basement, I was going to give it to daddy as a farewell gift."

"Right. Of course," Creed says sarcastically, "Why give him seven pieces of silver when you can give them a severed head."

"Ignoring that for now," Kaiden frowns, "Captain Collins, removing him means our father will lose the power of law enforcement. That'll give us more room to move. Luckily for us, he's already all tenderised and waiting for our visit."

"I want to finish him," I interrupt. "We have unfinished business."

It's more than just Paul, he's been corrupting everything I'd cared about for years.

"Very well. Creed, I moved your bike to the playhouse, that's where I've stashed Collins. Take Jason with you and bring back all the supplies."

"Yes, boss," Creed replies.

Kaleb scoffs.

"Who's a good little puppy? You are, oh yes you are," Kaleb teases.

Creed jumps up out of his chair ready to fly at Kaleb.

"Creed!" Nyx barks. "Sit. We have more to discuss. You can play together later."

Weirdly enough, Creed sits back down.

"I'll be waiting, sweetcheeks," he jokes, blowing a kiss to Kaleb. Nyx giggles, breaking the tension between them, and drawing both sets of eyes back to her again.

She can really control a room. She's fearless and inspiring, with a dash of Maria's temper. You really didn't want to fuck with her.

Warmth radiates in my chest, something which can only be described as fatherly pride. She really is the best of both of us. The sense of justice, the empathy, the way she's so free with her emotions.

Granted, I'd prefer she didn't hang around with a bunch of criminals, but the situation being what it is I'm starting to see them in a different light.

Well, maybe not Kaleb, pretty sure that fucker is just crazy.

"Getting back on track, all that's left is the money. Then he's just a nobody."

"Where does your money even come from?" Nyx asks curiously.

Yeah, I'd like to know that too.

"Not good places, Wildcat," Kaiden replies.

"What he means to say is the Ryker fortune was built on extortion, drugs, prostitution, guns, general blood money—" Kaleb explains before Kaiden cuts him off.

"Thanks for that," he snaps.

"What, scared Nyx will see through the prince in shining armour routine? Give me a break." Kaleb rolls his eyes.

"I swear, Kaleb, if you don't knock it off I—"

"You'll what, dearest brother? Trust me, you've had your free shots. You won't get anymore."

"I have no idea what you're talking about," Kaiden's voice turns to steel, "I don't know what you think I've done, I didn't even fucking know we were twins before yesterday. Whatever you think I've done, it wasn't me. I've never seen your face in my life. Just whispered words about a little brother. I think I would have remembered us meeting."

"You don't need to see someone's face to hurt them, to leave your mark," Kaleb snarls back.

Creed looks at me, and then looks at Nyx. I know what he's thinking. The twins need to clear the air, they need to get all this shit out of the way, but they won't, not with Nyx sitting there. She'd put herself straight in the middle and get caught in the crossfire.

Nyx stands up, trying to placate Kaleb, but every step closer to Kaleb fuels Kaiden's rage.

Fuck. Things were simpler when he was a cold-faced bastard who didn't give a shit.

I pull Nyx to my side, she looks up at me about to argue, but with a shake of my head she decides against it and turns to watch the brothers. Creed edges towards us so we sandwich Nyx between us, just in case anything goes south.

"Oh woe is me, get over yourself."

"Easy for you to say, you were always the favourite. The golden child. I was the spare, the whipping post. The fucking experiment."

"Golden child? Ha, don't make me laugh. All I've heard is how much of a disappointment I am for my whole fucking life. Hell, even my own mother left me in the hands of a monster instead of taking me with her. Discarded like some—"

"Is that what he told you?" Kaleb interrupts.

Kaiden doesn't reply, and just frowns at his twin.

"You stupid, self-centred, egotistical . . . it was never about you. She was going to take both of us with her, but father got wind of her plan. Someone sold her out. She just woke me up first. It was luck, nothing more."

Silence reigns between them as Kaiden absorbs that bombshell.

"It's true," Nyx says, "In Maria's box, there were two fake passports."

"Kai and Eve Marshall," Creed adds. "One for you, and one for your mother."

"But if her passport was there . . ." Kaiden murmurs, putting two and two together.

"She never made it out of the forest alive," Kaleb finishes.

"Your dad told me what happened," Nyx explains.

"Tell me please, my mother told me to run, and I did, like a coward. I always wondered if I could have stopped it . . . I need to know," Kaleb pleads.

"You really don't, trust me," Nyx argues, "Don't make me say it."

"Look, guys, does it really matter, I mean there's no bringing back the dead," Creed tries to interject.

Kaiden looks at Nyx, with a somewhat tortured expression.

"Tell us, Wildcat. You're the only one who can, and if he used it as a weapon against you, you can be sure he'll use it against us. It's better to be prepared."

"Listen, if she doesn't want to—" I start, not wanting her to be forced into anything, but her hand on my arm stops me.

"Only if you are sure." She gives them one last chance to back out. Creed's expression is grim. Both the twins share a look and nod. It's almost creepy how in sync with each other they can be when they aren't trying to rip each other's throats out.

"He chased her through the woods, he hunted her. He said he loved the panic and . . ."

"And what . . ." Kaleb encourages.

"He strangled her," Nyx explains.

"What else?" Kaiden asks. "We need to know, Wildcat, I know you don't want to say it but we need to hear it. I'd rather hear it from you."

"He said her panic made her . . . cunt tight," she trails off, looking at the floor.

Kaleb roars with anger, throwing a fist into the wall and Nyx flinches. I pull her to me, and rub her arm. I can understand her hesitation but I can also see why Kaiden needed to know. He just stands there, stoically. Not a single emotion registering on his face. Kaleb storms off, clearly done with the situation for now, but Kaiden has the opposite reaction, it's almost like he shut down.

"I'm sorry," Nyx mutters.

"It's not your fault, Wildcat, you have nothing to be sorry for. Creed, do you think you can take Jason to the playground, clear it out? I think me and my brother need to work out just how much our father has poisoned our lives. At the moment he has too much power over us, and we have too many blind spots he can exploit."

"Sure thing, boss. Jason, you ready?"

"Are you going to be okay, Spitfire?" I ask, looking down at Nyx.

"Yes, I'll be fine. You go do what you need to do, Dad."

Dad.

I was expecting to see judgement in her eyes, but there is none. It doesn't matter to her what title I have. Cop or Criminal. She doesn't see the world as good and bad, or right and wrong. She sees the shades of grey. She can see the darkness inside me clambering for a hold but she doesn't shy away, she doesn't seem ashamed of me. She just offers me a reassuring smile and I know no matter what I choose, as long as I choose it for the right reasons, she'll support me. Just as I'll support her.

"Okay, we won't be long," I say, pressing a small kiss to her head.

"Take the SUV," Kaiden orders.

"Isn't it too flashy?" I ask, I thought we were going under the radar.

"At this point, safety is more important. That SUV is a tank of wheels. It could buy you enough time for reinforcements. Take the SUV," Kaiden insists.

"Yes, boss," Creed replies, pulling me towards the door.

"Be careful," Nyx calls from behind.

I didn't realise how tough it would be to leave her again, the last time we split up we almost lost them.

But this wouldn't be like last time.

CHAPTER TWENTY FOUR

T hud.

I should have stayed.

Thud.

I should have gotten help.

Thud.

I should have done something.

Thud.

You.

Thud.

Fucking.

Thud.

Useless.

Thud.

Pathetic.

Thud.

Why?

Thud.

She was your mother.

Every hit on the punching bag does nothing to erase my anger.

Picturing *his* face instead of the bag doesn't help either, it's not enough.

It's too easy to blame myself.

I feel lost.

I think deep down, I knew what my father was capable of. I had heard the stories. I've seen the haunted eyes of the women who survived and the missing posters of the ones who didn't.

I know how cruel he can be.

My shirt clings to my back, the scars ache as they often do when my thoughts linger on my childhood for too long. I rip the shirt off, and press my forehead against the cool surface of the bag. My hands throb, but pain is my friend. I focus on it, trying to shut everything else out. The ache in my arms, the sharp stab of pain from my bruised knuckles, when I clench and unclench my fists. Me and pain are old friends, the clarity it gives me when the demons are overwhelming me has brought me back from the brink time and time again.

My breathing slows, my mind focuses, but my peace is short lived.

"Go away." I don't care who it is, I don't want to see anyone right now.

They already know how weak you are.

How pathetic.

"I said go away," I snarl, but the door doesn't shut, footsteps don't retreat. They're still here.

"Are you deaf?" I snap, turning around like some sort of feral monster.

Kaiden stands firm, putting Nyx behind him, a calculating look in his eye.

He's working out just how much of a threat I truly am.

I probably look like a monster.

Something akin to shame briefly flashes across my mind before it's replaced with rage.

Of course you look like a monster, you are what they made you.

You didn't get a choice.

Who are they to judge you now?

We should show them.

Show them just what they created.

Hurt them just like they hurt us.

"Shut up, shut up, shut up," I scream, clutching at my head.

I crouch down, curling in on myself.

"Leave me," I shout, not sure how long I can hold my shit together. I reach for one of the gloves that'd long been discarded on the floor, and throw it towards them.

They need to get away.

Please.

"You're bleeding," Nyx's concerned voice filters through my spiralling thoughts.

You deserve to bleed.

Why should you be the one who lived?

I'm cold, the darkness swallowing me up.

The feel of a hand over mine is almost scalding, such warmth . . .

You don't deserve it.

I try to snatch my hand away.

"Let me look," comes a no nonsense tone.

Kitten. It could only be her.

"Nyx." This voice is different, warning, danger.

I growl low, warning it to stay away.

They always hurt you.

Hurt them first.

"No," I bark. Not sure who I was even talking to.

"He won't hurt me. Will you, Kaleb?"

Kaleb.

That's me.

I am Kaleb.

I'm not a monster.

"Kitten?" my voice is weak to my ears.

"It's me. I'm here. I'm so sorry, Kaleb. It's my fault." Nyx kneels down beside me and wraps her arms around me.

"No," I snap, flinging my eyes open.

I could never let her blame herself.

"It's not your fault, you did nothing. I ran, I left her. It's my fault." I let a tear fall down my cheek, I hadn't cried since that day.

Without hesitation, Nyx brushes it away.

"Idiot," Kaiden mutters.

"What did you call me?" I snap.

"Kaiden, I don't think this is the time—" Nyx interjects.

"I said you're an idiot," Kaiden repeats.

"And what do you know, Golden Boy?"

"Apparently I know more than you, I know that now, as fully grown men, taking out our father is a long shot, as an eight year old boy, you didn't have a hope in hell," Kaiden snaps back.

"I could have gotten help, I could have made a distraction, helped her get away," I argue. I've been through the scenario so many times in my head. Over and over until it drives me crazy.

"And Keith could have had a heart attack, got struck by lightning, got bitten by a poisonous snake, but he didn't. What is done is done, there is no changing it."

"Don't you think I know that? I know there's no bringing her back."

"So what are you doing? Crying like a baby? What's that going to do?"

"I'm going to kill the son of a bitch, that's what I'm going to do about it."

Kaiden smiles, and I realise I've been played. Nyx has reached past my demons, and stopped me from drowning, and Kaiden has reminded me of my purpose, reminded me who truly deserved my rage.

"Well played," I mutter reluctantly, hiding the smallest of smiles.

Nyx helps me to my feet. I feel weak, vulnerable, but for the first time in a long time the monster lurking in my head isn't swirling on the edges, whispering, tormenting. Even when it's silent I can usually feel it, like a dark cloud, but for now at least, I feel free.

I hug her tightly, ignoring Kaiden completely.

"Thanks, Kitten, you saved me again." I give her a final squeeze before letting her go.

The colour has drained from Kaiden's face, his smile absent.

"Look, I know she's your girl and everything, she's made that clear but—" I start.

"Where did you get that?" Kaiden asks, and I know what he is referring to, but after what just happened I choose to play dumb.

"No idea what you mean," I reply, picking my shirt up off the floor and pulling it back on. But the damage has already been done. I don't care about my scars, not really, but I hate the response they garner, the pity.

Kaiden's look isn't a look of pity. It's haunted. Tormented.

I sigh, I can already tell he knows, and he isn't going to let it go.

"That's what you meant, wasn't it? When you said you didn't need to see someone to leave a mark . . ."

"What's he talking about?" Nyx asks.

"This." I lift up the corner of my shirt and show her what Kaiden had seen. No one would notice what it was unless they were looking for it.

"I never knew, I—" he starts to explain.

"Stop. I know. It was all part of his sick, twisted plan. It seems like he left brands on both of us. I tried to cover it, but every time he'd carve it back in deeper."

"K. R." Nyx says, tracing the letters with the tip of her finger.

"Kaiden Ryker," Kaiden explains.

"No, Keith Ryker," I correct him.

"Your cries, they gave me nightmares for weeks, I tried asking about you, I asked everyone, no one would tell me. I—"

"What's done is done. What is it you told me? What's crying about it going to do?" I smirk as anger flashes in his eyes.

Nyx giggles beside me drawing our attention to her.

"Wildcat?"

"It's just . . . You guys are complete opposites but when you do the same thing, and you look the same I just—" she laughs harder. "You're both so stupid." She doubles down on the laughter causing us both to smile along with her.

I look towards my twin, really look at him for the first time, and for the first time I realise somewhere down the line I'd stopped hating him. He isn't part of the problem. He was a child, who did his best to survive just like I did.

"I'm clearly the handsome one though," Kaiden retorts, clearly teasing.

Dick.

Just because he's not part of the problem doesn't mean he needs to be part of the solution.

"Oh my God, you guys should totally pretend to be each other next time we see Creed, it would be freaking hilarious," Nyx suggests.

"No fucking way," We both snap in unison.

Nyx just breaks down into another fit of giggles.

"Fuck," we both mutter, our eyes widening in alarm.

"Stop guys . . . you're . . . killing me . . ." Nyx gasps out between hysterical laughter. Clutching her stomach, barely able to stand.

It isn't that funny.

Me and Kaiden scowl at each other, not risking saying another word.

As Nyx starts to calm down she wipes the tears from her eyes, and looks at us.

"What am I going to do with you guys?" Nyx asks hypothetically.

Well I can think of a few things.

Nyx must feel the tension in the room shift as she looks towards us both. We watch her cheeks flush with colour as she realises just what she'd said, how she lumped us both together, and how we could take it. Take her. She can probably see the lust in my eyes as my thoughts go straight to the gutter.

Kaiden clears his throat.

"We should probably clear the air, and share everything we know. Make sure our father can't blindside us any further. Are you up for that?" Kaiden asks.

"I think I can manage."

"Let's go back to the kitchen, and I'll make us some breakfast. I have a feeling it's going to be a long morning," Nyx suggests.

"It's as good a place as any," I agree.

Soon the smell of bacon is in the air, and we're sitting around the kitchen table sharing information. It's almost homely. It almost feels like . . . family, you know with added scheming, hostile takeovers, and how to get away with murder. So pretty darn close to perfection.

Chapter Twenty Five

We drove in silence for a while. Both of us are meant to be dead men, so everytime we stick our neck out it's a risk. I was expecting jokes and quips, but Creed remains silent.

"We're here," he says, pulling up to a small warehouse. It's deep within the industrial part of town, near the docks to be practical, but far enough away from everything it makes me nervous. Creed obviously notes my discomfort, much to my annoyance, as he gives me a condescending smirk.

"Come on," Creed says, opening the driver door and getting out. I follow his lead. He stops outside a plain metal door, it doesn't look like much, covered with various graffiti and phone numbers to call for a good time.

I hear a gun cock, and spin around to find the source. Creed shows no conflict, no remorse, the gun in his hand remains steady.

"For fuck's sake, what's with everyone pointing guns at me lately?" I sigh. Thinking about it, it's probably not the most normal of responses, and if I ever dared to see a therapist they'd probably have a fucking field day. I clearly have more issues than even a millionaire could afford to pay for.

"Maybe because you're a cop?" Creed replies.

"Is that your excuse?" I snap.

"Excuse?" Creed spits. "So you think the incorruptible, hero cop of Blight with a badge more spotless than a stripper's pussy after a bikini wax, suddenly joined the dark side? You just happened to have this secret relationship no one ever heard of?"

"Nyx proves—"

"Nyx proved you did. At some point. Feelings change, people move on. You've managed to cuddle up to Kaiden and get a target on his back. Nyx put herself in danger all because of some piece of paper . . ."

His hand trembles slightly as his rage grows.

"It's all so easy, so clean. You've talked a big game, said big words, but what have you actually done? You could easily run down to the police station right now and hand Kaiden to them on a silver platter, but I won't let you. You're a liability."

"Kaiden and Nyx don't seem to think so," I reply

"Maybe, but Nyx always wants to see the good in everyone, and for the first time Kaiden is actually trusting someone . . . I can't let you hurt them."

"I would never, Nyx is—"

"Your daughter, yeah I know. But parents can betray kids, I mean look at Keith going for father of the year."

"Don't fucking compare me to him," I spit. My entire body vibrates with anger, my ability for rational thinking is getting swallowed by my rage.

"How fucking dare you, Creed." I storm up to him, forgetting all about the gun until I feel it poke me in the chest. "You know I've put up with a lot of shit from you, your childish quips, your lame ass jokes, the whole ridiculous tough guy act you put on, but you do not get to pull this shit. I've missed out on Nyx's entire life. She was kept hidden from me, I didn't know anything about her. If I had done, I would have been there. Every . . . Single . . . Time . . . She needed me." I poke his chest with every pause, driving my point home. "Maybe if I'd been there she wouldn't have such low standards for men, and you and the psycho musketeers wouldn't even be given the time of day. Keith, fuck. It takes a special kind of psycho to do even a fraction of what he's done to his kids. Kids he watched grow up, kids he actually had a chance to know. If you think I'm capable of hurting Nyx, even the tiniest fraction of what that monster has done, pull that fucking trigger. Right . . . Fucking . . . Now," I demand, fire in my eyes. "I'd rather be dead than ever hurt her."

If I can't convince him with words, there's nothing I can do to prove my sincerity.

I suppose that's the problem with love, it isn't tangible, it isn't something you can prove on the spot. People have used love like a weapon too many times. Some people just have too many scars to ever trust in words again. Sometimes it is easier to believe a lie, than to take the risk that a person's love is real. Love and pain are too closely intertwined.

Creed looks at me, and I stare right back. We're at a stalemate.

"Not today," Creed sighs, lowering the gun.

"Thank you so much, how will I ever repay you?" I reply sarcastically. Brushing off the non-existent dirt from where the gun rested on my chest.

"Shut up. I'm still not convinced. I'll be keeping my eye on you. The moment you step out of line, I'll be there seeing what the inside of your skull looks like," Creed grumbles, pushing past me. He walks over to a banged up electric meter box, it's clearly seen better days.

What the fuck was he up to?

Creed removes the panel, revealing a lot of tech that shouldn't be in there. He scans his thumb and when a robotic voice asks him for his password he replies "Yippee-Ki-Yay."

I fight back a snigger, as Creed turns around to face me.

"What?" he snaps, "It's a classic."

I hold up my arms in mock surrender.

"No denying it," I agree. *Die Hard is a classic.*

"Okay then," Creed grabs hold of the door, a sceptical look in his eyes, like he doesn't quite believe me. This guy has trust issues upon trust issues, and I am really getting fed up with his hot and cold attitude.

"My baby!" Creed shouts, seeing the rainbow coloured monstrosity flicker as the fluorescent lights come to life. He runs over and starts to coo over the . . . I reluctantly call it a machine, but it's like an abomination for the eyes. I'm shocked Kaiden chose to save it, maybe he did just save it to set it on fire.

The way Creed's whispering to his bike and running his hands over it is borderline obscene, but I feel like I can't interrupt despite wanting to throw up.

Just how attached is he to that thing?

"I'm sorry, my baby, soon we must part once more. It's not safe to take you with me, so you stay here and be a good girl for daddy. I'll take Stabbifer with me for luck, that way you'll be with me in spirit," Creed coos. "It's okay baby, this won't hurt." He slides one of his curved blades from his hidden holster at the base of his back, and slips it around the weird little plush freeing it from the front of his bike. With his trophy in hand, he slips the blade back into the holster and tucks the little brightly coloured horse-knife thing in his jeans pocket. He keeps the head poking out, and gives it an affectionate pat.

He turns to look at me, and my feelings must show on my face.

"Oh, I forgot my manners, Stabbifer, this is Jason. Jason ... Stabbifer," Creed makes the introductions, while I just stand there very fucking confused.

This man just pulled a gun on me, and now he's prancing around with a plush that looks like it was made by a disturbed little girl.

"Okay, now you're just being rude," Creed snaps.

"Erm ... I'm sorry?" I reply, not really sure what the hell is going on anymore. Even if you take *Stabbifer* out of the equation, this place is almost unsettling. I was expecting blood, a dungeon, something dark, not this bright clean space. Sofas to relax on, a pool table, a bar, everything looks sophisticated and high end, which I have come to expect from Kaiden. It's clear to see he's the brains behind this place.

"Pretty sweet, isn't it?" Creed says with a smirk, finally registering my wide eyed curiosity. "This is the relax area, we have a locker room and showers through that door there. Spare clothes and all, a small incinerator for any clothes we don't want to keep. The door next to the bar, that's the armoury. Guns, knives, explosives. All the fun stuff. Probably better kitted out than the BPD, but you need a thumbprint to open it, and it has a fail safe so nothing can fall into the wrong hands. Through that big padded door over there is . . . I don't think we came up with a special name for it, but open that door and that's when the screaming usually starts. Fire proof door, switch on the outside incinerates everything within, so don't get any ideas about bringing your cop buddies here." Creed is acting like a weirdass tour guide.

"I wasn't going to. Get it through your head already. I want to stop Keith just as much as the rest of you."

"Mhmmm." Creed still sounds sceptical though.

I'm getting really fucking fed up with having to defend myself every two seconds to him.

"So Collins?" I ask.

If Creed thinks I'm just going to keep my hands clean, that I'm not fuelled by the same darkness, the same sense of revenge as the rest of them. There's only one way I'm going to prove myself to him.

"Sure. Let's go pay him a visit," he says, as if we're going to visit his grandma in hospital, as if it's just an everyday occurrence. It really annoys me how nonchalant he is about all this. We're talking about someone's life. Collins isn't a good man by any stretch of the imagination, but there's still a small part of me clinging to the good vs evil facade, the ridiculous lie humans made up to make themselves feel better than others.

Good and evil is a concept born out of fear, it's primarily driven by the weak and cowardly. It gives the 'good' the excuse of never fighting back, taking the safe path, if you don't hurt anyone then you aren't going to be the victim of revenge. If you get hurt, you justify letting it go as being the 'better' person. But there's no such thing. There's only fear. Fear of judgement; what would the neighbours think? Fear of retaliation; what would they do back to me to make it hurt worse? And fear that you'd have to face the realisation you aren't as tough as you thought you were when you're beaten into the ground.

So good is safe.

Until it isn't.

It wasn't safe for Paul.

It wasn't safe for his flatmates.

It wasn't safe for the women at Haven.

And it wasn't safe for Maria.

If anything, the last few days have proven to me I can't play it 'safe'. I can't hold on to this stupid idealism of good. The good in storybooks isn't real. There is no white knight coming to knock Keith Ryker off his throne. All we have now is a dark and twisted fight for survival, and in every war there are always going to be casualties. Paul and his friends are going to be the last people I lost. Every drop of blood, every pound of flesh from here on out will be carved from Keith Ryker and anyone sick enough to follow him.

I follow Creed down the dark corridor, this area did scream dungeon. You can feel the violence in the air, the tang of metal that'd never be erased no matter how many times fire licked the walls. As we pass rooms, I peek in, relieved to find them unoccupied, but horrified by their contents.

Tables that look like a mix of operating theatres and morgue slabs with drains in the floors and multiple gleaming surfaces.

An almost medieval looking room, with devices I can't even begin to fathom what they can be used for.

Another one is empty, save for manacles bolted to the floor and a discarded bucket in the corner which looks like it had scratch marks in it.

Eventually we come to the end of the corridor.

"Here we go, in the finest accommodations the play-ground has to offer," Creed announces, as if he's a tour guide at the circus.

There's Collins, all right.

If I didn't know it was him, I might not have recognised him hanging by his wrists, his feet barely scraping the floor.

"Just how long has he been here?" I ask.

"You'll have to ask Kaiden," Creed says with a shrug. "You said you guys had unfinished business . . . So what are you waiting for?" Creed narrows his suspicious eyes on me once more.

"Can we get him down from there?" I ask.

"Why?"

"Because he's clearly exhausted, his feet barely touch the floor, and when was the last time he drank something? If you and Kaiden are the only ones who know about this place then no one has been to—"

"Who the fuck cares?" Creed snarls.

"This isn't right," I reply.

Creed laughs.

"I knew it. You can't do it, can you? All talk. What was it you said? You want to stop Keith as much as the rest of us? Well clearly fucking not if you're worried of getting your hands dirty," he sneers.

"Is that what you think?" I snap, "You think I worry about his comfort, that I'm trying to save him?"

"Well aren't you?"

"Fuck no," I answer, "I don't want to save him, I just want him lucid. I want him to know what he's done. I want him to have to face his crimes, the lives that have been sacrificed to save his fucking job of all things."

"Well why didn't you say so?" Creed snarks, pressing a button on the wall. The cuffs instantly release, causing Collins to fall to the ground with a pained cry. I must look puzzled.

"What? We aren't in the middle ages. What were you expecting? A big ring with iron keys on it?" Creed jokes.

"Well, kind of," I reply.

"I know, right? It would totally add to the whole aesthetic, but Kaiden said no," Creed pouts. I roll my eyes.

Creed's mood changes so fast it could give me whiplash but honestly, it's probably all part of his gimmick. The guy isn't stupid, Kaiden wouldn't have kept him around and had so much faith in him if he was.

"Oh, Jason, you found me." Collins finally notices my presence and gets to his knees looking at me with wide-eyed hope.

It's sickening.

He looks from me to Creed, who is leaning nonchalantly against the wall as if he doesn't give a shit. Collins has seen better days, that's for sure, but I can't muster up pity for him. Seeing his swollen eyes, and purple bruises doesn't even begin to feel like justice.

"Where's the back up?" Collins asks, his voice shaking.

"Probably still dealing with stuff down at the station. With you missing, and me not there to issue orders, it wouldn't surprise me if the precinct was on fire and they were merrily roasting marshmallows telling scary stories."

"Hey, Creed," I address him without taking my eyes off the disgusting creature in front of me, "did I ever tell you the latest story of the mystery box on the detective's desk?"

Collins frowns, his fat face resembling a scrotum trying to collapse in on itself.

"It was a bomb, wasn't it?" Creed says gleefully.

"No, not a bomb. Good guess though, it was my first thought too. What about you Collins? Want to guess?" I ask.

Collins shakes his head. I'm not sure if he knows about the people who were sacrificed for him, I doubt it though, someone as entitled and lazy as him probably doesn't have the stomach for it.

"Oh go on," I encourage Collins.

"Guess," snaps Creed, causing Collins to jump. I fight to suppress my laughter. I can see why it's rare to see a rehabilitated criminal, the power is intoxicating.

"Er . . . Er . . ." stutters Collins.

"Any day now." I make a get-on-with-it motion with my hands.

Maybe he's been hit around the head one too many times.

"You know what? I'll just tell you," I say impatiently. Collins looks relieved, as if I'm helping him out, but in reality being in his presence is making my stomach churn. He reeks of piss, and sweat, and yet still the horrible stench of his cologne clings to him despite him not seeing the sun in days.

"There was a matching pair of ears."

Collins gulps.

"A set of eyeballs, perfectly removed," I continue.

"Wow, that's tricky to do, that is. Pro stuff," Creed adds, making Collins turn green.

"And there was also this big fleshy mass, which I could only presume was a tongue. Have you ever seen what a severed tongue looks like, Collins? One that's been ripped from the skull? It's longer than you'd think," I explain.

I've barely made it to the end of my little speech before Collins face plants the floor, out cold.

Creed laughs at the thunk his head makes as it hits the floor and I find myself smiling.

Yeah, safe to say he never handled any of the dirty work. He probably isn't even aware of the sheer amount of bodies he's indirectly responsible for. But he soon will be.

"Let's move him before he wakes up." I move towards him, grabbing an arm.

"Just what are you planning, Detective?" Creed asks

"Don't call me that, not here," I snap.

"Okay, no need to get touchy, just tell me where you want to put him."

"The tables looked good."

That isn't exactly the truth, the tables look like the place you'd either build a body, or take one apart, but that suits my plan perfectly. He'll know exactly what pain he's caused, one excruciating lesson at a time, it's the least I can do. Hopefully then I can absolve myself of some of the guilt I carry for Paul's death.

The next hour or so passes in a blur of blood, and screams. At least I think it's an hour. It could have been five minutes, or five days. Looking at Collins I should feel horrified by what I've done, but I feel nothing.

Collins makes a noise that sounds like he's slowly drowning. I can only presume he's wishing for death. I'm just not sure if I should give it to him. Death is freedom, it's final, but I can't keep him in this perpetual state, there is only so much a body can take, after all. His eyes are long shut, never to reopen. Robbing him of his sight was one of the first things I did. I knew it would make the other senses work harder, every sound and touch so much more threatening and painful. His hearing had gone next, ruptured eardrums. Painful, but not life threatening. That's when the begging turned into something more raw, animalistic sounds instead of words, as the blood from his eyes mixed with his tears. He's broken, bruised, and bleeding, and even now it doesn't feel like justice has been served.

"It's time to end it," Creed interrupts.

"Not yet," I snap.

I can't let him off this easily.

"We've already been here for too long," Creed explains.

"You said no one knew about this place"

"Nyx will worry," Creed reminds me.

Nyx. Shit.

I look at Collins and feel something akin to shame.

I was so focused on revenge, and the dead, I completely lost track of what's actually important.

"You're right. Let's finish up here."

Collins lets out a sound which is somewhere between a wheeze and a moan. I'm not sure if it's relief or panic, it could just be him surrendering to the inevitable. He has to have known there's only one way his life was ever going to end.

I turn around and walk over to the tools.

How to do it?

There's still a small part of me warning me, crying out to stop, to notice how far I'm falling. But that naivety is what got Paul and his friends killed in the first place. Maybe in an alternative world, or a different town, it could have been different. Here I don't have the luxury of holding onto my morals so tightly. I need to adapt. I have to. It's the only way to survive now.

I grip one of the bowie blades from the side, and turn around to face Collins once more. The knife is surprisingly heavy, with an eight inch blade.

Pull it together, Wyatt.

Think of Paul.

Think of all the innocent people.

I grip the hilt tighter.

I'm hyper aware of Creed's eyes on me, watching me closely.

Fucker was probably judging me, thinking I can't do it.

Well he won't be thinking so for long.

I stand over Collins, wondering where to deliver the final blow.

Shall I make it quick? Clean? Messy? Slow?

Stop overthinking it.

Just do it.

I'm waiting for Creed to make a snide comment, it's so much easier to act when I'm angry. It's easy to lash out. If I'm being honest, I didn't even know Paul well, it was a working relationship, if you could even call it that. He was just one of the first people I thought of.

I don't have friends. After Maria left, I retreated, wallowed in self pity, built walls to keep people out. Saying I'm doing it for the people, his victims, blah blah, it's harder than I thought when they aren't here. When he didn't actually pull the triggers. He didn't even know about them. My hand starts to shake with my wavering resolve but I grip the hilt tighter, feeling my nails bite into my flesh.

Get angry.

Just think of all the times he blew you off.

He undermined everything you stood for.

Ridiculed you for doing the right thing.

It didn't matter how many times I tried to justify it, the anger just wouldn't come.

So I have to do it without the anger.

Rationally.

Intentionally.

271

I nod, and bring the knife up and over his stomach, blade pointing downwards. I place my other hand palm down over the other to provide maximum thrust. Taking a deep breath in . . .

In three . . .

Two . . .

Before I can finish counting down, Creed's blade comes out, I hadn't even heard him move closer. His knife sinks into Collins's abdomen like butter, and he slices to the side. Collins opens up like a steaming jacket potato, but what falls out of him isn't potato.

I drop the knife, and run out of the room.

Creed finds me throwing up a little bit further down the corridor, and pats me on the shoulder.

"Why did you do that?" I rasp, my throat raw from bringing up this morning's coffee. "I was going to—" I'm cut off when another load of bile wants to say hello.

"I know," Creed replies, not teasing, but sounding surprisingly sombre. "I know you were going to, which is why I couldn't let you."

"What do you mean?" I'm so confused, just a while ago he'd been complaining there was no dirt on me, surely killing my own Captain would give him the ammunition to destroy me if I ever moved against them.

"Look, him dying wasn't worth you killing him," Creed replies

"That doesn't even make sense."

"It will do, one day. Besides, now you owe me." He smirks, Creed's normal happy go lucky, cocky expression firmly back in place.

"What the fuck for?"

"For not telling everyone how you threw up like a little bitch," he teases. Remembering the sick squelch and the way—

Creed leaves me throwing up, as he sauntered down the hallway laughing. "When you're finished being a baby we have a car to load up," he calls over his shoulder.

I feel a little wobbly, and still very green, but I'm pretty sure at this point I have nothing left to throw up. Picking up the last shreds of my dignity, I go to catch up with Creed.

Chapter Twenty Six

"Took you guys long enough," is the first thing I can think of to say, when Creed and Jason finally drag their asses through the door.

"Aww, K, I missed you too," Creed teases, blowing me a kiss. "It's nice to know I still have a special place in your heart and that Nyx hasn't kicked me out entirely."

"I've got a special place for my fist," I mutter, but Creed hears me and starts to howl with laughter. Even Jason sniggers. "I meant your face. Fucking perverts the lot of you."

Nyx chooses that moment to walk in with Kaleb, while I'm blustering and trying to regain some resemblance of control over the situation.

Fucking hell, what happened to my god-damned respect?

"What's going on?" Nyx asks, frowning at Creed who's barely standing from laughing so hard.

Come on, it wasn't that funny.

I scowl at him.

"Loverboy . . . wants to . . . fist me," Creed gasps out in between laughter.

Nyx looks at me and sniggers.

"I think this is the first time I've seen you flustered," she teases, "It's cute."

Kaleb joins in laughing at my expense and honestly I'm contemplating shooting the lot of them. Well, excluding Nyx. I have other punishments in mind for her. Nyx must notice my mood as she comes over to me, planting a small kiss on my lips. The small gesture is enough to calm me and remind me that they aren't being malicious, and I don't have to prove anything to anyone.

"Once you ladies have finished, me and Kaleb came up with a plan."

"Huh, I didn't think the psycho twin did plans," Creed snarks.

"It's less of a plan, more . . . organised chaos," Kaleb replies.

"Sounds fun, I'm guessing that's why we raided your bunker," Jason replies

"Urgh, don't call it a bunker, you make us all sound like old men, not just you. It sounds like some weird dirty talk from '*back in the old days*'," Creed says, rolling his eyes, back to his teasing ways.

"Regardless, it's empty now," Jason replies, not rising to Creed's bait.

"Not empty, my bike's still there," Creed mutters.

"Focus, Creed," I snap. "Do you want to know the plan or do you want to sit and sulk about a piece of metal?"

"Take. That. Back!" Creed hisses, getting his fucking knickers in a twist.

"He's sorry," Nyx answers on my behalf, shooting me a glare.

I'm not fucking sorry, he's acting like a baby.

"So the plan?" Jason prompts before whatever this is, could dissolve into chaos once more.

"There's a shipment coming in, a big one," I explain. "Any of you heard of the Jula family?" Everyone apart from Kaleb shakes their heads.

"I've only heard rumours" Kaleb explains, "Distribution experts, if you've ever moved something, even so much as posted a letter, it passes through them, or someone owned by them. But they're like ghosts, just getting a meeting takes years, and some heavy collateral."

"He's not wrong. It seems like daddy dearest has been trying to get in their good graces for a while. I had the pleasure of meeting with the Deus, and his psycho spawn and I have to admit, I've never met anyone like it. The men were theirs. Both the ones at the safe house, and the ones at Haven."

"Wait . . . The Jula were behind the attack on Haven, I thought you said your dad was to blame?" Jason asks.

"The Jula gave my dad the men, that's why they were hard to identify. He said he was unhappy that he lost them all, and to not lose this set."

Kaleb chuckles.

"I'm guessing you had something to do with the extra bodies at Haven?" I ask my twin.

"Daddy dearest is going to be in so much trouble," Kaleb answers, completely ignoring the question, "it's rare for someone to get this many chances. Just what is he giving them to make them this interested?"

"It's not important", I threw a hesitant look at Nyx. If I tell her I was what's been promised she won't let it go, and I need to keep her as far away from that psychotic female as possible. "We'll be severing that connection, it's the easiest way to put him on the back foot. There's a shipment coming in, safe to say it's his last chance with the Jula's. No matter how much they want something, no one will tolerate being made a fool of three times. The Deus warned as much."

"So we're going to have a party at the docks, a few fireworks, shit tons of chaos, a party worthy of the death of an era," Kaleb adds, smirking like a psycho. I don't even think I could twist my face into that shape, he looks predatory and unhinged.

"Sounds like my type of party," Creed replies, his voice vibrating with excitement.

"There's not enough time to come up with a fool-proof plan this time. It's going to be messy, and it's going to be crude. There's too many variables."

"Variables, schm-ariables," Kaleb scoffs.

"We don't even know what the shipment is," I snap back, recklessness is going to get us killed.

"Doesn't matter, everything burns," Kaleb argues.

Fucker had an answer for everything.

"It's not . . . *people, is it*?" Nyx asks.

I sigh, hating that she would imagine the worst, but honestly . . .

"I don't know, Wildcat, but I hope not," I answer.

"How do we plan for something that could be people, could be drugs, weapons, explosives? It could be exotic fucking animals for all we know. It's a logistical night-mare." Jason sees the problem, at least one other person can see the risk we'd be taking.

"Honestly? There's only so much we can do. We're going to need to be very flexible, which is why Nyx you will be staying here," I say.

"No." Nyx already starts to get upset, shaking her head. "We are not splitting up, not again. Can't you see that's what keeps letting him get the upper hand? It's like a cliche horror movie. We are not splitting up."

"Kitten, as adorable as it is watching you rip into him, hear him out."

I don't know what to make of the pet names, or his clear interest in her. Nyx is certainly a tamer of monsters, and at the moment the only priority I have is keeping her alive. The more monsters who are in love with her, the safer she is.

"Did you pick up the surveillance stuff or just the toys?" I ask Creed.

"You said to clear it out, we cleared it out. Including the boring stuff," he replies.

"It's not boring if it keeps us alive," I snap. Taking a deep breath I continue, "Nyx, I need you here, being our base, it's you who will have to watch our backs, co-ordinate us."

"Why me? That sounds like something Jason would be better at doing," Nyx argues, and yes I can see her point. I mean Jason has the experience, and he has been practically running things at the station as far as I can tell.

"Because, Kitten, I trust you with my life. Everyone else not so much," Kaleb answers.

"Plus, you know how to bring Creed to heel and that's not an easy task. We all listen to you, Wildcat," I explain.

It's more than just placating her and keeping her safe. This is honestly the best chance we have at success.

"I mean, if I'm going to have someone nattering in my ear, I'll take a lady over an old grouch any day of the week," adds Creed, never missing a chance to wind Jason up.

"The feeling's mutual, pip squeak," Jason quips.

"Pip squeak? Who uses that anymore?" Creed laughs.

One day that guy will piss off the wrong person, I swear.

"And that's why," I point out. "Realistically it can only be you, Wildcat."

"And the fact it keeps me nice and safe here, doesn't factor into it at all," she deadpans.

"Well, I don't hate the idea," I answer honestly.

"We know you can take care of yourself, Kitten, but we need you here. It's as simple as that," Kaleb adds.

"You guys promise you will be in contact with me the entire time? This won't be some stupid 'let the men handle it' shit?" Nyx asks, looking between me and Kaleb sceptically.

"Cross my heart. I've never lied to you, Kitten. I'm not going to start now."

I remain silent, hoping she'll believe us. It's the only way working together is going to work. It's already fifty-fifty if Creed follows my orders in the heat of battle. Jason I think would follow orders, as he is used to it, but he's also easily angered and can be unpredictable. I don't know when he'd suddenly go all martyr or do something reckless based on his morality. Kaleb, well I'm still not sure. He doesn't seem like one to play nicely with others, even if we have reached some kind of truce.

"Okay, I guess I'll stay behind, but I really have no idea what I'm doing."

"Which is why Jason will be staying with you to assist."

"I don't need a babysitter," Nyx argues.

"Princess, you just said you had no idea what you're doing and Jason would be better for the job. Make up your mind," Creed teases.

"Well, I—"

"To be honest, Nyx, I almost lost you once. I'd rather not let you out of my sight for a bit. It was one thing to have you stay with Kaiden, but I only just got you back. Please let me stay with you," Jason asks, surprising me. I knew he was upset when she was missing, but I had no idea he was still struggling. Leaving him with her is the right call. It also means what needs to be done will be done. I know Collins took his toll on Jason, and I can't afford him getting a crisis of conscience now.

Until I know for sure what happened at the playground and where his head's at, it's best to keep him out of this.

"Okay so we'll set up the computers here, Jason and Nyx will run point. We'll cover the exits with the cameras giving them eyes, and have comms in so we can stay in touch, then it's just a case of reacting once we know what the shipment is. Not sure who will handle the shipment, it's usually left to Uncle so we'll have to be sneaky, set up too soon or if he discovers anything in his sweeps we're fucked. He will call the entire thing off if he thinks he's in danger. If it's my father—"

"We kill him," Kaleb finishes, cutting me off.

"I don't think it's that simple but if we get the chance, we take him out."

"No," Nyx interrupts, surprising us all.

"Princess, some people you just can't save," Creed tries to reason with her.

"Yeah I don't think just arresting someone like that will work," Jason adds.

"I said, no."

"Wildcat, I'm sorry but—"

"Let her finish," Kaleb interrupts again.

I'm getting sick of him always undermining me, always fucking interrupting and trying to have the last word.

"Thanks, Kaleb," she smiles at him and I find my trigger finger getting itchy.

He's your brother, he's your brother.

Yeah that wasn't calming me down.

"I don't want to save him, I don't want to arrest him and let him live in a comfy little cell for the rest of his days," she explains, "I want to make him pay, I want my pound of flesh, I want to carve him up, and make his last moments on this planet agonising. I want to watch the blood run from his veins and the light vanish from his eyes. I want him to crumble, and I want him to know who's fucking responsible."

We shouldn't be surprised by now, we've all seen her bloodlust, but every time she seems crueller, colder, more like what I used to be. Kaleb beams at her like he's proud of her or some twisted shit. I can't let her lose herself, and I vow to kill the son of a bitch as soon as possible. The sooner our vengeance ends, the sooner we can start to heal and move on.

"Okay, but no promises. If we can capture him, we do so. But that fucker does not get to breathe for a second longer than necessary. We can't capture him, he dies. Fair enough?" I ask, I can't let her hate me for robbing her of her kill, but at the same time I can't risk her safety. My dad wants her, and I can't let him have her.

"Okay," she grumbles, reluctantly.

Has she always been this bloodthirsty?

"Okay, if no one has any other objections, let's get a move on. The shipment arrives at nine tonight, and we have a lot to do."

"Team on three?" Creed says, putting his hand out palm down in the middle.

"Nope," Kaleb is the first to refuse.

"I'll get the surveillance stuff out of the car," Jason excuses himself.

"Not happening," I state.

"Aww come on, Princess, you won't leave me hanging will you?" Creed pleads.

She giggles but walks over to him, putting her hand over his.

"3 . . . 2 . . . 1 . . ." Creed counts down

"TEAM!" they both shout, raising their hands in the air.

I smile at them, I just hope there'll be more smiles and more moments like this in the future. I look from my sworn brother to my twin. It seems with every move I make in this chess match, the stakes get even higher, and I can't afford to lose.

CHAPTER TWENTY SEVEN

I give them all a kiss on the cheek for luck, but I hate them going without me. Don't get me wrong, I'm not delusional. I know even with my little training session I'm more hindrance than help. The headshot was a complete fluke, adrenaline and fear made the shot go wide. I can't imagine what it'll be like for them at the docks.

"It will be okay, Nyx, they know what they're doing." Jason tries to soothe my worries.

"Probably," I reply. It's the closest I can feel to positivity at the moment. After everything they've been through they have to be okay. For them to fail now isn't an option.

"As soon as the cameras are set up, you'll feel better." I know he's trying to be encouraging, but I feel like my heart is being strangled in my chest. I've seen the haunted look in all of their eyes, I know how much this means to all of them, I just . . .

You're just being selfish, I scold myself, trying to shake off my feelings. It's selfish. I've always been selfish. When Kaiden didn't want me to go back to Haven, I insisted. When Creed didn't want to take me along with them to the safe house, I insisted. Every single time, I have just thought of myself and my feelings.

"Wildcat, you there?" Kaiden's voice comes through the comms device in my ear.

"Yeah, I'm here," I reply. Hearing his strong calm tone makes me feel a little better. "Creed? Kaleb?" I ask, my voice wavering a little.

"Yep, I'm here, Princess, missing me already?" Creed teases.

"Maybe," I confess.

"Don't worry, we'll all be reunited soon. This will be a piece of cake." Even with Creed's signature confidence, he can't convince me this is going to be easy.

I scoff.

"Sure it is," I deadpan, "All sunshine, rainbows and unicorn dicks."

"Aww, Princess, you remember . . ."

"Of course I do. I also remember punching you in your big, stupid face, so do not do anything stupid and just come back to me," I warn.

"Me? Stupid?" Creed makes a little sound of outrage and I find myself smiling. That's Creed alright, forever the jokester.

Kaiden's dark chuckle came through my earpiece causing goosebumps to spread over my arms.

Damn that sound.

"She's got you figured out, Creed," Kaiden teases.

"Whatever," Creed replies, but there was no heat to his words.

"Kaleb?" I ask, "Are you there?"

Static.

"He'll be on any minute, I'm sure," Kaiden replies, but I can hear the tension in his voice. My stomach twists.

"Oi, dickhead, answer the girl," Creed says.

"How is that going to help if he's not got his comm in?" Kaiden asks.

"But he should have it in by now," Creed replies.

The line goes quiet as those words sink in.

"I'll go look for him," Kaiden offers.

"Just give him a minute, I'm sure it'll be fine," Creed replies, but even his optimistic tone has dropped a little.

"Kaleb, please." I'm not above begging as my mind automatically starts to think the worse.

"Look, if he's been spotted, there'd be movement, right, but everything's quiet. Would you two stop worrying? He's a big boy," Creed snaps, it's rare for him to be the serious one, but he does make a good point.

The line crackles.

"Kaleb, is that you?" I ask, hoping with every fibre that it is.

"Expecting someone else, Kitten?" A cool reply came through.

Thank fuck!

"What took you so long?" Kaiden snaps. Clearly, I wasn't the only one affected by his radio silence.

"Fuck you, brother," Kaleb offers as an explanation. "I'm wearing it now, aren't I?"

"It's like working with fucking children," Kaiden mutters, but the microphone picks him up perfectly.

Before Creed and Kaleb can argue, I think it best to defuse the situation.

"Play nice, you guys."

"Oh I can play nice, Kitten," Kaleb purrs, which sounds a lot more intimate when it's whispered directly into my ear.

Jason coughs, and looks embarrassed.

"Oh yeah, Kaleb? Maybe later hmmm? I'll let you bend over for me and I'll tell you what a good job you did," Creed teases.

"Try it and die," Kaleb spits back.

"As stimulating as this conversation is, we have jobs to do," Kaiden interrupts, before it can disintegrate into playground insults.

"Kaiden's right, the sooner you get eyes on the docks, the better. We're blind here, and we don't have much time left until the shipment arrives," Jason explains, the urgency in his tone makes them shut up and listen.

"Good luck, guys," I add.

"You know what to do, meet by the car to load up for part two. Only use the radio if necessary," Kaiden orders.

There isn't a lot I can do, apart from nervously pace while the three of them go to work. I'm full of jitters and can hardly sit still, my knee bobs up and down restlessly whenever I try to. My mind keeps spinning, thinking of all the ways this could go wrong.

Jason's given up telling me to calm down, trying to reassure me it'll be okay, and a million other ways you can rehash the same platitudes.

It will be okay when they are back here.

All three of them.

It will be okay when I can see for myself that all three of them are safe and sound, far away from Keith's toxic reach.

Jason keeps scowling at the blank computer screens. His expression is hard to read, is he scowling because they're taking too long? Does he think they're in trouble? Suddenly one of the empty squares on the computer screen flickers to life. Creed's look of concentration is almost unnerving, the way he looks around, and the tension in his body language.

Urgh, I hate this. I hate knowing they're in danger and there's really nothing I can do to help. I don't even have any idea what type of numbers they'll be up against. There are only three of them.

They handled the safe house just fine.

I try to convince myself that Creed being wary is a good thing, he's being careful. He looks at the camera and gives it a little wave. He must know I'm watching. A warmth settles in my heart, Creed's always been so supportive. Always thinking of my happiness, even now when he is in a risky situation he's focused on how to cheer me up. I have to be stronger than this, I have to be better.

Despite the peptalk, my heart clenches with fear as he leaves the scope of the camera, and I have to fight back the urge to break radio silence.

Distracting them will help no one.

One by one the cameras come online. Each time I see their faces, the tightness in my chest eases, only for panic to strangle me once more when they leave my vision.

Get a fucking grip, woman.

When they're all back at the car they break radio silence to check in. The relief is immediate.

"Nyx? Jason?" Kaiden calls.

"We're here," I reply eagerly.

"Camera's all working?" he asks.

"Yes, we have visuals on all the entrances and over the loading bay. It's just a waiting game now." Jason replies.

"Hopefully we won't be waiting long." I can hear the smirk in Kaleb's voice, the way his words drip with the promise of violence.

"Just be careful," I remind them. "Please."

I will never be above begging if it means bringing them home safely. I will pray to every star, and sell my soul over and over if it means I know they'll be okay.

"Of course, Wildcat," Kaiden promises.

Creed made a 'wa-chuss' and I can imagine him miming being whipped.

"Ow," Creed exclaims, as Kaleb chuckles.

I can't help the giggle, picturing Kaiden cuffing Creed around the head.

"We have movement," Jason interrupts.

"Time to load up," Kaiden orders.

"Finally," Kaleb sighs.

"We're off to see the wizard . . . the wonderful wizard of boom . . ." Creed starts singing excitedly.

Cases are opened, the tell tale click of guns being cocked, the sound of bullets being counted, and things being shoved into holsters. Minutes later the sounds stop.

"Ready?" asks Jason.

"Ready," the three of them reply simultaneously.

I open my mouth to give them another warning, a reminder to be careful, but I bite my tongue. I need to trust they have this, I need to have faith in them.

They will come back to me.

They have to.

"Any visual on the bastard yet?" Kaleb questions.

"Er . . . Nothing yet," I answer.

"Honestly, I'd be surprised if the bastard shows up. I mean he thinks he's untouchable. Even if Kaiden is MIA and the men are dead he wouldn't be expecting us to hit the shipment," Creed theorises.

"Really hate to say it, but Creed is probably right," Kaiden agrees.

"Don't sound so surprised, it's not like it hasn't happened before," Creed sounds smug.

"Guys, keep it on track," I remind them.

All we needed was Creed being well . . . Creed.

"I was," replies Creed in a butter won't melt tone.

"Creed," I warn.

"Yes, ma'am, whatever you say, ma'am." I can actually picture the salute, I roll my eyes. Even now it's kind of cute the way he always tries to keep my mind focused on anything other than my worries.

"Ow, what the fuck was that for?" whines Creed.

"Felt like it," replies Kaleb.

"Will you two focus?" Kaiden snaps at the pair of them.

"You all know your positions? Creed, you're going to get close to that shipment, find out what the hell it is. Kaleb, you're our ace, no one knows about you. Stay hidden for now. I'll try and figure out what's going on, if my father's not here I might be able to control the situation. It'll be better if we can avoid a fire fight."

"You want me to hide? That's not fucking happening," Kaleb snaps, "I'm not a pussy."

"I didn't say you were," Kaiden replies with a sigh. "We have no idea what my father's told them, they might not see me as friendly, I'm trusting you to pull my ass out of the fire and cause a distraction if need be."

"Well when you put it like that, how can I say no to causing chaos to save my big brother?" Kaleb teases.

"I'm going to die," Kaiden deadpans.

I know he's joking but I can't help the sharp intake of breath.

"Way to go, dickhead," Creed mutters.

"I'm sorry, Wildcat, I was only joking," Kaiden replies, "Forgive me?"

"I'll forgive all of you for scaring me half to death when you drag your asses back here. If any of you joke about dying again, I'll kill you myself," I snap.

"Meeeeeow," Creed mocks.

"Creed," I warn . . . again.

"Yep, got it. No more jokes."

"Apologies again, Wildcat, I was careless. I love you and we will be home soon."

"I love you, too," I answer. It gets less and less embarrassing every time I say it. "Seriously, guys, please be safe . . . all of you."

"It's time, guys. Now or never," comes Jason's reminder to everyone that we're on a deadline.

"Let's do this," Creed replies excitedly.

I study the cameras, waiting to get a glimpse of them. It seems like the Ryker men are out in force tonight, but I can't tell who's leading them. I spot Creed first, working his way along the loading dock, trying to get into a good position to see what the cargo is. I'm hoping it isn't people, people are messy, unpredictable. They will complicate matters. It's easier if it's just 'us' and 'them'.

"Okay," comes Creed's whispered voice. "I'm as close as I can get, but without going on the boat, but I still can't see what the shipment is."

"You are not getting on that boat, Creed, you have no idea when it will leave," I snap.

"I'm a good swimmer," even when whispering he manages to sound like a cocky son of a bitch.

"Stay where you are, they'll be unloading soon, and without knowing the layout of the boat you'll be too exposed. You have no idea what you'd be walking into," Kaiden warns. "I suppose it's my turn."

"Kaiden," Jason interrupts, "I don't think this is a good idea, what if they have orders to shoot you?"

"They won't. My father doesn't work that way. If he's going to kill me he'll do it in such a way my death will serve as a warning to others. A bullet from a no-name grunt wouldn't do," Kaiden explains.

"But—" I start.

"Kitten, I'll keep him safe for you, okay?" Kaleb cuts me off.

"Okay." I let it go, reluctantly.

"Just remember, I love you, Wildcat, no matter what."

Why did it sound an awful lot like a goodbye?

I watch the cameras intently. He can't just go strolling up to a group of armed men, but who am I kidding. This is Kaiden. He walks across the open space as if he owns it.

Hell, he probably does.

"Stop," one of the men shouts as he notices Kaiden's approach, "who are you?"

The other men, alarmed by the first guy's shout, spin round at the intruder, guns raised.

"Who am I?" Kaiden's voice is like ice. Almost all of the men point their weapons away, a few need a little extra encouragement from their buddies. On the cameras I can see the panic on their faces as they understand just who Kaiden is.

I can't help but feel smug. This is my Kaiden, and seeing the way he controls the situation makes me squirm in my seat a little. He oozes power, and I love it. I admire his control, his domination, his ownership. It doesn't matter what situation he walks into, it's all his kingdom.

"Princess, I can hear you drooling from here," Creed teases.

I instantly blush at being caught staring.

"Focus," Jason growls. I'm not sure if it's aimed at Creed or myself but my cheeks are positively on fire.

Fuck. Fuck. Fuck.

I scramble for unsexy things to think of, aware of Jason keeping a close eye on me.

Could this be any more awkward? Fuck you, Creed, I swear to God, I'm going to punch you so hard in the nutsack your grandkids will feel it.

"Status," Kaiden barks, as the men scramble to accommodate him.

"I'm getting cramps, Kaleb's playing Batman, and Nyx is being a pervert," Creed explains rather unhelpfully.

"He wasn't talking to you, Dickmunch, shut the fuck up," I hiss.

Thankfully the line remains silent.

"Trucks parked, just waiting for the—" the man starts to explain but is cut off with the sound of a crane starting up.

We watch as a shipping container is lifted off the boat, and lowered near the awaiting men. As soon as the container touches the ground the men spring into action.

"Wait!" someone shouts. The voice belongs to a gangly looking man who looks a little out of place amongst the muscled up help. He looks like he should be teaching a class at the community college, or something, not running around the docks late at night with a bunch of criminals. "What are you doing here?" The man is making a beeline for Kaiden.

"Oh shit," Kaleb mutters.

"Who's he?" I ask

"What's going on?" Creed asks at the same time.

"That is Uncle," Kaleb explains.

"But Keith's an only child, isn't he?" I question.

"Kaiden warned me about him, he's paranoid, and likes to handle the business and numbers side of it. A bit like an accountant," Jason explains.

"Pretty much," Kaleb confirms.

I scoff, "Is that it? Kaiden can handle an accountant."

"Evening, Uncle," Kaiden is all manners and manages to maintain a poker face while we're all yammering on in his ear. "Don't let me stop you, I just wanted to provide support, just in case."

"In case of what, boy? What do you know?" The man referred to as Uncle looks around, eye's narrowed as if he's expecting people to come jumping out of the shadows.

"Nothing, I just want to be on the safe side," Kaiden explains, trying to calm the guy down.

"I don't believe you," Uncle hisses, and my heart sinks. "You've never paid attention to this sort of thing before, and last time I heard you were playing 'catch the detective'. No . . . I don't believe you for a second."

Kaiden laughs a cruel laugh, one which sounds twisted and forced.

"And just how long do you think one little detective would take me?" Kaiden boasts, his tone is all wrong, not like the Kaiden I know.

Out of the corner of my eye I see Jason tense, but he remains silent.

Uncle closes the distance between them, circling him like a shark. Something is very wrong. Kaiden stands under his gaze, rigid, but still. He doesn't even turn his head to follow the guy into his blind spot.

"There's something different about you. I don't like it." Uncle seems to be getting more and more twitchy. I wait for Kaleb to create a distraction, we need to get him out of there, before everything goes to shit.

"I don't trust you," Uncle spits, "You've planned something, this a trick."

"Kaleb," I whisper angrily, "get him out of there."

"But the shipment, we still don't know what it is yet," Kaleb replies.

"Creed, have you seen anything, a single clue?" I ask.

"Not yet, we need someone to open it, but the old guy needs to give the order. At the moment it's a pissing match."

"People don't get shot in pissing matches," I hiss.

"Nyx, calm down. I know you don't like this but we only get one shot," Jason tries to reason.

"Fuck you all, if anything happens to him—" I rip out the earpiece before I say something I'll regret, and go to take a walk.

Chapter Twenty Eight

T he constant nattering in my ear is annoying, but they're right. We only get one shot which means we need to get that crate open. I wish I could break character, reassure my little Wildcat, but I have faith she'll be okay. She doesn't need to have her hand held, she's stronger than she realises. As soon as this is over I'll make it up to her.

"There's no trick, I assure you." I try to calm the old man down. "Dad just introduced me to the Jula's that's all, and I wanted to make sure this went perfectly. Put my best foot forward, so to speak."

"You expect me to believe this is all some brown nosing? Fine. But you can't expect me to believe you walked all the way here. Which means you drove. But there's not been a single car engine, so you were early. Now why would you show yourself all of a sudden, if your intentions were pure?"

Shit. Shit. Shit.

"I don't know what to tell you," I reply. "Maybe I wanted to avoid Dad."

"And please pray tell, why would you want to do that?" Uncle replies, his beady little eyes missing nothing.

Nyx forgive me.

"Because he's trying to auction me off left, right and centre, and seeing him fawn over the Jula's is uncomfortable," I explain honestly.

"Ah yes, I heard of your . . . Situation. Women . . . messy things. I always let your father deal with them, numbers never lie, or cheat, you can trust numbers."

That's the thing about Uncle, he's very smart, very quick, his IQ was probably higher than anyone else I know, his people skills though are non-existent. He'd be able to calculate every angle, every risk, every probability, but put him in a poker game with the human element and he'd lose everything. That's what makes his paranoia so dangerous, innocence is something he doesn't recognise, he can't tell the difference between the truth or a lie, so it's safer to think everyone is lying. I have no idea who'd hurt him, but whoever it was fucked him up royally.

"Yeah, more trouble than they're worth," I agree.

Technically, she's a lot of trouble, but she is totally worth it.

"You're lucky Nyx took a walk," Jason growls in my ear.

Shit.

I can't tell if this is better or worse.

Nyx's wrath I can probably deal with, but Jason, that's almost scary.

He has to know I don't mean it, right?

"Hmmm, still if you were wanting to avoid your dad you wouldn't be here. If you don't want to cosy up to the Jula and live happily ever after with your pretty little wife, you wouldn't be here," Uncle snaps, getting a little irate.

So much for calming him down and finding the middle ground. He really misses nothing.

"Wait, wife? Creed snaps.

"Now it makes sense," Kaleb knew our father had offered the Jula something but he didn't sound happy with me.

"I'm going to kill you," promises Jason

I flinch as all the voices shout at once in my ear.

I suppose with the revelation that my father killed Maria, I forgot to share that little tidbit.

My flinch didn't go unnoticed.

"You're not alone, I see." Uncle narrows his eyes, his hand travelling to his pocket.

Fuck.

"No, I'm not," I confess, "So think carefully about what you want to do."

"Take it out." He gestures to the ear piece. I remove it and toss it over.

I had to hope Jason would know what to do, they'd listen to him.

Uncle crushes it underfoot.

They still have visuals, it'll be okay.

"I don't need to communicate with my team, they know what to do. You want me to call them off, you need to stand down." I eye the way his hand is holding something in his pocket, it's too small to be a gun, but a switchblade seems unlikely. I'm bigger, stronger, more experienced, a knife fight would be in my favour, but I doubt Uncle will play a game he can't win.

He laughs at my threat.

"I'm suspicious of the Jula family. You know, too much one sided power in a relationship is just . . . unfair. It gives one ideas, ownership. But your father has been so insistent. We need this, he said, it will bring us big things, he said. The numbers are good, yes, but the risks, the power balance, it's just wrong, it wasn't balanced, it's not even. Things need to be even, there needs to be order." Uncle is ranting, getting irate. My eyes are still firmly focused on his hand, irate people are unpredictable, it's why I had always avoided the madman. "Order is everything, order keeps you alive, safe. Safe is good. Numbers are good, but as soon as things tip—" he tilts his head to the side dramatically and holds it there while he continues, "it's broken. It's not safe. You can fix something that's broken, but it's never fixed. It's different, it's known what it's like to be broken, got a taste for it. It never leaves, the broken becomes a rot, it eats and it eats and it eats. Until everything is gone."

Still he rants, getting more and more out of control to the point I can barely follow the logic, that's if he's even making sense anymore. How did my father ever calm him down?

"Luckily, I'm smart, see—" he taps his temple, "I plan, and I think. I don't trust the Jula's, your father convinced me to see, but no, with you here too. Something's very wrong. I don't like it. Not one bit. But your dad said to be good. Are you a good boy, Kaiden? I don't think you are. I think you are naughty. Naughty. Naughty." Uncle starts to pace back and forth, muttering to himself as the men around us look confused, still awaiting further orders.

"I have decided," Uncle exclaims, coming to a sudden stop. "Keith won't be happy, I won't be happy, but this is your fault, Kaiden, you and the greedy Jula wanting to take, take, take. So broken, so greedy. Only one way to stop that." He smiles a cold smile, a calculating one that is logical, detached, lethal. He pulls his hand out of his pocket and in his hand is a phone. "Make it burn."

He presses a button and all hell breaks loose.

Chapter Twenty Nine

"Hello? Hello? Can anyone read me? Someone come in, please," Jason's calling over the comms.

Holy fuckballs.

I cackle like I'm unhinged, my ears ringing from the explosion. Heat from the flames licks against my skin. I shake my head from side to side, trying to clear the colours from my vision, trying to stumble to my feet.

I need focus. I ignore my pain, and the rapidly forming bruises.

I'm fine.

I'd been crouched on top of a set of shipping containers, with a decent view overlooking the place. I remember seeing the ear piece get crushed and then Uncle pulling something out of his pocket. I look over towards where my brother was moments before, but I can't see him. Bodies lay scattered all over the dock, some burning, a few men are screaming, but most are unmoving.

Please be okay.

The thought is surprising to me, last week I wouldn't have pissed on him if he was on fire, and here I am worried about his safety.

I promised Nyx.

Yeah, that's why I'm worried. I promised her I'd keep him safe.

Lies. The traitorous voice whispers in my head.

You care.

Weakness.

Something else to be taken.

Gone.

Gone.

Gone.

"Fuck. You," I hiss, instantly shutting up the voice. I've noticed it seems weaker, less convincing somehow.

"Fuck you too, asshole," cames a groggy reply.

"Creed?" I ask hesitantly, worried I really have gone crazy this time.

"No, this is the devil, time for your enemia. Bend over."

"We both know I'd be on top," I quip back, horrified the words had even left my mouth.

Since when did I banter?

"I dunno, if you feel anything like I do right now, I've been fucked, daddy, fucked hard, and I don't like it," Creed mutters.

"Fucking hell you two, I think you gave me a heart attack," Jason sighs.

"I think I'm okay . . ." I reply, checking everything's still attached.

Two arms, two legs. Feet, hands.

Yep all good.

"What happened?" Jason asks.

"Look, Jason, not meaning to be a dick, but we'll fill you in when we fill you in. I don't know what the fuck's going on, and I don't know what happened to Kaiden. The explosions . . ." he trails off. "He will be okay, he's got to be, but well, I had to duck onto the boat to avoid the explosion, and now the door won't open."

"Aww, is the poor little meerkat stuck?" I tease.

My teasing is met with just the crackle of static.

Maybe I did it wrong.

"Yeah, we kinda have another problem," he reluctantly admits, "Looking at the rapidly growing paddling pool around my feet, the boat is sinking."

"Like sinking sinking?" I ask

"Like last time I checked I can't fucking breathe under-water and it's either you get me out of here or I have to do my best impression of a fish. I don't think optimism will make me grow gills do you?" Creed snaps, panic lacing his voice.

"I mean are we talking about Titanic, and I need to get you out of there in a couple of hours, or is it—?"

"It's like get me the fuck out of here now, or I'm going to haunt you," Creed snarls. The line goes quiet for a little while before he speaks again. "Wait . . . You've seen Titanic?" Creed asks, a teasing tone to his voice.

"Fuck you man, it's the first boat I could think of," I snap back.

"Mhmm, and you know it took hours to sink how?" he asks.

"I've changed my mind. Go die."

"Okay, I'll take it back. Save me, please," Creed pleads.

"No. Good luck with the whole aquatic thing." I'm already trudging my way over to the boat which is leaning dangerously on its side.

"You guys play nice, and I'll be right back, I need to help Nyx." Jason's voice sounds far away, but Kitten always comes first. I can imagine her freaking out, and honestly I'd hate to be Jason right now. Kitten has some real claws on her. We need to get back.

I fight the urge to look for my brother, Creed needs my help now. Without knowing where Kaiden is all I can do is hope he's okay.

One. Rescue the meerkat.

Two. Rescue Kaiden, wherever that prick is hiding.

Three. Never let the fuckers forgot it. EVER.

Four. Accept all the gratitude my Kitten will give me for saving her useless pets.

Five. Tell everyone I told you so, and that plans are stupid.

I manage to get to the boat quickly, dispatching the dying on the way. Last thing I need is to be shot in the back.

"Where are you?" I ask, hoping Creed could narrow down where he is. It's a big fucking boat.

"On a beach in the tropics, with an umbrella drink in hand. Where the fuck do you think I am?" he snaps.

"I'm not playing fucking hide and seek with you on a sinking ship. Tell me where you are?" I roll my eyes.

Forever the drama queen, I swear. Abyss help me.

"Look, I just darted in here, I didn't take the scenic route," Creed replies, "Look, if I don't—"

"Oh shut the fuck up with that shit, do I look like a priest to you? I am not listening to your last confession. If you want to give up, fine, but save all the sappy shit for someone who cares," I snap.

I am not hearing anyone's final words. Ever a-fucking-gain.

Think, Kaleb, think.

Thinking is what your brother does.

You're not a thinker.

You do things.

Yeah, well, punching ships isn't going to help.

I argue with myself, racking my brain for ideas.

Kaiden would know what to do.

But Kaiden isn't here, I am.

And unless I do something Creed will drown.

That gives me an idea, when drowning people, you submerge them. You always have to hold them below the water level. I start to scan the ship, focusing on the water line.

He has to at least be at it or below.

"How deep is the water?" I ask, hoping to narrow it down.

"Deep enough that soon this radio is going to stop working. Please tell Nyx—"

"Save it. I'm not listening."

"Fucking listen to me, it's important. Tell her—" Creed shouts.

"There," I say to myself, it has to be that door. It's the only one that makes sense. It looks like some sort of loading door, but the explosion must have thrown something heavy against it as it's warped. There'd be no removing it.

"Are you listening? Tell – "

Nothing.

Silence.

"Creed?" I ask, hesitantly.

No response.

Fuck.

I run to the mangled door, and bang against it.

I wait for a moment.

Please.

A knock answers, and Creed's eye appears in a little fist sized hole.

Thank fuck!

I need to get him out of there, I need a plan.

"You got a plan?" he pants, he's treading water. If the boat sinks much lower it will come through this door too and drown him quickly. While the door is still above the water line we have a chance but the more water the boat takes on, the lower it sinks. It's pure luck the explosion on the dock had pushed the boat, causing it to list to the side, or he would have drowned already.

"No, but I'm thinking," I snap. "Unless you have any bright ideas, save your breath."

No, you know what. Fuck plans, what have they ever done for me anyway.

Chaos. Chaos was mine.

The boat is going down, no if, but's or maybe's.

What would another hole hurt?

I smile.

If explosions got us into this mess, then they might get us out, and if it doesn't I can honestly say I tried.

"Oh no, I don't like that look, stop smiling," Creed demands. "What are you thinking? Tell me. Tell me right now."

"You might want to get back," I warn, pulling a grenade from my pocket. I had seen it sitting in the SUV and I don't know why I took it, it certainly didn't fit in with Kaiden's plan but they're like a swiss army knife, handy to have, and it's better to have one than not.

Case in point.

"What the fuck? Why do you—No, there's got to be another way." Creed shakes his head frantically, causing the water to slosh about.

"It's either boom or drown." I toss the grenade up and down while Creed panics.

"I'm going to die," Creed mutters.

"Maybe." I shrug.

"And you still won't take a message for Nyx?"

"Nope," I reply popping the P

Without giving him any more time to argue I pull the pin and shove it in the gap, holding down the spoon.

"Oh shit," Creed shouts, swimming as far from the door as possible.

After I count to three, I let go, and run like hell.

I duck behind some cover, but I'm still close enough to the explosion for the shockwaves to rattle my teeth.

I can't help but feel a little like things were easier on my own. No worrying, fussing, almost getting blown up. Just a bit of violence, a bit of wallowing, a bit more violence. It was a simple life. I sigh, getting to my feet and brushing the dirt off me.

Better go see if Creed's been barbecued, but hell, it beats drowning, I guess.

Looking over at the ship, the door certainly isn't going to be a problem anymore. The explosion has forced the fist-sized hole wide open.

"Here, meerkat, here, boy." I call, tapping my knee like a dog.

No response.

Well shit.

For a second I think about going and looking for my brother instead. I mean it was a lose lose scenario so I should get points for trying, right? No, after what Kaiden went through there'll be no convincing him of Creed's death without a body.

Time to go fishing.

I look into the hole, the water swirling underneath.

"If you're alive in there, Creed, now would be a great time to come out," I call on the off chance he's just being a bit of a prick.

No answer.

Fuck it.

I take a deep breath and dive in. The space is pretty small, with a hatch leading to elsewhere in the ship. I don't have to look far to find Creed floating, his eyes closed, his limbs waving about with the water. He looks like a bad Halloween decoration.

I wrap my arm around his middle and drag him to the surface, pulling him from the boat and on to the dock.

"Come on . . ." I mutter, feeling for a pulse.

"If you think I'm giving you mouth to mouth . . ."

Fuck's sake.

I pinch his nose and take a deep breath.

Just think of Nyx, think of her gratitude.

Think of how Creed will never live this fucking down, ever.

I breathe into his mouth, and pump on his chest before repeating the cycle.

"I swear, Creed, if you're dead, I'm going to kill you," I snap, glancing a look around to make sure I don't have company. That is the last thing I need. "I'm going to shove you in a pickle jar, and bury you in a hole like some creepy time capsule."

Creed coughs up a mouthful of water, and finally takes a big gasp of air.

Thank fuck!

CHAPTER THIRTY

I wake and quickly shove the heavy weight off me. He probably had a name but I don't recognise him, he must have been a new hire. Just another no name caught in the crossfire. My anger flares, just how many lives would be taken due to needless violence? This was meant to be a simple transaction. A delivery so to speak, but because he put it in the hands of a madman, it turned Blight's dock into a warzone, and took out Jula and Ryker men alike. Explosions don't care who they rip through.

I look down, trying to memorise the guy's face, so I can maybe find his family. It could have easily been me, if he hadn't taken the brunt of the blast. I check myself over, apart from some grazes and some bruises I'm okay.

"I'm sorry," I whisper, wishing it didn't have to come to this. It was a lot easier being around all this bloodshed and senseless violence when I didn't have emotions, when I managed to ice out such things as empathy.

"You're alive," I snap around at the sound of Uncle's voice.

"Yeah, sorry about that. Turns out explosions aren't as predictable and safe as you thought," I tease.

His scowl is almost comical, what with how it pinches his features into something that resembles something more rat-like than human.

"Maybe, but it's something easily rectified," Uncle snarls.

"Well, last time I checked, looks couldn't actually kill. So it looks like you're shit out of luck." I smirk. I swear his face actually starts to turn purple as his anger starts to consume him, but that's what I need. I need to bait him into doing something rash.

"What are you waiting for? Numbers can't help you. If everything was perfect, every last little calculation, I wouldn't be standing here. You . . . Messed . . . Up," I tease, attacking the order he's clearly so reliant on.

Splutter, splutter, come on you old badger. Do something.

I watch him struggle with himself. Reluctant to close the distance just in case he does actually have something up his sleeve, the last thing I want is to walk into another trap he's set.

It doesn't take him long to lose himself fully to his rage. My smirking face seems to have that effect on people. He pulls a switchblade from his pocket and fumbles it open. He crouches over, ready to rush me. He looks a little bit like a goblin, and I struggle to hold back my laughter.

Let the knife give him power, let him think he can actually do something.

It doesn't take long for the false sense of power to seep into his body, bringing him to life. His charge is almost laughable, I'm half expecting him to trip as he runs clumsily, almost tumbling over his own feet. I dodge easily as he runs past me, blade extended.

He growls his frustration. Turning for another pass.

This time I tuck my hands in my pockets and shrug.

He charges again, this time more controlled, but no more effective than the last one.

I laugh this time as I spin away.

He trips, the blade flying from his hand and skidding away. I roll my eyes in annoyance. It's too easy. It barely takes the edge off my stress. I let my mind wander, I hope Creed and Kaleb made it out okay.

Uncle must sense my wandering thoughts as he gets up, picks the knife up from where it fell and tries his luck at throwing it. It misses completely, of course. The guy has the athletic ability of an armchair.

"Oh, I'm sorry, I wasn't paying attention there," I tease, bending over to pick up the blade. I walk slowly up to him and place it in his hand. "Here, one more go." I dodge the angry swipe as he snatches the blade away from me. "That's not very nice, you didn't even say thank you."

He screams his frustration, and I laugh.

With the knife firmly in hand, he rushes me one last time but honestly by this point I'm getting bored. I need to find my brothers, if he killed them I'll make him wish for death. As he closes the distance, I stand my ground. I don't dodge, I merely smile. His footsteps stumble, confusion briefly crosses his features, before my fist and his face connect with a crunch. Uncle falls to the ground, an unconscious heap at my feet.

Worthless worm.

"Ouch, I think I felt that one," comes a cocky voice from behind.

My face breaks into a genuine smile. I spin round and there's Creed and Kaleb, I glance over them, checking for injuries, but they seem okay.

"Why are you guys wet?" I ask, puzzled.

"Because someone went on the boat, and needed rescuing," Kaleb shrugs.

"I thought I told you to stay off the boat," I scowl at Creed, he's going to get himself killed one day if he keeps ignoring my orders.

"Yeah well, I've been punished enough. Kaleb kissed me," Creed dramatically cringes as if he is reliving a nightmare.

"It was CPR, fucker, and you know it," Kaleb snaps

"Tomato, to-mar-to, still pretty sure you copped a feel," Creed teases.

"I really regret saving you," Kaleb growls.

I chuckle.

"It seems you guys are getting on well," I comment.

Jealousy flares briefly, but I lock it down. If they get on surely that's a good thing?

Creed doesn't miss anything though, he walks over to me and slings an arm around my shoulder.

"Don't worry, boss, you'll always be my first love," Creed teases.

I shrug him off and roll my eyes.

"Dickhead," I mutter.

"As touching as this is, what are we going to do with him?" Kaleb asks, kicking the unconscious mass.

"Leave him. I think when the Jula comes to visit, wondering where their boat is, they'll have lots of questions for him, don't you think?" I smirk. It's the least he deserves, just how many men have been lost tonight, killed just to justify his paranoia.

Kaleb chuckles, and Creed looks down at Uncle with malice in his eyes.

I definitely wouldn't want to be him when they come calling.

Noise coming from the direction of the boat catches our attention. Shouts from men about securing the area, and saving the cargo echo around the dock. We take that as our signal to leave.

"Let's get home to Nyx, she's going to be freaking out." I smile thinking of the warm welcome we'll get. Me and my brothers are safe, and there's only one piece left on the board. It's almost time for the endgame. Soon this entire thing will be over. At least I hope it will be.

CHAPTER THIRTY ONE

G uilt is eating me alive, but I'm trying to remain strong. Nyx came running in when she heard the explosion, collapsing to her knees when she saw all the cameras were either destroyed or burning. There was no way of knowing if anyone was okay, until I heard Kaleb's voice. I knew it was him after watching Kaiden's comms get destroyed, but the more time I spend around them the more I'm able to tell them apart. Kaleb is rougher and gruffer somehow, and lacks Kaiden's more refined manner. Creed's voice soon followed.

At the sound of their voices Nyx seemed to pull herself together a little but there was still one voice missing, and without hearing Kaiden's voice I doubt the haunted look will leave her eyes.

"No, this can't be happening," she mutters, still on her knees, "Kaiden, he can't be . . ."

I mute the comms, they don't need to hear this, it will just distract them. I've seen the way they all look at her when they think no one is watching, hearing her upset would be something they wouldn't be able to ignore. I need to deal with this before I can help anyone.

"I'm sure he'll be fine, Spitfire, you know what he's like." I try sounding positive, but it comes out sounding forced. I'm worried too.

Why did I let them leave me behind when they went into danger?

"You don't know that," she screams at me, tears falling down her face.

"No, I don't," I agree, "but here's what I do know. Kaiden is a resourceful guy, he's seen the worst of people and has always come out swinging from the other side."

"But . . . the fire," she whines, the glimpses of unmoving bodies didn't help aid my argument as the last camera flickers and dies. The fire finally consuming it too.

"I know, but I know nothing will keep him from you, he loves you, remember. He might be a little singed when he comes back, but Kaleb and Creed will bring him home to you. You know they'd do anything for you." I wrap an arm around her, pulling her to her feet.

"I know, but . . ." she sniffs, wiping her eyes, "after Ma
. . . I just can't lose anyone else. Not you, not Kaiden, not
Creed. Even Kaleb. I can't lose anyone else."

I close my eyes against the wave of pain the mention of
Maria always brought, holding our daughter tight, hugging her close. I can't help but feel the anger and betrayal
which comes with memories of her. I have no idea how I
can even begin to reconcile with a ghost. I'll never have
answers, never be able to understand her reasoning. I'll
never get to tell her how I really feel about this, about *her*.

The detective part of my brain demands answers, needs
the truth, but it's something I'm never going to get. How
could I possibly? Maria is gone, the truth and answers
along with her.

Still, underneath the bitterness, anger, and heartbreak,
is something else. Holding her, letting her cry into my
shirt, I feel whole, I feel like I have a purpose. I don't care
if Nyx is in her twenties, and a fully grown adult. I don't
care if she has men clamouring for her attention, willing
to do anything for her. I'm going to be the best damn dad
to her I can be.

"Thanks," she says, wiping the tears from her eyes, and
putting on a brave smile.

"Anytime, Spitfire," I reply, pressing a hasty kiss to her
head.

It's too soon to confess loving her, too weird and awkward, but I hope the little peck conveys the things I'm too much of a coward to mention.

"Let's get going," she says, stepping out of my arms.

"Going?" I ask.

"Yeah," she replies with a frown, "To rescue them, obviously."

"Hold up a moment, we can't go there."

"We have to."

"You saw what it's like down there, it's a warzone. It won't be long before the place is crawling with cops. We'd never find them." I tried being the voice of reason.

"Well we definitely won't find them sitting here, will we?" she snaps at me.

"You're not listening to me, we can't go."

"And you're not listening to me, I am going, I'm not just going to sit here—"

"I said no," I snap at her, startling us both.

"Where the fuck do you—" she snarls, getting angry.

"I am your father, and it's my responsibility to keep you safe."

She scoffs and rolls her eyes.

"You really want to play the father card now? Well fuck you. I have spent the last twenty plus years just fine without you, I don't need you telling me what I can and can't do. I made it this far by myself, didn't I?" she snaps, going straight for the kill shot.

I didn't realise just how much of a heart I had left, but that shot, fucking destroyed it. My pain must show on my face, as Nyx's expression floods with guilt.

"I would have been there . . . I would have . . . If only I had known," my voice is quiet, detached, it feels empty.

How could she not know that?

How do I prove myself?

My heart breaks as I thought she knew me better than that, but I'm kidding myself. I mean, when have we talked? What do I actually know about her? If it wasn't for Maria dying, would we have ever found each other? The only reason I can think of for keeping Nyx away from me was that I'd be a bad father . . . I know I'm not going to win any awards, but still. Wasn't my love enough?

Ha.

My love isn't worth shit. It wasn't enough for Maria, and Nyx clearly doesn't want me.

"Look, I didn't mean it—" she starts to explain, maybe even apologise.

I put a hand up, silencing her as I shake my head.

I don't want to hear it. Not yet.

I'm angry and I really don't want to say something I'll regret. I'm not even sure who I'm really angry at. Maria for robbing me of those years with my daughter? I mean if she didn't want to be with me, fine, but she shouldn't have kept her from me. Am I angry at Nyx? I couldn't be, I can see the remorse there, and the pain. She's scared and she's lashing out. I recognise those feelings, and I understand, but I'm just not ready to hear her apology just yet.

Luckily I'm saved by the bell, so to speak.

Ring. Ring.

Nyx sprints over to where my burner phone is, there's only one person with that number and I find myself smiling.

Three for three.

I don't need to hear his voice to know Kaiden's okay. Of course he was, the resourceful son of a bitch.

I'm not expecting the overwhelming sense of relief as I hear Nyx chatting away. They're fine, all of them. They are a family all of their own it seems, and an unstoppable force at that. I feel something resembling pride for them, they went up against some insane odds and won. As a detective I should be horrified part of our city was destroyed, that the morgue will be trying to identify bodies for a week, but honestly, the town can be rebuilt, people will grieve, but the world will keep turning.

With a final check on Nyx to make sure she won't be running off, I decide to slip out into the cool night air. Looking up at the stars, I take a seat on the stairs. My head is full of thoughts, and I finally have a moment to breathe.

"Maria?" I call hesitantly into the sky. I laugh at myself and shake my head, I'd never get a reply, so what's the point? I feel like I'm barely holding it together. It's like I'm in an ocean treading water, it seems easy, and after a while it becomes second nature. Until the moment you stop. At that moment you realise just how bone weary you are. How long you've barely been keeping your head above water.

Now the adrenaline is wearing off, all that's left is a bone deep ache, a lingering pain that won't leave. It just suffocates. A tear runs down my cheek, followed by another, and another. I catch one on a fingertip.

I'm crying.

I chuckle to myself, after everything, getting yelled at by my kid is the one thing that pushes me over the edge. Ridiculous.

"I don't know if I will ever be able to forgive you, taking those years from me . . ." I take a deep breath needing to get the words out, even if it's just to the empty air. "I don't think I can ever forgive you. I loved you, I will always love you, on some level," I confess, "but I don't think love will ever erase this pain. Every memory, every smile I remember feels tainted, like a lie."

"Once upon a time I was content to live in a lie, as long as it meant you could be happy. I have to believe you had your reasons, but I can't do it anymore. I can't console the woman I love with these lies. I feel . . . Angry. Hurt. Betrayed. My Maria didn't have a malicious bone in her body. Just who were you?" my whispered words are carried away in the wind.

"This is stupid," I mutter to no one in particular.

Here I am, ranting to the memory of a dead woman, when I need to clear the air with Nyx. She was hurting and I pushed. Just the thought of her being in the firing line scares the living fuck out of me, and I'd reacted. I could have handled it better, I should have handled it better.

Time to face the music, I guess.

I stand up, brushing off my trousers before heading inside.

"Hurry back, I love you. Be safe," Nyx says into the phone, before hanging up.

She notices me, and holds the phone out for me to take.

An awkwardness hangs in the air, and then I realise she's waiting on me. If we're going to have any hope of clearing the air, I have to make the first move.

"Look," I say, rubbing the back of my neck, it does nothing to erase the awkwardness I'm feeling, "I shouldn't have snapped at you. I was just . . . Scared."

"Scared?" She looked surprised, "I thought you were just mad at me, I know I have a tendency to be . . . strong-willed is probably the most polite way of putting it."

I chuckle.

"Spitfire, when have you ever worried about being polite," I tease.

"Touche, okay . . . I'm stubborn," she explains, with a shy smile.

"Like me," I reply

"Impulsive."

"Like me."

She smirks.

"A bit of a brat," she continues.

"Must get that from your mum," I say with laughter in my voice. Her face lights up and she smiles. I wait for the wave of pain, but it doesn't drown me this time.

"She could be a brat, I guess. I mean, she was all for helping people, but God help anyone who tried to make her do something she didn't want to do," Nyx agrees.

"Oh tell me about it, for years I begged her for dates and the like. All I got was quiet nights in." I sigh. "I thought she was probably just embarrassed of being seen with a cop. I mean a lot of people would come to her for advice and help. Me lurking about would have hindered that."

"No, I don't think so. You should have seen her at Haven. The way she was with the girls, the way she'd tell them to find love again, she'd get this look in her eye and you could tell she was thinking about someone." she explains, a mischievous twinkle in her eye.

I gasp.

It wasn't possible.

"Have you heard about the Haven parties?" she asks curiously.

"Oh I've heard of them alright, I know a few times people have needed escorts home." I raise an eyebrow like a disappointed parent but I can't hide the smirk.

She laughs and it's a lovely genuinely joyous sound.

"Well one time she seemed down about something, so we threw a smaller family party. Still gets a bit mental but it's a great way for all of us to wind down. Well one thing led to another, there may or may not have been shots involved, and as I wanted Ma to relax, I let her drink mine. Well safe to say she got wasted. When the truth or dare started, we asked her if she'd ever been in love. She said yes, and told us a little bit about him. Even drunk she wouldn't tell us his name, but if she was in love with someone . . . who wasn't you . . . well, she wouldn't have given you the time of day." Nyx pins me with a knowing look.

"You think she loved me?" I ask, not daring to hope.

"Only one who'd know for sure is Ma, but if I had to put my money on it, I'd bet on you." She smiles. "I'm sorry, I tend to be selfish, and focus a lot on my own pain, but I know this isn't easy for you either."

"No it isn't, finding out you have a daughter. I mean everyone has parents, but not everyone has kids. Do you know what I mean?"

"Yeah, I know. I used to imagine my parents growing up, and would make these fantasies in my head . . ."

"Oh?" I ask.

"You know, ice creams, theme parks, family dinners. Don't get me wrong, Haven was like a family, but when you're little, and different . . . well kids can be cruel."

"I'm sorry I wasn't there." I'd give anything to have made it easier on her. I briefly consider trumping up some charges, so I can at least scare the fuckers now.

"I know." She smiles up at me, with such sincerity.

She believes me.

Slowly it feels like the scraps of my heart are pulling together, this is our first real time connecting and it makes me so happy. Anxiously, I decide to risk it all.

"But . . . I mean . . . If you'll have me . . .I'd like to be there for you now." I can barely look at her, afraid to see her reaction.

"I'd like that," she replies, and warmth engulfs my chest. I won't screw this opportunity up, I'll be worthy of her trust in me.

"I have a lot of learning to do, and I won't always get it right. I'll get scared, I'll make mistakes, I'll snap and we will butt heads more often than I'd like," I admit, hoping she'll understand.

She chuckles.

"Yeah, the family stubbornness," she replies.

"Yeah that," I laugh.

"I'm not the easiest to get along with, I know. I can be snappy, and I . . . have this darkness . . . I'm not a good person. I suppose the reason I've been so angry and kept you at a distance was it was easier. I feel like if you get too close, you'll leave," she admits, looking vulnerable.

"Nyx, I loved your mother, everything you are came from us. How could I not love you?" I confess.

"But the darkness . . ."

How can I make her understand?

"That's my fault," I admit, though the more I'm starting to understand Maria, she must have had some darkness too, or at least secrets she felt she couldn't share.

"You're a cop," she instantly dismisses it, blinded by the badge.

"Maybe, but trying to get you back, there's nothing I wouldn't have done. I was ready to kill Collins, Creed killed him for me, but I tortured him . . . I—"

I expect her to flinch and pull away at my words.

"Is it weird I find that comforting?" She blushes at the confession, and I just know we're going to be okay.

I laugh.

"You've been hanging around *that* lot for too long," I joke.

"Probably, but hey . . . I love them," she says with a shrug.

"Aww, Princess. We love you too," Creed calls from the other room.

Her eyes widen with alarm, and she instantly turns red. "I . . . I mean . . . er." Her brain short circuits as the three of them, bedraggled and looking a little worse for wear, walk into the room like conquering heroes.

CHAPTER THIRTY TWO

N *o, no, no.*

My eyes instantly look to see Kaiden's reaction. I've seen what guys can be like in the club when the girls would bring their boyfriends around. The possessiveness and the alpha posturing, they never lasted long, but I've seen what men are capable of. Kaiden has called me 'his' with such surety, I'm initially worried, until I see the mischief sparkling in his eyes.

"Already planning on replacing me, Wildcat?" he teases.

"No, of course not. It's not like that, it's—" I reply, getting flustered.

"I know, Wildcat, besides," Kaiden stalks up to me, and places a finger under my chin, tilting it towards him,

"Who else can do this?" He purrs a hairbreadth away from my lips before he kisses me, in that all consuming way he does, and it's all I can do to remain standing. His arm snakes around my back holding me to him, as he invades my senses. Taking, owning.

Yeah, Kaiden isn't the type to be insecure. He has no fucking reason to be.

He kisses me until I'm breathless, and all I can think about is him. The smell of smoke clings to him, the reminder of danger and violence, but having him pressed against me, he's very much alive. Forever dominating, the same hands which kill, wring out every lustful desire from my body. There's something very wrong with me, but as Kaiden's tongue dances with mine, I don't give a fuck. Let the shadows swallow me whole, we will own them together.

Jason clears his throat and I instantly sober up.

"That's my sign to make myself scarce, be good to her, you hear me?" Jason threatens, and I honestly want the ground to swallow me whole.

After our talk, his words of concern warm me, gone is the defensive feeling. Clearing the air was the best thing we could have done, and I realise just how much he means to me already.

"Goodnight, Dad, don't worry about me, I'll keep the boys in line."

He's initially shocked but recovers quickly, but it feels right calling him dad.

"I know you will, Spitfire, but I don't want to have to help you hide bodies in the morning," he replies, throwing me a wink, before leaving.

I'm grinning like a loon when I turn back to the boys, but it soon drops.

The looks in their eyes . . .

It's positively primal.

I suddenly feel a lot less sure of my words when they all look at me like that.

Like a rabbit among the wolves.

I can't help but imagine what it would be like, to have them chase me, catch me, devour me as I writhe in pleasure under their hands, their tongues, their cocks—

My body tightens at the mere thought, fuck. I shouldn't be even thinking about it. I have Kaiden.

"Care to share your thoughts, Princess?" Creed teases.

Hell no!

"I don't think she needs to," Kaiden replies, "Just look at her."

He slowly runs his nose up my neck, inhaling my skin.

"Mmmm delicious," he purrs against my throat.

My eyes connect with Kaleb's over his shoulder, the lust in his eyes is unmistakable, but there's also something else there. Some kind of torment. I want to ease his frown, make him feel better. My eyes trail down his body hungrily noticing the differences between them, there is something wilder about Kaleb. He rearranges the obvious bulge in his trousers drawing my eyes southwards. When my eyes reach his again he seems angry. Conflicted. He looks like he wanted to rip Kaiden off me, and take his place. I instinctively mould myself to Kaiden, wrapping my arms around him so no one will be able to take him from me. Kaleb narrows his eyes, before he storms off, slamming a door somewhere in the house.

"I'll go check on him," Creed says, hastily, before going after him.

"Wildcat?" Kaiden's voice brings my attention back to him, and I feel ashamed. How can I be thinking about anyone else?

"I'm sorry." The words sound weak but what can I say without confessing everything?

"You care about them?" he asks. I nod, burying my face into his chest. I'm waiting for him to push me away, tell me I'm too greedy. I don't want to hurt him, but I don't want to lie to him either.

"You meant what you said earlier, didn't you? You love them?" his voice is steady, not angry or disappointed, just Kaiden.

"I don't know." The words feel like sawdust in my mouth.

Did I?

I know I care, the mere thought of losing any of them makes me go out of my mind.

"You know what?" he asks, "You're pretty incredible."

I look up, meeting his gaze, surprised by his words.

My shock must be clear on my face as he chuckles at me.

"You have so much love in you, so much light and goodness."

I scoff.

"Yes, you have a darkness in you too, but you are light. The way your emotions are clear as day, and the way no matter how much you've been hurt, you create these infinite amounts of love, and compassion. A lot of people would see us as monsters, but not you."

"You aren't monsters," I snap.

"Don't get the wrong idea, we are monsters. We own, we take, we reduce fully grown men to weeping, broken piles. We are the men people are warned about. We're killers all of us. We'll never change, never be tamed, or be good little boys working in offices from nine to five. We are monsters down to our cores. We've seen too much, been broken too many times to be anything else."

"I don't think you're broken," I whisper, feeling like if I speak louder it will shatter whatever this fragile thing is.

"Of course you don't, it's one of the reasons I love you. You see me. All of me, and you accept me just the way I am. I think my brothers deserve the same love, the same happiness."

"What are you saying?" I'm so confused.

"What I'm saying is, I've seen Creed take a bullet for you. I know how hard it was for you, but you went back into hell to find him. You worry about Kaleb too. If you have feelings for them, you don't have to hide them from me. All three of us would die for you, and with your ability to attract trouble, I don't think having more bodyguards is a bad thing. All I want is for your happiness."

"I love you," I say with utmost sincerity.

"And I love you, Wildcat."

"I might love Creed," I confess, "when he got shot—" a tear ran down my cheek, the thought of losing him, seeing him so still is a raw ache in my heart.

"I know you do, and I appreciate the honesty, Wildcat. Your ability for love is incredible, and you take my breath away."

I can't believe this, I would have never thought Kaiden would be okay with something like this, but looking into his eyes, the love he has for his brothers is clear. He really believes I can help heal their hearts like I did his, and he's willing to let me love them to do it.

"Kaiden, you are everything to me, and your love for your brothers makes me love you even more," I confess. "You really are unlike any man I've ever met."

"And I'll spend every day reminding you of it," he murmurs against my lips, before claiming them once more. His kisses are powerful, and rob me of my ability to think. I claw at his shirt, wanting him. I Need him. I mewl my frustrations and he chuckles against my lips.

"So impatient, sweetheart," he teases. He lifts me up and I instantly wrap my legs around his hips. His hands are squeezing and kneading my ass, fanning me higher as I seek his mouth again. He walks me over to the wall, and pins me against it so I'm helpless against his continued assault. This man's kisses are positively sinful, and I melt against him. I rub against him shamelessly, feeling his hardness so close but not close enough. I bite his lip in my frustration.

"Enough teasing already, fuck me. Please," I beg.

"Mmmm, sweetheart, you sound so fucking good when you beg. On your knees," he commands, sliding me down his body. I eagerly get to my knees, looking up to him.

"Yes, sir," I surrender my control to him, that one word giving him ownership of me. I don't fight it, not when I need this, I need to feel him, I need to know he's alive and with me. I need him to chase the demons from my mind. I want to forget everything, I want to let go and be consumed by him.

"Fuck, Nyx, I've imagined how good you'd look on you knees, but you're more perfect than I could imagine. I need inside that sassy little mouth of yours. Now," he demands. I eagerly undo his belt, and remove his cock. My mouth waters at the sight, and I lick him from base to tip as he moans his pleasure.

"Fuck." He moans as I wrap my lips around him, sliding him down my throat. His thighs tremble against my palms as he gathers my hair up so he can watch me. Feeling his eyes on me, watching, makes me feel powerful. I meet his gaze as I run my tongue over the tip, and give him a few lazy pumps with my open mouth, before licking the precum away. I feel like a goddess seeing the lust in his eyes, the edge of crazy. The barely restrained passion contained there makes me so unbelievably wet. I take my hand off his thigh, I need to take some of my own pleasure. It's all too much.

"Hands on me, sweetheart," he snaps, and I moan my frustration around his cock, causing him to gasp with the sensation.

"You're not complaining are you?" I meet his eyes again, the frustration slowly leaning to defiance. My hand starts moving down my body, almost as if I can't control it. He watches as my eyes soften when my fingertips finally brush against my clit. My gasp at the sensitivity as electricity fills my body. His grip on my hair tightens to the point of pain.

"What did I fucking say?" he growls, and I find myself growing wetter at the aura of power radiating off him. I can't answer with his cock in my mouth but I slide my hand from my trousers and put it back on his thigh.

"Oh no, sweetheart, you want to rebel, you have to take the punishment." He smirks down at me. Slowly he slides his cock to the back of my throat, robbing me of air and causing my eyes to water.

"If you need me to stop, pinch my thigh, you won't be able to use your safeword this time." He slides from my mouth so I can answer. "Understand, sweetheart?"

"Yes, sir," I reply, already missing the feeling of him.

"Good girl, now take a deep breath and open that mouth of yours." He smirks, his eyes full of challenge. I know he is going to push my limits, push what I'm capable of, but I don't feel anxiety, or self doubt, I'm all for it.

"Use me, sir. Fuck my mouth," I open my mouth, but he brushes his cock over my lips, teasing us both.

"Even on your knees, you're a sassy little brat trying to give me orders." I smirk against him, I can't help it, this game we play is addictive. He shoves a thumb in my mouth and I start to move my tongue against it.

"One day that mouth of yours will get you in trouble, fortunately for you I want to fuck the sass right out of you. You going to gag around my cock, sweetheart? Be a good girl?" I nod eagerly at his words. "I'm going to make a mess of that pretty little face of yours, make your eyes water as your throat tightens around me, screaming for air."

He slides past my lips once more, his fingers gripping my hair. When I think I can't take anymore, he slides out, and back in, pushing just a little bit further, a bit deeper, until I've taken all of him. My eyes water, as he holds himself there, robbing me of air.

"You take me so well, sweetheart," he praises me, even as my lungs start to burn. My eyes water freely, but I'm so fucking turned on, I don't care. I try swallowing as my instincts scream at me for air. He moans at the sensation, before pulling out.

"Fuck, you do that again and this won't last as long as I want it to." He composes himself as I suck in lungfuls of air, my pussy flooding itself. I never thought much of blow jobs before, but when it comes to Kaiden I'm starving for him. I love seeing him barely in control of himself, being helpless to resist the call of my mouth.

"I'm going to need you to remember I love you, Nyx, because I'm about to fuck that bratty little mouth of yours like I don't," he growls, his shackles loosening and I can see the monster in his eyes. The one who demands he take, he own, and fucking hell, I want it. "Now open up," he demands.

He's a man of his word. He fucks my mouth with reckless abandon, it's all I can do to hold onto his thighs as I focus on his rhythm, stealing air when I can. My tears are running freely, my hair a tangled mess in his hand, but all I need is to look in his eyes and I don't feel like a mess. I feel beautiful, powerful, even on my knees letting him take his pleasure, it's the pleasure I allow him to take. It's me who's making him almost feral. His pace is punishingly brutal in his need.

"Fuck . . ." he moans, as he gets closer and closer to his release, "You feel so good, I'm going to come down that throat of yours, and I want you to drink down every single drop." I squeeze his ass, pulling him to me, eager to taste him. I want to see him crack, and fall apart. I need it. I want to see him lost to the pleasure only I can give him. He comes with a moan, the grip on my hair tight, as he holds himself deep. My pussy clenches in protest, wanting more. As he slides out of my mouth, a drop of cum falls on my lips.

"I said every drop, sweetheart," he orders, catching the drop on his thumb and pushing it in between my lips where I lick it off eagerly. "Good girl," he praises, as his cock twitches in front of me. He gives it a lazy stroke, while smirking down at me.

"What?" he teases. "You can't think we're done already. Get that sexy little ass of yours upstairs. I want you naked, and spread on your bed." He cups me through my trousers, grinding his palm, "Mmmm, I want you to play with this pretty pussy of mine, but you aren't allowed to come, not until I say so. You think you can do that for me?" he growls against my throat.

Lost for words, all I can do is nod.

"Good girl," he murmurs before he kisses me. If the taste of him on my tongue bothers him any, I wouldn't have known, he kisses me like a man possessed, fanning the flames of my desire higher and higher.

Fuck, this man can kiss.

When he pulls away I'm breathless and dazed.

"Upstairs. Naked and spread. Now," he orders, and I scurry off, my pussy clenching in anticipation, my underwear drenched with my need for him. I can't get up the stairs fast enough.

Chapter Thirty Three

W atching her practically run out of the room makes me chuckle. My earlier words about my brothers had caught me off guard. I've never been the type to share, and honestly, if anyone else lays a finger on her I'll end them in a heartbeat. But when I look at my brothers, I see their pain, and the secret looks they throw her way when they think I'm not looking. They aren't fooling anyone. I know Creed will never act on his feelings, out of loyalty, respect, and our friendship. I'm grateful to him for that, all those times he flirted, he didn't do it for him, he did it to help me pull my head from my ass. I can see it clear as day now, and I think it's time to return the favour.

Nyx is one of a kind and we were lucky to find her. I mean it when I say her capacity for love is endless. I know her loving my brothers won't take away any of her love for me. It's a weird feeling, but I know the truth of it. We all bring something different to the table, something which makes her happy. Nyx deserves every pleasure, every scrap of happiness, but I know she'll never act on her own if she thinks it might hurt me. It's time to prove to her, I'm man of my word, while simultaneously returning the favour of pulling Creed's head from his ass.

I go upstairs, following Nyx's steps, until I come to her bedroom door. If I listen closely I can hear her little moans, her little gasps of pleasure as she plays with herself. I want to burst in there and feast on her like a starving man, coming down her throat didn't sate my hunger for her at all. I don't think it's possible to ever get my fill of her.

I leave her door, and walk down the corridor to where I know Creed has claimed a room. I find him sitting on his bed. He doesn't notice me at first, lost in his own thoughts. He looks so broken, more than I realised. He's always there with an easy smile, or a joke whenever I'm feeling down, but he's very guarded with his own feelings. He'll always sacrifice his feelings, and prioritise the people he cares about. It's the main reason I both love him and want to throttle him.

"Creed?" I announce my presence, causing him to jump.

"Yes, boss." I cringe internally, he always calls me boss to try and distance himself and remind himself of his supposed place, and I hate it, but if I correct him he'll laugh it off. I gave up trying to change him years ago, but that doesn't mean I like it any better now than I did then.

"Nyx's room," I order, giving little information.

"Is something wrong? What happened?" He rushes to his feet, tension lacing his body. I fight the urge to laugh, he can deny it all he wants, try to downplay his feelings, but it's clear to everyone with a set of eyes just how into her he is.

"She needs help," I offer as a way of explanation, trying to keep my face neutral.

"Okay," he replies, not even questioning why I'd be here if she needed help. He's too worried about her to think straight. Seeing him like this is kind of cute. In a way, he 's kind of like a puppy.

I follow him to the room as he opens the door, when his eyes fall on her he stops dead in his tracks, Nyx's moans can be heard clearly now, so I step in behind him and close the door. At the sound of the door closing, Nyx opens her eyes and gasps, instantly closing her legs.

"I didn't tell you to close them," I tell her, and she looks confused before reluctantly opening them again, blushing the most delightful shade of pink. Creed's gulp is audible as her hands trail back down her body, eyes on us. As her fingers slide through her wetness, Creed reaches his limit.

"You don't have to rub it in my face," he hisses at me, tearing his eyes away from her. Nyx frowns and stops her teasing, but her legs remain open.

"I'm not," I state, annoyed with myself at having hurt him. I walk over to Nyx, praying he won't bolt. I can see his conflict in his body posture, I know how badly he wants her, how much he's holding back.

"This is cruel," he murmurs, but we hear him.

"Creed," Nyx calls, and he partially turns around to look at her again, before catching himself.

"Tell him, sweetness," I encourage her. I know he'll never act unless he knows what I do. Her eyes widen as she understands what I'm asking.

"Creed, I—"

"Don't, Princess, not unless you mean it," he interrupts, his voice pained, but he doesn't turn around.

"Do not interrupt her," I growl, I'm all for self-preservation but the guy's being an idiot. He spins around at my tone, fire burning in his eyes.

There he is. The fire and strength, he isn't one to cower, and he needs to face his feelings.

"What is this, some sort of sick game? I thought . . . I thought—"

"Creed, shut the fuck up," Nyx snaps, closing her legs, and getting to her feet. I fight the urge to control her again, but I'm also curious about what she'll do.

She stands before him naked, totally unashamed or bashful. She reaches up to grab the hair at the back of his neck. Seeing her control someone bigger than her, I have to admit is hot. I love the way she submits to me and gives me control, but seeing this side of her. Dominating and taking, I smirk knowing there's no way Nyx is letting her prey escape.

She looks over at me, and I give her a reassuring smile, rearranging myself. It's all the permission she needs. Knowing I'm okay with it. Honestly, I hadn't even considered just how hot it would be to watch this. Voyeurism hadn't ever been a kink of mine, yet watching her command Creed is something else.

She pulls his head back, forcing him to bend at the knees unless he wants to lose a handful of hair.

"You listen to me, Creed, and you listen fucking good," she snaps.

I chuckle, when his eyes open wide, I don't think any woman has owned him like this before, but it doesn't take a brain surgeon to figure out he likes it.

"I love you, you idiotic, self-deprecating asshole. If you need someone to put you down, make you feel like a little bitch, fine. But you dare question my feelings," she looks at me, and I nod, "Our feelings," she corrects, "You will regret it." I love that even now, with a man under her control, she's still including me subconsciously, with the little glances she throws my way. She is my Queen, through and through, and seeing her like this, fucking hellfire. Just remembering the way she was on her knees, so pliant, so responsive as I took my pleasure from her, and now the same sexy little mouth is cutting my brother down to size.

When she claims his lips with hers, his eyes widen before glazing over with lust, and closing as she deepens the kiss. You can hear Creed's defences shatter, as she batters straight through them. When she breaks the kiss, he looks up to her, wide eyed, but there's still a look of confusion in his eyes.

"Come here," I command, catching Nyx's attention, she smirks down at Creed before releasing him. He stumbles to his feet, bringing his fingers to his lips as if he can't believe what just happened. "I think you got through to him, sweetheart." I kiss her, and she yields under me. Her submission tastes so much sweeter after seeing her display of dominance.

"Remember your safeword?" The question serves as a reminder and a warning of what's to come.

She nods.

"Out loud, sweetheart, so Creed can hear you too," I command.

"Bagels. That's my safeword."

"Good girl. Now what did I ask you to do?" I ask, her eyes widen as she remembers my instructions. She looks towards Creed and then back to me, questions in her eyes.

"Problem?" I ask.

She shakes her head, throwing Creed another glance as she crawls back on the bed. This time when she spreads her legs and starts to play with herself, Creed doesn't look away. He looks at her like a man lost in the desert and she is his only hope at survival. Her eyes dart between us, unsure where to focus. But it isn't long before her eyes drift closed as her pleasure grows, our names whispers on her lips, with breathy wanton moans. I wait for any jealousy, but there is none.

"Creed," I call, getting his attention. He grunts an ac-knowledgment, but can't seem to tear his eyes away from our girl. I can hardly blame him. "I think you should show her just how sorry you are for interrupting her, and doubting her."

His eyes snap to mine, needing to see the sincerity there.

"She tastes so sweet, it's so good you want to drown in her. Show her how sorry you are with your tongue on her sweet pussy. I want to hear her scream." I smile wickedly and it's permission enough for him. He prac-tically throws himself across the room in his eagerness to get to her. As soon as his lips close on her she gasps, squirming under his attentions. I take her hand in mine and lick her taste off her fingers.

So fucking good.

I kiss her, letting her taste herself on my tongue. Creed owning her pussy, me invading her mouth, she's squirming, uncontrolled, her kisses getting sloppier as she loses herself to lust. Her orgasm is right round the corner, but it's too soon.

"Stop." And just like that Creed stops, ignoring her whines of protest. She tries to grab a fistful of hair and grind against his face, chasing her orgasm, but I haven't given permission yet so Creed holds firm, allowing me to run the show.

"I take it back, I hate you both," she mutters, causing us both to chuckle.

"Now now, Princess, you don't really mean it" Creed teases.

"Make me come and I'll take it back," she demands.

"All in good time, sweetheart," I promise.

She huffs her frustration and Creed bites her thigh, eliciting a moan from her lips.

"How wet is she?" I ask Creed, already knowing the answer.

"Fucking dripping," he replies, licking his lips as if he can't get enough of her. "Such a dirty, greedy girl."

"Sweetness, how about you show him how good you are with that mouth of yours?" She smirks up at me, and I know she has mischief planned. I get up, moving away, giving her space to play her games. It amuses me how different she is with us both, she stalks Creed with a wicked smile on her lips.

She pounces on him, pinning him under her. I don't think any of his conquests have ever been so in control of him, it's almost comical the way he is with her. You can see him holding back, trying not to frighten her with his size, but he's underestimating her. And if there's one thing she hates, it's to be underestimated. She pulls his clothes off him, stripping him bare, he doesn't stand a chance against her sheer determination, not that he wants to resist. I can still feel the remnants of his awkwardness, his eyes keep floating to me, unspoken questions, and a wariness that I'll snatch her away at any moment.

She kisses down his body; he lets out a pained moan as she torments him with her tongue, pressing kisses down his chest and stomach, nipping with her teeth every so often causing him to groan and arch. She has her ass to me, waving it in the air, a blatant invitation. She spreads her thighs, giving me an unobstructed view of her drenched pussy.

"Fucking hell, Wildcat, I need to bury myself in you."

She moans, her pussy desperately clenching, needing to be filled. Creed flings his head back as he starts to thrust gently into her mouth. I strip eagerly, ready to give her what she needs. I run my hard cock through her wetness, coating myself fully before thrusting deep into her. She gags on Creed's cock as I push into her, forcing her tight pussy to stretch around me. My thrusts force her to take him down her throat, pushing her limits. Every time she chokes on him, her pussy grips my cock in the most delightful way.

"You're so beautiful, Princess," Creed praises. I don't need to look at her to know tears are running down her cheeks.

"She is," I agree, "You're taking us both so fucking well." I run a finger over her clit causing her to make borderline animalistic sounds as she loses herself to carnal pleasures. Creed's hands are in her hair, as he fucks her face, and I bury myself deep. "Come for us, sweetheart," I demand, sending her over the edge.

"Fuck, Princess, I'm going to come," Creed moans as he shoots his load down her throat. When he slides from her lips they both have glazed looks on their faces, but I'm not done with her yet. I still want at least one more orgasm from her.

I move my fingers away from her overly sensitive clit, and pound into her relentlessly, her head is on Creed's stomach as she fights to keep herself upright. My hands on her hips are the only reason she hasn't fully collapsed on to him. Every thrust I pull her back onto me, forcing myself deeper. Her moans soon turn to screams, my name on her lips.

"Yes, Kaiden, more. Yes, fuck me, sir. Fuck me hard," she begs, her words barely coherent, as she's consumed with pleasure. I fuck her, my pace punishing and brutal. I gather her cum on my fingers, bringing them up to slowly circle her asshole.

"Tell me, sweetheart, have you ever been fucked in the ass before?" I ask, curious as she pushes against my finger. Begging for more.

"Yes," she whispers. Jealously flares up inside me at the thought of her being touched by anyone else, them getting to use her sweet fucking body. Creed growls his annoyance, it seems like it's something we agree on. She's ours.

"You better not fucking tell us who, Wildcat. You do and you'll be signing their death warrant. You... Are... Ours ..." I punctuate every word with a violent thrust of my cock, as if I can carve my name on her soul.

"Yours." she agrees.

I pushed my finger into her asshole causing her to moan in delight.

"Yes," she moans, "more" she demands and I slide another one into her. Working my fingers in time with my cock. She's writhing against Creed, bucking into me, taking everything I have to give.

"So fucking good," I moan, getting close to my own release. I pull out of her, needing to see her eyes as I fill her. I turn her over, laying her down on top of Creed. His cock rubs up against her ass, and his hands come up to hold her thighs wide, baring her to me.

I rub my cock against her, delighting in the way her eyelids flutter closed at my teasing. But I can't resist for long, I slide into her, my eyes rolling back at the sensation. How can she be so fucking perfect? Sliding into her is like coming home. Creed's fingers find her swollen clit, rubbing it in time with my thrusts. I put her legs over my shoulders, forcing myself deeper. She squirms, sandwiched between us, Creed's palm covers her breast, his fingers pinching one of her nipples, toying with it, pulling and twisting until she's panting between us.

"Come for me, sweetheart, one more time," I demand, wanting to feel her come all over my cock. Having her come undone is addictive, her moans, and gasps, the way she writhes under me.

"I can't," she murmurs, "It's too much." But I'm not accepting no for an answer.

"Come on, Princess, do it, I want to feel you drench us both. Own us, mark us as yours." He squeezes her clit, as he bites down on her shoulder. Leaning over them both, with her legs still over my shoulders, I sink my teeth into the other shoulder.

"Yes," she screams, the border of pleasure and pain drawing out her elusive orgasm, causing me to fall right over the edge with her.

CHAPTER THIRTY FOUR

I wake up ridiculously hot, sandwiched between Creed and Kaiden. This bed isn't made for three, and as much as I don't regret the events of last night, I need some air. I wriggle out from between them, careful not to disturb them. Firstly, I need to pee. Secondly, I need a drink. Between the two of them, I'm surprised I'm not a mummified husk with the amount they managed to ring out of my body.

I vaguely remember one of them cleaning me up and tucking me into bed as I dozed. I was completely exhausted, both mentally and physically. Even now my clit aches, their relentless attention too much, but at the same time perfect. I smile watching them sleep, Kaiden frowns briefly sensing the empty space, and reaches out and pulls Creed closer to him, before drifting back into a deep sleep. I fight to contain my laughter at imagining his face when he wakes up.

I head to the bathroom at the end of the hall and when I leave I almost feel like a semi functioning human, one that's been pounded to the point her soul left her freaking body, but at least clothed.

It's too early for anyone else to be up and wake. Honestly, I'm not sure why I am. It's not like I've ever been a morning person but I just feel restless. It's probably just my brain trying to decompress, I mean the last twenty-four hours have been absolutely ridiculous.

Who would have thought?

I fill up a glass of water in the kitchen, and head outside to sit on the steps. The chill of the early morning air is pleasant against my skin.

Thinking about last night makes me blush, but it's better than I ever imagined. I can still feel their touches on my skin, as if they've branded me. I smile, filled with happiness, but there's still . . . something. Kaleb's reaction hurt, I don't want to see him upset. I feel guilty for not going after him. I'm really not a good person.

I can still remember his face, he's going to forever compare himself to Kaiden, but can't he see, he's special in his own right? I don't want to make him feel bad, but I'm also not going to feel ashamed of my feelings for Kaiden, either.

Sigh.

Adding Creed to the mix will just complicate matters further. Last night was positively primal, all-consuming. My throat still feels raw, the sounds they managed to ring from me, the way they played my body. I have never known anything like that.

Argh why is everything so complicated?

The door opens behind me, and I turn to find out who's awake so early.

"Room for one more?" Kaleb asks.

How did I ever get them confused before? How could I have been so shallow?

"Of course," I say, patting the stone slab next to me.

"I think I owe you an apology—"

"Look, I'm sorry about—"

We both start talking at the same time, before stopping, and sharing an awkward laugh.

"Let me go first, please, Kitten," he asks, and honestly I am happy to let him. I'm not exactly good at talking to Kaleb without sticking my foot in it.

"I'm not very good at sharing my feelings, hell, I'm not very good at talking full stop, but I have to come clean with you."

Dread curls in my gut when he looks away refusing to meet my eyes.

"It was my fault Maria died," he confesses.

"What do you mean? It was Keith's fault," I ask, confused.

"She phoned me the day she died. If I'd answered, then maybe—"

"No," I snap. "You don't get to claim what happened as your own. That's not your sin to carry, it's his."

"I could have stopped it, I mean, if I'd arrived earlier than maybe not everyone would have died," he argues, his expression riddled with guilt.

"It was you, wasn't it? Who killed the men?" I whisper.

He nods.

I throw my arms around him, hugging him tight. His entire body goes rigid, and he holds his arms away from me.

"Thank you," I murmur against his neck.

It seems to be the right thing to say, as he relaxes.

"But I left you there," he admits, his voice full of regret. "I left you alone to wake up in that mess."

"Maybe," I agree. "But you didn't know I was there, did you?"

"No. But I was there when Creed kidnapped you, and I just let him. I thought protecting my identity was more important."

I laugh.

"Well, if there's something to be sorry for, it would be that, but I gave as good as I got. Keith took my family from me. That's unforgivable. What you're talking about— the kidnapping, and everything that followed—well, it was just steps along the path which brought me here to you guys, and I wouldn't change it," I confess. I briefly feel guilt at my happiness, remembering all I've lost but denying myself isn't going to bring anyone back.

"Well, I guess. I mean, I heard you last night. It took all my self-control not to come rip them off you. I always thought—" he trails off, "It doesn't matter. I was clearly wrong."

"Kaleb." He closes his eyes, seeming to savour his name on my lips.

"Don't," he looks at me, "I don't need your pity, or your excuses. I'll be your monster as long as you want me. I'll protect you and slay your enemies. All I ask is you don't push me away. I . . ." He swallows, emotions and pain swirling in his eyes, "I can lose anyone else. I can't lose you, Kitten."

"You're not a monster," I whisper, taking his hand in mine. "You're a lot of things, but a monster isn't one of them. But you barely know me, half the time I feel like you can't stand me."

"It's not you I can't stand, it's me," he confesses. "It's even worse seeing you with someone who has the same face as me, it just drills in the fact I'm the spare, I'll never measure up."

My hand is in motion before I realise, the sharp sting against my palm the only warning. I look at my palm in horror, but you know what? Fuck it. He deserved it.

He raises a hand to his face, and rubs at the red palm print.

"Careful, Kitten. I like it when it hurts," he growls.

"You stupid, egotistical, self-destructive psycho," I snap, finally reaching my limit. I've never been known for my bedside manner and I've officially reached my level of bullshit. I stand up, creating distance between us, so I won't be tempted to kill the masochistic asshole.

"You just don't get it do you? To busy wallowing in self-loathing to open your fucking eyes. The only one who thinks you're a spare is you. The only one comparing you to Kaiden is you. The only one standing in the way of you finding anything resembling happiness is you." I stand there glaring at him, wishing my words would just sink in. "Kaiden wants you to be happy, he even told me how he thinks you deserve love. You know he counts you as his brother, even when you act like a colossal dick, always throwing temper tantrums."

He sits there speechless, processing my words. My anger fizzles out a little, and I go to sit down next to him, taking a softer approach.

"Look, I care about you. Ever since you told me who you were, I've cared about you, and I'm grateful for your help. But you are so much more than some attack dog.

I've seen it. Hearing the way you rip into yourself hurts, I know it hurts Kaiden, too. Creed, well he's in his own world half the time so try not to hold it against him. I know you have kindness in you, I've seen it in your eyes, even when you pushed me away. All I'm asking for is if you can spare a little bit of kindness for yourself, and stop hurting someone I care about."

He lets out an agonised sigh, and with it I can see the pain he's clinging to uncoil from his shoulders.

"I can try," he promises, the words difficult but sincere.

"That's all I ask." I smile at him and press a chaste kiss against his jaw. "Sorry for slapping you."

"How's your hand?" he asks.

I hold it between us, flexing my fingers.

"I knew you were hard headed, but never would've guessed your face would be hard too." The skin still prickles from where I struck him. He gently takes my hand in his, pressing delicate kisses to my fingers, and palm. I watch transfixed at the way his eye lashes flutter with every connection, the slight sharp inhale as if he can feel the same sparks of electricity between us. Heat flares at my core, and I clear my throat, trying to extract my hand.

Since when was I this fucking greedy?

I scold myself, after last night I should be able to hold it together, yet I still find myself rubbing my thighs together, as his eyes meet mine.

Fuck.

He gives me a knowing smirk but releases my hand. Still, I know whatever this is . . . it's far from over.

"How do you do that?" he asks, leaving me completely confused.

"Do what?"

"You always know what to say, what to do. You always make me feel better."

"I just see you, that's all. I'm not anything special." I shrug. It's true, my empathy is a gift. I've seen people, studied them so much at Haven, seen their masks, and eventually the masks always slip. Eventually you just get good at reading people to avoid pain, or drama, or in the case of the girls, to get better tips.

"I disagree. You are special," he murmurs, looking at me with such open adoration, it makes me squirm under his gaze. His eyes fall to my lips, and I instantly think about him kissing me.

Did I want him too? Was it okay to want it?

I start to pull away, knowing I need to talk to the others first, I need to make sure we're all on the same page.

"Aww, isn't this sweet," a female voice, dripping with sarcasm, breaks whatever moment we're having.

Kaleb growls, pulling me close.

Just who is this woman?

"So, this is the reason why you've been . . . resistant."
She glares at me, with venom in her gaze. It's like she's
trying to incinerate me.

"You take your eyes off her," Kaleb snarls.

"Feisty." She chuckles. "I knew you had it in you. You
just need the right motivation it seems." She licks her lips
in a predatory way which makes me feel sick. She looks
him up and down as if he is a piece of meat. I see Kaleb
physically cringe under her gaze. I step in front of him,
forcing her gaze back to me. She sneers in disgust.

"What do you want?" I spit, wanting to rip that disgusting look off her face.

"I don't *want* anything. I'm here to collect what's mine,"
she snaps.

"He's not yours," I snarl back.

"Oh, you naive little girl, did he not tell you?" I growl
at her tone. "His father sold him to me, the Ryker heir.
A little bit below my paygrade, but worth it, wouldn't
you agree? If I'm going to be bred like a prized mare, I'm
going to have fun with it. That coldness, that way he acts
all aloof, it's delicious. I can't wait to see him break." She
smiles wickedly. "I barely got my fingers on him before
father pulled me off, but you see . . . Daddy is very very
angry with the Ryker's, and there's no way I'm losing my
prize to a pissing match. I've worked too hard to get this
close. Come, Kaiden, say goodbye to your whore, we've
wasted enough time here."

Kaleb flinches at his brother's name.

"He's mine," I hiss through gritted teeth "You're not taking him from me".

Over my dead fucking body

She throws her head back, laughing maniacally.

"Oh, I really don't think you have a choice, little girl. He's not yours to keep," she replies, with a self-assured smugness that really grates on my fucking nerves. "Oh, boys?" she calls into the trees, and Kaleb's eyes narrow, as he steps in front of me.

"Get behind me," he whispers, and my heart sinks, this is like Creed all over again.

Slowly a group of heavily armed soldiers come slinking out of the trees, guns raised, pointed directly at us.

Okay, I take it back. This is worse.

Those guns will rip us to shreds. They're the ones you see in movies. They belong in the army, not in Blight. There are eight assault rifles pointed directly at us, and I'm shit out of ideas on how to save us. I study the men carefully, looking for any signs of compassion, but their eyes are hard, almost vacant. She walks up to the one closest to her and pulls a knife from his belt. His attention flickers as she draws the blade, but his expression remains blank.

"Take a good look, Kaiden, my love. These were all strong-willed males once. Now they're helpless slaves to my will. I'm their addiction, and they'll do anything for another hit." She grips another by the dick and squeezes, he lets out a pained moan but tries to hump her hand regardless. "Shameless, uncontrolled, my own army of perfect fuckboys. Breaking the ice and claiming the heart of the untouchable Kaiden, that will be my ultimate trophy. Maybe I'll lend you to my friends once you've been properly broken in," she snickers.

"You're a monster," I spit.

"Ha, they feel good, crave it. How many women are left broken, screaming in pain, terrified after men have had their fun? This is nothing compared to that," she snarls at me. "You think you know what it's like, you have no idea. You think living here in your little *'gangster'* town, you've seen darkness? This is a fucking kiddy pool. So shut the fuck up and let the grown ups talk."

"And if I refuse?" Kaleb asks. I watch him as he slowly morphs into the version of Kaiden I 've seen before, the one where he pushes me away, the lonely one, the perfect poker face which makes my heart weep.

"You can come willingly, be my little puppy. Or you can pretend you don't want me, and become a slave. I'd prefer it if you come willingly, I'd like to watch your ice walls crumble as I milk you for all you're worth." The way she speaks makes it sound like she actually believes what she said is reasonable.

"No you can't," I cling to him, begging him. "You're worth so much more than being a toy, I won't let you do this."

"I'll be able to protect you all," he whispers softly, so only I can hear. "That's all I ever wanted. You don't need me to stop Keith. Kaiden's the brainy one, even Creed is useful."

"Take. That. Back," I hiss. I thought I'd gotten through to him . . . I thought we'd turned a corner.

"Awww, I don't think your little plaything is very happy, Kaiden. Should I bring her with us? I'm sure I can find some sort of use for you. Maybe I should let my men toy with you while I take what's mine," she sneers at me.

"Over my dead body," I snarl.

"That can be arranged." She smiles, closing the distance between us. She draws the blade up over my stomach, pressing gently, not enough to draw blood but enough I can feel its bite. She draws the knife over my breasts and up my neck, holding it against my throat. Still I glare at her. I wasn't scared of this bitch, if she killed me it would be a lot less painful than losing any of them.

"I don't think your plaything wants to play nice with me, Kaiden," she teases, her voice light, almost musical. "If you want to spare her life, I suggest you show her what manners look like." She pulls a collar out of her pocket, and with horror I notice the men surrounding us had the telltale metal peeking out from their clothes.

"Don't!" I hiss. That one word causes the blade to cut into my neck, but I'm not backing down. For him to humiliate himself like this . . . I don't want to see him suffer.

In slow motion he reaches out to take the collar, hatred burning in his eyes, but he can't act, he won't, not with all these guns trained on us.

Why did I come out here?

How could I have been so careless?

As his fingers brush the collar, she drops it.

"Oops," she says with a chuckle. "I'm so careless, good thing my other hand didn't slip. Now, on your knees, pick it up," she snaps.

Kaleb kneels in the dirt to pick the collar up, before fastening it around his throat. He stays there on the ground, his body practically vibrating with anger.

"Who's a good boy?" She coos, pulling the knife from my throat to pat him on the cheek. She pinches his chin, forcing his eyes to meet hers. The hatred and fire there is explosive, I can see the demons thrashing behind his eyes.

"Your hatred is clear as day, but no worry. There's a fine line between love and hate, you'll see." She waves the men off, and they slink back into the shadows. She turns on her heel, and beckons for Kaleb to follow.

"Now," she hisses, "or she dies."

I want to do something, scream, scratch her evil little eyes out.

I can't let her take him.

He gets to his feet, and rushes over to me, hastily claiming my lips with his. It's messy, and I know he's kissing me goodbye. I grab hold of him, as he tries to pull away, pouring my feelings into it.

I will find you.

I will get you back.

We will burn down the world looking for you.

At the click of a button, Kaleb's collar tases us both, my grip on him tightens involuntary, as the current races through my body. We're gripped in its power, unable to break apart, or breathe until she releases the button.

The last thing I remember before the world goes black is a comforting shade of icy blue, and whispered words against my lips.

"I will always love you, Kitten."

TO BE CONTINUED . . .

Note from the Author

I know, another cliffhanger, please put the pitchforks down haha. I know this was initially a duet but Creed and Kaleb's mischief was too much to handle. I promise Keith will get his comeuppance in the last book. But with the Jula family getting involved the story just started to spiral.

It was never my intention for Creed to be involved romantically, but when they shared that special moment, it didn't feel right to cheapen it. I love seeing how their relationships are all growing, but my heart really does bleed for Kaleb. The poor guy doesn't get a break.

So what did you guys think? Did anyone picture Uncle as Uncle from Jackie Chan Adventures or is it just me? I'd love to hear your thoughts and theories about book 3. At this point, I'm just as much in the dark as you guys but I'm sure it will be an adventure.

If you could leave me reviews I would appreciate it, it's the most motivating thing for an author.

The story will pick straight up again in Blood Bonds.
Which will be due for release in October 2023

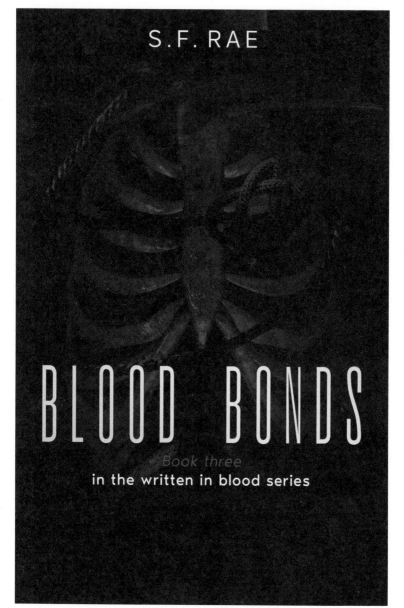

BLOOD TIES

Keep in touch

I would love to hear from you, and there are plenty of ways for you to get in touch. You never know, you might be able to spot teasers, and take part in giveaways, or you even might be lucky enough to bag an advanced reader copy (ARC).

All my socials can be found here:
https://linktr.ee/sfrae
Sign up for my monthly newsletter:
www.sunsetwrenpress.com
Email me:
SFRaeAuthor@gmail.com

Acknowlegements

Thank you reader, for continuing with me on this journey. This one has been my favourite yet and as I'm writing this the series is almost complete. Blood Bonds is shaping up to be something special, and I am so incredibly grateful for all the love and support I have received. I'm trying to not make this a repeat of thank you's from the previous book but I can't do this without the support from my family and friends. You join in on my excitement, even when you don't know what you are being excited about. I'd be lost without you guys.

Big special shout out to Alicia, my amazeballs editor, who helps make my scatterbrained ideas into something that actually resembles a lick of sense.